breathe

Doctor Nell Northam is abducted by jihadists to help them launch a weapon. The President asks his top security advisor, Donovan Rourke, to stop the attack. But when Donovan and Nell are finally ready to stop it, they realize they've been deceived – and that thousands of Americans are about to die.

breathe

A suspense thriller.
MIKE BROGAN

Lighthouse

Business to Kill For

Dead Air

Madison's Avenue

G8

Kentucky Woman

This book is a work of fiction. Names, characters, businesses, organizations, places, events, and incidents are either the product of the author's imagination or are used fictitiously. Any resemblance to actual persons, living or dead, events or locales is entirely coincidental.

ISBN 978-0-9980056-7-6

Library of Congress Control Number: 2017941349

Printed in the United States of America
Published in the United States by Lighthouse Publishing

Cover design: Vong Lee

First Edition

This book is dedicated to the men and women
of the FBI, CIA, Homeland Security, Police, and US Military
who risk their lives…to protect ours.

Acknowledgments

To Andrew Manning, former-FBI Special Agent, for his helpful suggestions and insights into the challenges facing FBI agents each day as they protect our citizens.

To the experts at the US Military's Aberdeen Proving Ground for their helpful counsel on weapons of mass destruction and related subjects.

To my fellow novelists and writing colleagues for their suggestions that made this story better.

To editor/translator, Brendan Brogan, for his insightful review and improvements to the rough draft of BREATHE.

To author, Rebecca M. Lyles, for her comprehensive final edit and enhancements to the manuscript of BREATHE.

And to my wife, Marcie, and the family for their endless patience with the distracted writer in residence.

ONE

MANHATTAN

Nell Northam thought her sister, Lindee, looked good.
  Eight months ago Lindee looked dead.

A man had attacked her in her apartment and left her to bleed out. Nell found Lindee with no pulse and did CPR until an ambulance rushed her to Mount Sinai where her heart stopped twice in the ER. But she was resuscitated.

Days later, she emerged from a coma and began a slow recovery. Her doctor called her "The Miracle Girl."

Today, the Miracle Girl seemed almost back to normal, if you forgot about the three dead-bolt locks on her apartment door, two alarm systems, and her sweat-drenched nightmares.

Nell had flown up from Virginia for their annual Sisters-Shop-Till-We-Drop-Athon. She had her eye out for a few items, but really wanted to make sure her younger sister was recovering physically and psychologically. So far it appeared she was.

Nell turned and looked in a shop window and couldn't believe her eyes. "Found it!"

"What?" Lindee said, two shops ahead.

"That beautiful Michael Kors purse I've been lusting after."

"In brown?"

"Brown and on sale!"

"Look at what else is on sale!" Lindee said, pointing in her window.

"What?"

"Those Cole Haan shoes you've also been on the prowl for!"

"No way!"

"I'm looking at them!"

Nell was amazed. They'd been shopping for only four hours and she'd already found the two items she wanted most just a few feet apart. On sale! What were the odds?

She looked back at the attractive leather purse. Why 50%-off? She couldn't see any flaws. Even if it had a flaw, it was good enough for her.

She heard footsteps come close. Suddenly two men grabbed her from behind.

She tried to scream, but a huge male hand clamped her mouth shut. She struggled against arms that felt like steel bands. The big man and a short man dragged her quickly toward an open van.

This is not happening! Nell thought, as they lifted her into the van.

Lindee turned, saw her, and shouted - "*STOP! LET HER GO! HELP!*"

But a truck horn blasted, drowning out Lindee's cries.

The big man pushed Nell down on the van floor as the van sped away from the curb.

* * *

Lindee slumped against a parking meter, watching the van disappear into heavy traffic. *I'm having another nightmare!*

But then she saw Nell's earring near the curb.

My God - Nell was taken! She grabbed the earring and called 911.

"My sister was just taken by two men in a van!"

"Where are you ma'am?"

"On Broadway near 67th. Not far from Barneys."

"What kind of van?"

"Long. White. Big windows along the side. It looked new."

"Did you see the license plate?"

Lindee paused. "The last number was maybe a . . . nine."

"Which direction was the van driving on Broadway? North or south?"

"I don't know."

"*Away* from Columbus Circle?"

"Yes."

"What was your sister wearing?"

Lindee told her.

"Remain there, ma'am. Keep your phone on. We're sending a police car immediately."

"Please *hurry!*"

Her mind spinning, Lindee stared at the spot where they grabbed Nell. She prayed it was just another one of her crazy nightmares.

But she knew it wasn't.

Her sister was just abducted.

TWO

Donovan Rourke sat in his CIA office in Manhattan, one of the CIA offices scattered throughout Midtown, Lower Manhattan, and Brooklyn.

He was relaxing between meetings and gazing out at the sun-drenched leaves in the nearby park. He liked how the leaves blended from lime green to emerald. The greens always calmed him until the next crisis, which looked like it might be walking into his office right now.

Mamie, his smart, organized, fifty-something, Nigerian-born assistant, had that something's-up look on her face. She pointed at his phone.

"God's on one!" she said.

"Tell Him I'm busy."

"Everyone's a comedian!"

"What's the Director want?"

"No idea. Meanwhile, here's more stuff for you." She smiled

as she dumped a stack of paperwork and folders in his inbox, and walked out.

More stuff, how nice. He had enough. Nine months ago the Director of National Intelligence, Michael Madigan, and the President appointed Donovan as a Special Advisor on terrorism, and head of a new secret covert group affiliated with the CIA. Donovan had been honored by the appointment. He coordinated closely with the FBI and other Manhattan-based anti-terrorism groups because Manhattan was the golden magnet for terrorist groups.

But each week he had to fly to Washington, sometimes twice or more, to huddle with various national security groups and DNI Madigan. The weekly travel was starting to wear thin with him and Maccabee, his wife. They'd been considering whether relocating to Washington would make things easier for their family.

Line one buzzed.

DNI Madigan, the most powerful man in the United States Intelligence community, was a long-time friend and a tough but fair taskmaster . . . who was about to task him again! *And possibly screw up our wedding anniversary trip this weekend. Already postponed twice.*

Donovan picked up. "Director . . ."

"Donovan, we have a situation."

"What's up?"

"A top government scientist was just grabbed off a Manhattan street."

"Where?"

"A few blocks from you."

Donovan heard the soft drone of an engine and assumed Madigan was flying somewhere to check one of his many intelligence groups: the CIA, NSA, FBI, Homeland Security, and all sixteen US intelligence agencies, or whatever number the congressional idiots decided on this week. Madigan visited the agencies to insist they share information and to kick ass when they didn't.

"What happened?"

"Pentagon says one of their chief scientists, a woman named Doctor Nell Northam, was abducted near Broadway and 67th. Two men dragged her into a white van and sped off. Her sister, Lindee, saw it happen. She gave NYPD a brief description."

"The FBI on this?"

"Yeah. Special Agent Drew Manning's heading it up for the FBI."

"Manning's excellent."

"Agreed. But we want *you* to work with Manning."

"Why me? Kidnappings and abductions are *FBI* stuff."

"Yeah, but we . . ."

"The President and I."

"Ah, the *Royal We.*"

"Yeah. The President wants you heading this up, Donovan."

Donovan paused. "Why?"

"Because of Doctor Northam's job. Which is highly critical to our national security. Like your job."

Donovan said nothing.

"He also wants you because of who Nell Northam is."

"And who is she?"

"The President's first cousin."

"Ah, the *Royal First Cousin . . .*"

"Yep. Check in with Drew Manning and call me when you guys know more. I got a real bad feeling about this because of what Doctor Northam does. And whoever took her, knows what she does."

Madigan gave him a brief overview of her work. As he did, Donovan's stomach churned with the horrific implications of her skill in terrorist hands.

They hung up.

Donovan started to call FBI Special Agent Drew Manning when Donovan's personal phone rang. Maccabee, his wife.

A year ago, she'd transferred from the Princeton faculty to NYU as a full professor in the Foreign Languages, Translation, Interpreting Department. She enjoyed NYU's academic-urban environment better than she'd originally thought she would.

"I'm packing your white linen suit for St. Thomas," she said.

"I thought we were just going to loaf around on the beach. You know, make sand castles with Tish . . ."

"We *will*. But one night we should get gussied up and dine in a fancy restaurant for - "

"- our first wedding anniversary dinner," he said quickly.

"Who's a caring, thoughtful male?"

"What can I say . . ."

"You can say what sweet gift you're getting me? Remember, the first year wedding anniversary gift is paper."

"Our boarding passes are paper."

"So are 5,000 certificates of Apple stock."

"Hey - I'm a lowly government employee."

"Gotta go - Tish just spilled her mac and cheese! See you later."

As Donovan hung up, he hoped he did see her later. He also hoped this new assignment would be resolved before their flight to St. Thomas. They'd both been working too many hours. Maccabee needed time away from students as much as he needed time away from tracking jihadists and ISIS sympathizers.

He pictured their family strolling along sunny Megan's Bay, admiring the Caribbean's serene blue water.

But something told him the only water he'd see for a while was the East River, gray as a slab of lead.

THREE

Nell felt the muscular, bull-necked man push her down hard against the van's cold steel floor. Each pothole banged her head and brought a grin to his face.

Bull Neck reeked of garlic and sweat. His bulging brow, puffy face, and his skin-tight suit suggested steroid abuse. His thick black eyebrows had grown together over small olive-pit eyes. His left ear was mostly gone - replaced by a thick gray scar that squiggled down his neck like a worm and disappeared into a beard as black as the gun he pointed at her face.

Beside him sat a small, thin man. Black hair, pencil mustache, narrow face with dark, deep-set eyes. He looked intelligent and intense. His thick, wire-rimmed glasses gave him a scholarly appearance. He dabbed his left nostril with a clean white handkerchief.

The small man looked down at her. "Do what we say and you will not be hurt."

Nell didn't believe him.

"Take my money. And credit cards."

"No thanks. But I will take your phone!"

She handed it to him. He smashed it with a hammer and dropped the pieces out the window.

"Please, I have a young daughter and a husband . . ."

"I know."

How could he know?

"You will see them again *if* you do as I say."

Again, something told her not to believe him.

The van hit a deep pothole and Bull Neck's gun bounced hard against her temple. He smiled, revealing a green substance between his teeth.

"What do you want from me?"

"Obedience," the small man said.

"Where are you taking me?"

He said nothing.

She glanced out the windshield. The sun's position told her they were driving north, parallel with the Hudson River.

What's Lindee doing? She saw them grab me. She shouted for help - but a truck horn blasted over her cries. But by now she would have called the police. And maybe the young saleswoman inside the purse store saw the men grab me.

"We don't have much money."

"We don't want money. We want something else," the small man said, dabbing his nose again.

Please God, not sexual predators . . .

"Relax. We don't want what's between your legs either."

Bull Neck's expression suggested he didn't agree with that.

"We want what's between your ears, Doctor."

Now she got it.

They knew who she was. What she could do. And they wanted that. But how could they possibly have learned what she did? Very few people knew – and they held the highest security clearances in the US government. She trusted them all. But then, the US government trusted Robert Hansen and Edward Snowden and two million other people with high security clearances.

The small man nodded to Bull Neck. Before she realized it, Bull Neck grabbed her right arm with both hands and held it flush against the van floor. The thin man swabbed her arm with something that smelled antiseptic. Then he removed a long wand like device, which she recognized as an ultra-sound wand.

The small man placed a damp cloth over her nose. She smelled kerosene scent and realized it was ether. Her vision faded, but she saw the thin man move a surgical scalpel along her forearm. She felt a sharp pain.

Then everything went black . . .

FOUR

Donovan stared out the narrow office window at a guy on the street below. The guy was aiming something long and black up toward him. A telescopic camera? A scoped rifle? Donovan moved to the side. The rifle followed him.

As Donovan grew more concerned, the guy turned, revealing his long black selfie stick.

Paranoia. Perk of the job, he reminded himself.

He was in the FBI Manhattan headquarters located in 26 Federal Plaza, the massive, charcoal-gray, forty-one story fortress at Broadway and Worth. He wondered if the windows were narrow so employees wouldn't waste time gazing outside like he was – or so snipers couldn't easily shoot someone inside?

FBI Special Agent Drew Manning walked in with Lindee Langstrom, the sister of Dr. Nell Northam.

Dr. Northam had been abducted an hour ago, but Lindee's red, mascara-smudged eyes looked like it just happened. She sat down and stared at the floor.

———

Manning handed her a bottle of Evian.

Donovan liked Drew Manning. They'd worked together to help prevent several terrorist threats in the city. The six-four, thirty-five-year old ex-University of Dayton Flyer basketball star was intelligent, compassionate, and professional. Even more important, he liked Jameson whiskey, which Donovan suspected would be their medication of choice after this crisis, and maybe during. Manning wore his usual: blue blazer, tan slacks, aqua shirt, and a disarming smile.

When Donovan told him the President asked for Donovan to head up this case, Manning laughed and said, "Great! They can fry your sorry ass if it goes wrong."

Lindee leaned forward and asked, "What are my sister's chances?"

Donovan nodded for Manning to answer since Manning had handled several abductions and kidnappings successfully. Donovan had handled two in Europe. Both victims died.

"If they want ransom money, our chances are probably better," Manning said.

"What if they don't want money?"

"We don't think your sister's abductors do," Donovan said. "They want her expertise from Aberdeen Proving Ground."

Lindee nodded.

"You saw them take her."

"Yes. They stepped from the van. A big muscular man with a black beard, and a small thin man with glasses. Both wore dark business suits. They walked down the sidewalk, grabbed Nell from behind, pulled her into the van and drove off. It was over in like ten seconds."

"Did you see the driver?"

"No. His black hoodie was pulled up."

"What color van?"

"White. A long white van."

"Like a plumber's van?"

"Yes, but different."

"How?"

"It had big side windows."

"Like a van for a school or church group?"

"Yes, like that."

"Remember anything else?"

"The last number of the license was a nine."

Lindee's eyes widened as though she just remembered something.

"What's wrong?" Donovan asked.

"Nell's husband. Jacob. I have to tell him."

Donovan saw fear in her eyes. "You want me to notify him?"

"No . . . I should . . ."

Donovan knew about *notification* of next of kin. *He'd* been notified the night his wife, Emma, was murdered by an assassin in Brussels. *Murdered because I wasn't there to protect her. I'd been the target.* Donovan eventually killed the assassin, Valek Stahl, in a bloody scene at a Dutch windmill. But revenge didn't ease the pain. Time had eased the pain. A little at a time.

"I'll call Jacob," Lindee said.

She dialed with trembling fingers.

"Please hit the speaker button, Lindee," Donovan said, "so we can assure him we're doing everything to find her."

She punched the button.

Donovan also wanted to hear the husband's reaction. The husband is always a person of interest in the disappearance or murder of a wife. For good reason. He's guilty sixty-six percent of the time.

Jacob picked up on the third ring.

"Hey Lindee, please don't tell me Nell maxed out our credit cards!"

She paused. "Jacob . . . I . . ."

"What is it?"

"Ah . . ."

" - is something wrong?"

"Yes . . ." As Lindee explained what happened, Donovan heard Jacob's genuine shock and disbelief, and then his anger.

Donovan looked at a photo of Nell Northam. She was a tall, attractive woman with thick brown hair, light-brown eyes, and a friendly, professional demeanor enhanced by large horn-rimmed glasses. She wore a white lab coat and smiled up from a microscope. She looked like what she was - a skilled scientist. And her abductors wanted her skill.

Lindee hung up. "Jacob is taking the next flight from Baltimore."

"Good," Donovan said.

Manning asked, "Lindee . . . is everything all right in their marriage?"

Lindee seemed surprised by the question. "They have a wonderful marriage. Surely, you don't suspect Jacob?"

"No. But we check all possibilities."

"They love each other. And they have a beautiful young daughter, Mia."

Drew Manning's cell phone beeped. He looked at the text message, and frowned.

"State Motor Vehicles just gave me the approximate number of white vans just in Manhattan."

"How many?"

"Over a thousand."

FIVE

Nell tried to open her eyes, but couldn't. Were they glued shut? Was she drugged? She moved her arms and legs a bit. They felt stiff, as though they hadn't moved in hours.

She remembered the two men grabbing her and dragging her into the van, the big Bull-Neck man pushing her down on the steel floor, banging her head on it, smelling his vile sweat, then smelling the sweet scent of ether, seeing the scalpel, then blacking out.

She managed to open her eyes. She saw a small room. The bull-necked man sat a few feet away ripping greasy meat off a kebob.

She saw knotty pine walls, a stone fireplace and wood floors. A cabin maybe. Through a small window, the moonlight hit the swaying branches of some evergreens.

Where am I? Upstate New York? How far from Manhattan? How long was I unconscious?

What time is it? Her watch was gone. Why'd they take it? Obviously, to disorient her. The watch, embedded in a mother-of-pearl bracelet, was an anniversary gift from her husband, Jacob. She treasured it.

Then she saw the bandage on her right forearm. *My God – they removed my microchip implant!* The chip had been her one hope. Now Aberdeen could not track her. How had her abductors known about the chip?

She thought about Jacob. He must know by now. Lindee would have told him. He'd be flying to New York after dropping off Mia with his mom.

They would have told the police where I work. The police would tell Homeland Security, the FBI, NSA, and anti-terrorism groups. Her Aberdeen bosses would tell the military chain of command and all federal authorities.

A lot of people were searching for her. Smart, skilled people. She just had to remain patient. Not her best trait. Still, she'd try. But what if the police and government security people couldn't track the white van?

She had to find a way to escape.

Obviously, they'd kidnapped her for her scientific expertise. The thin man said "we want what's between your ears." Her lab experience.

But she saw no hint of a laboratory in the small cabin. So they'd have to drive her to a lab. The drive might offer her a chance to escape.

The small thin man, who seemed to be the boss, walked into the room and punched two digits on his phone. He whispered, "*La moshkelah! La taqlaq!*"

She had no idea what he'd said, but the language sounded like it might be Arabic.

He hung up, saw she was awake, and walked over to her.

"My name is Mr. Smith. My colleague is Mr. Brown."

And I'm Queen Elizabeth!

"You will follow us now," Mr. Smith said. He dabbed his nostril with a clean white handkerchief.

She hesitated and Bull Neck pulled her to her feet.

They led her down a hallway to a painting of a mountain. Mr. Smith moved the painting to the side and placed his left thumb on a wall panel.

She heard a motor click on.

Suddenly the floor she and the men stood on began vibrating. Then an eight-foot-square section of the floor descended with them down into a dark underground shaft with concrete walls.

Fifteen seconds later, the floor stopped, and they stepped off. She couldn't believe her eyes. She was looking at a sprawling state-of-the-art laboratory brilliantly lit with LED lighting. She saw large centrifuges, vacuum ovens, three spectrophotometers, beakers, pipettes, round bottom flasks, Petri dishes, sterilizers. Other tables held Erlenmeyer flasks, gas burners, stands, and sophisticated, state-of-the-art microscopes.

Long windows overlooked an air-lock laboratory, a decontamination chamber and showers, a room with HazMat suits equipped with self-contained oxygen, plus a vacuum room and ultraviolet light chamber.

It looked as sophisticated as her lab at the US Military's top-secret Aberdeen Proving Ground in Maryland.

In fact, the lab seemed to replicate much of the lab equipment she worked with every day.

But this lab was *not* dedicated to better living through chemistry.

This lab was dedicated to better killing through chemistry.

SIX

"They did what to her?" Donovan asked.

"Sliced open her arm and dug out her microchip implant. Destroyed the chip so we can't track her!" said Brigadier General Greg Fowl, Nell's boss at Aberdeen Proving Grounds.

"Where'd you lose track of her?"

"Manhattan. Around 53rd and 9th. Minutes after they grabbed her."

"How'd they know she had a chip?"

"Ultrasound, I'm betting."

"Did she have a panic button?"

"Yes. Probably in her purse. But her abduction happened fast, she never had a chance to hit it."

Donovan said, "We can't track her phone either. Destroyed."

"Nell Northam is a terrorist's gold mine, Donovan. Highly skilled in biological and chemical weaponry. She was obviously betrayed by someone on the inside."

———

"Sounds like it."

"Money buys secrets. Threats do, too," General Fowl said. "I gotta go, Donovan. Keep me looped in."

"I will."

Donovan hung up and looked over his desk at Nell's sister, Lindee. His heart went out to her. The attractive young brunette stared out the window, looking more desperate with each minute, as though her sister might not survive this.

Donovan feared the same thing.

FBI Special Agent Drew Manning walked in. "The police are looking at videos of white vans on Manhattan streets, tunnels, and bridges. We're also looking statewide. The problem is - there are 40,000 vans in New York State, 90% of which are white."

Donovan figured as much. "Lindee, you mentioned the kidnappers had dark complexions."

"They looked Hispanic or Middle-Eastern. Black hair. The big muscular man had a black beard and most of his left ear was missing."

"Can you describe what your sister was wearing?"

"I can show you." Lindee opened her iPhone. "I took this photo minutes before the men . . ."

It showed Nell wearing a light-blue blouse, navy skirt, and black walking flats.

"May I have your phone a moment?" Manning said. "We'll blast her photo to all police authorities."

She handed him her phone.

"Your sister's Aberdeen experience should work in her favor," Donovan said.

"How?"

"Her abductors might be less likely to harm her until she helps them."

"What if she refuses to help?"

"Will she refuse?"

Lindee paused. "Nell can be *very* stubborn."

Donovan feared the possibility. On the other hand, maybe it would buy her time, enough time for us to find her.

Lindee checked her watch. "Nell's husband's flight should have landed at LaGuardia. Their daughter is at his mother's home."

Agent Drew Manning said, "Lindee, we have to be prepared for something."

Donovan sensed what Manning was about to say.

"To *make* Nell cooperate, the kidnappers may threaten to harm those close to her."

Lindee closed her eyes. "You mean Jacob and Mia . . . ?"

"Yes. And possibly you."

The color drained from Lindee's face. She crossed her arms and sat back.

"Can you stay with a friend for the next few days?" Manning said.

Lindee nodded.

The office door opened and an agent escorted a tall, broad shouldered, dark-haired man in his mid-thirties into the office. The man's frantic expression told Donovan it was Nell's husband, Jacob Northam.

Lindee hurried over, hugged him for several seconds, then introduced him.

"Any news?" Jacob asked.

"Sorry, nothing yet," Donovan said.

"He just called me," Jacob said.

"Who?"

"The man who took Nell. He said if I involved the police, Nell would die . . . right after she watched the video of our daughter being abducted."

SEVEN

Nell felt her hope sink as she studied the depth of sophisticated lab equipment – the kind that could create and weaponize a range of chemical and biological weapons capable of annihilating the population of a major US city.

She was trapped in her worst nightmare: held captive by terrorists with weapons of mass destruction.

The small, thin man walked in, sat at his desktop computer, and faced her. He stifled a yawn, revealing nubby, coffee-stained teeth. He dabbed his wet nostril with a fresh white handkerchief and gestured for her to sit on a lab stool facing him.

She sat down.

Obviously, he wanted her assistance with a weapon. She hoped it was one she might somehow disable or weaken without his realizing it. But doing that would be difficult since he seemed suspicious, intelligent, and vigilant.

And what if she refused to help? Obviously, they would torture her until she did what they wanted. But if she pretended to help, she might find a way to sabotage or weaken the weapon.

Something occurred to her. What if she did not know how to do what they wanted? What if she was not the right person for what they needed? Would they believe her? Would they pump her full of sodium pentothal to force information from her?

"Why am I here?"

"To help me enlighten America."

"About . . .?"

"Injustice against Allah's people."

"Caused by whom –?"

"Who else - America's people, especially your government . . . and Israel, and your pathetic European lackeys."

She said nothing.

"You've desecrated our lands by occupying them for decades. Millions of my fellow Muslims have suffered. Hundreds of thousands have died, including my wife, my daughter, and a brother."

"I'm sorry for your loss."

"Your apology is sixteen years too late! So, until Americans leave *our* land, Americans will die in *your* land. *Quid quo pro*, Doctor. Americans need a wake-up call."

"But American *citizens* did not slaughter Muslims."

"They elected presidents who did. And besides, your citizens are genetic DNA cousins of your soldiers who killed Muslims."

"We're guilty by *genetics*?"

"Of course you are."

She decided to turn genetics against him. "Then *we* – you and Americans, including me, are guilty."

He said nothing.

"As a scientist, you know that maternal DNA, mitochondrial DNA, never changes through the centuries and because of that, you and Americans like me are DNA-linked back to one common grandmother-ancestor somewhere in time. DNA can prove it. We are all linked by DNA genetics. So if you kill Americans, you're killing your own DNA cousins."

He blinked, but seemed to understand the genetic truth.

"DNA rubbish! Even if you were my sister, I would demand that you help us."

"And if I refused?"

"You would die!"

There it is! Help or die. She believed him.

She also believed she'd probably die even if she *did* help him.

He dabbed his nostril again.

"What do you want help with?" she asked.

"This!" He shoved a document across the table toward her.

She read the first page and slumped down in her chair.

She was looking at a weapon that could kill hundreds of thousands of people in excruciating pain in minutes. A weapon that could wipe out maybe ninety percent of the people in a large American city. A weapon that could cause a full-blown, no-holds-barred retaliatory war against certain middle-eastern countries.

A weapon that could ignite Armageddon.

He pointed to a page. "You will combine this weapon . . . with another substance."

"Which substance?"

"All in good time, Doctor."

"Why combine it? Your weapon kills in a few minutes."

His thin lips bent in a smile. "Yes, it certainly does."

"But I'm not experienced in combining - "

" - or in lying it seems."

She said nothing.

"Do not lie to me again, Doctor. I know your experience and resume intimately."

How could he know that years ago she'd assisted briefly with some combination experiments?

Her anger flashed. "What if I sacrifice myself to save thousands of innocent Americans?"

"They'll die anyway - even without the secret substance blended in. Even without your help."

He was right. They would die without blending the substance in and without her help.

"There are other reasons you will not refuse." He pushed a button and an enormous screen lit up the back wall.

She saw her daughter, Mia, playing with her Star Wars toys in front of Jacob's mother's home in Maryland. Nell stopped breathing.

"Mia's a beautiful little girl. Like my daughter was. To keep Mia safe, we'll soon take her into protective custody. If you do what I say, then Mia will be fine. If you don't, trust me, you don't want to know."

Nell's eyes welled up as she stared at Mia. She felt a sharp, physical pain in her heart.

The video cut to a tall man getting into a car. The man turned around.

"*Jacob!*" she whispered.

Hasham smiled. "Handsome husband, beautiful daughter. The perfect American family. You know my description of the perfect American family?"

She said nothing.

"A dead one."

Which my family might soon become. Because of my job.

"Nothing will happen to them if you do as I say."

She did not believe him.

His phone buzzed and he read a text message, answered, then turned back to her. "So, you will do as I say, understood?"

Nell paused, then nodded. She remembered an Aberdeen biochemist who did *not* do as her terrorist abductor demanded. They tortured her for days to reveal a new bioweapon formula. Finally, she gave them one. When they discovered it was false, they left her body floating in a ditch. Her head was never found.

So if I don't do what they want, they will kill my husband and daughter, and then me.

And if I do what they want – they will kill many thousands of innocent people. And then me.

EIGHT

Donovan felt his phone vibrate. He checked Caller ID and answered.

"Any breaks?" Maccabee asked.

"Not yet. Still pursuing the white van."

"Any chance we can still fly to St. Thomas this weekend?"

"Well, Mac, . . . I . . . ah . . ."

"It's okay, Donovan, if we postpone. I understand."

She meant it . . . which made him feel even worse. His job had already postponed the trip twice. And this assignment would probably postpone it again. They'd dreamed of lying on the beach, sipping Mai Tais, making sand castles with seven-year-old Tish, and watching the sun melt into the Caribbean. Tish was his beautiful daughter from his deceased wife, Emma.

But since losing Emma, his prayers had miraculously been answered. He and Maccabee had fallen in love with each other. Then Maccabee and Tish had fallen in love. They'd become mother and daughter in every way, bonding naturally and deeply. He kept reminding himself, every day, that he was the luckiest man on the planet.

"Postponing again is not okay with me, Mac. We've postponed too damn many things."

"Yes, but . . ."

"Back when Director Madigan and the President named me a special *advisor*, I thought I'd be *advising*. Turns out, my advising turns into *fixing!*"

"Which wasn't part of your original job description."

"Nope."

"So what's the answer?"

He paused. "I'm still working on that."

"We can reschedule St. Thomas, Donovan. No big deal."

"It'll be a big deal for Tish. She's been so excited about going. She'll cry if she can't make sandcastles."

"True, but she'll learn one of life's important lessons!"

"Which one?" he asked.

"Life isn't fair." She paused. "We all have to learn that lesson."

He heard something personal creep into Maccabee's voice. Or was it fear?

"What's going on, Mac?"

"Doctor Dubin called. My test came back."

He didn't want to hear this.

"I have . . . endometriosis."

He seemed to recall it. "What's endomet - ?

" - the lining of the womb is not right. It explains why I've been feeling cramps and pain around my period."

"Can you take something for the pain?"

"Anti-inflammatories. Ibuprofen, aspirin. But there's one other complication. Endometriosis makes it more difficult to get pregnant."

The news hit him hard. Her even harder, he knew. She wanted their child more than anything. *They* wanted their child more than anything.

———

"But . . . you *can* still get pregnant, right?"

She paused. "He thinks so, because my case appears to be mild."

"That's good."

"Yes, it is. Listen, Jane's calling in. We'll talk later."

"Okay . . ."

They hung up.

Donovan stared at the phone. Maccabee had been worried that her biological clock was ticking. Now, something called endometriosis might have *stopped* her biological clock.

NINE

Nell ran from the cabin – from the three men chasing her! Her lungs begged for rest, but resting meant death. She forced herself to run faster through the dense, hilly forest.

But the men gained.

Ahead, she saw a wall of huge boulders with a narrow opening. She squeezed through the opening and yanked a leafy branch over it. Then she moved back a few feet and leaned against the cold stone wall. She was in a small, pitch-black cavern. Her pulse pounded in her ears.

The men ran up and stopped a few feet from the opening.

She buried her mouth in her arm to hush her breathing.

The men whispered in Arabic. One man stepped close to the opening. She recognized his black shoes. Bull-Neck's shoes. He bent down, fingered the soft ground.

Does he see my footprint? Does he know I'm in here?

She pressed back hard against the wall.

———

He leaned in, squinted into the dark cavern, his gun glinting in the moonlight. He was too large to squeeze through the opening, but the small thin man could.

The thin man walked close, bent down and aimed a flashlight into the cavern. It lit up the wall opposite her. Then the light crept toward her, very slowly.

She froze, afraid to move or breathe.

The light stopped inches from her shoe.

Suddenly, lightning exploded across the night sky, heavy rain started falling.

The men mumbled something, stood, and took off running down the path.

She breathed a long sigh of relief. Tension eased from her muscles. She closed her eyes and began to relax. They were gone. She was safe.

She felt warm air.

Behind her.

Warm, moist, foul air . . . breath on the back of her neck.

She turned and stared at the four-inch incisors of a black bear.

Nell bolted awake in the cabin, drenched with cold sweat, trembling. Just a bad dream, she told herself . . . just a nightmare.

But now, she knew, *my real nightmare continues.*

TEN

Nell looked out the cabin window at the pine trees she'd seen last night. A pink sliver of dawn slid between the branches and warmed her face. She heard birds singing.

She also heard her abductors talking in the nearby kitchen. The bull-necked man called the short leader "Hasham." And Hasham called Bull-Neck "Aarif."

They spoke what sounded like Arabic. Hasham would say something and Aarif would answer with *na'am* or *laa,* which seemed to mean yes or no.

She started to get out of bed, but her arm yanked to a stop. They'd handcuffed her to the bed rail. The handcuff rattle froze their conversation. They walked into her room and stared at her.

"The Ambien gave you a pleasant sleep," Hasham said.

"It gave me a nightmare!"

"Still you rested, and I need your brain well rested." He unlocked her handcuff.

She rubbed her wrist, then checked the bandage around her forearm incision where they removed her microchip implant. The bandage was clean and her arm seemed fine. But she wondered about infection.

"We've got coffee and Egg McMuffins in the kitchen," Hasham said.

They walked her into the small rustic kitchen and she poured herself a coffee. She sipped some. It tasted like tar. She bit into a cold Egg McMuffin. Maybe a day old.

The big man, Aarif, stared at her. Everything about him frightened her. His small black eyes and missing left ear creeped her out. No wonder he was in her nightmare. He looked at her like she was last week's garbage.

And she saw something else in his eyes – *he,* Aarif, would be the one who made sure she did not leave this cabin alive when her work was done. Some eyes can't hide evil intentions.

Hasham sipped coffee and read *DABIO,* an ISIS propaganda magazine she'd seen before. The cover showed machete-wielding jihadists praising Allah by beheading two kneeling orange-suited prisoners. She wondered how people's thinking got so warped and perverted? And whether she would soon join the beheaded?

"Time to work!" Hasham said.

He and Aarif walked her to the eight-foot floor section and they descended to the underground laboratory.

In the lab Hasham ushered her to the Hazmat suit-dressing chamber and pointed for her to put on a biohazard suit. She was relieved to see the suit was a new, fully encapsulated Tychem TK Deluxe. The Tychem would give her excellent, Level-A protection against biological and chemical agents up to Biohazard Level 4.

"Suit up. It's your size."

She started checking the suit for tiny holes or slits.

"The suit is safe. I checked it," he said.

"I always check my suits."

"You think I brought you here to poison you?"

"No, but my colleague missed a suit hole and died from Marburg days later."

Hasham shrugged. "Go ahead. Check it."

She did and found no holes or slits. She put it on. Hasham wore an identical suit.

He unlocked the airtight pressure door with a loud whoosh. He then led her into the bio-lab and over to rows of large round stainless steel canisters stored on racks. He turned a canister around and pointed to its label.

She read it and her blood stopped. Her worst fears were now confirmed.

"I see you recognize this product," Hasham said.

She nodded and feared the coming disaster.

"You've worked with it and its antidotes on several occasions."

He knew she had, so she nodded.

As Hasham showed her several more rows of the same gleaming canisters, she realized she had to get him talking so he'd reveal more details about his attack.

"You have so much. Where'd you get - ?"

"Allah provides for the righteous."

"With help from Iran?"

"Maybe. Or maybe from North Korea. Or Russia. Remember when Russia closed up its biological and chemical weapons factories and stopped paying the workers? Imagine Russians workers without vodka money! A crime against humanity! So we did the brotherly love thing. We kept their vodka flowing."

She said nothing.

"These weapons are also available right here in America, Doctor! Money buys information."

"Like what I do at Aberdeen?"

"Like that."

She couldn't think of a single colleague who would betray her. But an angry or fired employee might sell information. Or be coerced to, or be so pathologically deranged he would gladly slaughter a few thousand Americans for money or revenge.

Somehow, she had to stall Hasham, find a way to sabotage the weapon. Which meant she had to discover what his delivery system was. Which meant she had to work with him. Play along. Keep him talking.

"But how'd you get so many containers into the country?"

Hasham laughed. "Open your eyes, Doctor. America's borders are Swiss cheese. Lots of holes . . . like your 5,500 mile US-Canadian border. Some rural border crossings only have sensors."

"But those sensors work!"

"Not if we disable them. And your Mexican border is a joke. Forty *tons* of marijuana moved through just one tunnel last week! There are even underground railways."

She knew about the tunnels and railways.

"And an even bigger joke is sea containers! Fifteen million shipping containers arrive here by sea each year? Guess how many are thoroughly inspected?"

She waited.

"*Three percent*! That means *fourteen million* shipping containers are *not* inspected closely!"

"Why not?"

He smiled. "Could it be because many major US shipping ports are owned, controlled, and operated by Saudi and United Arab Emirates companies? Did you know that?"

She didn't and wondered if the containers she was looking at came thorough an Arab-controlled American port?

He led her over to another chamber and pointed to a rack stacked with smaller black steel canisters.

"You also know the product in these containers."

"They have no labels. What is it?"

"Let's call it medicine for Americans. You're going to help us combine the two."

"But why? You don't even need this mystery product to kill people. As you know, your weapon will cause excruciating pain and death in a few minutes."

"Quite true."

"So why the second mystery product? Dead is dead."

"All in good time, Doctor. All in good time."

Why was he not revealing the mystery product? Because it would suggest the weapon delivery system? Somehow she had to identify the mystery product. Knowing that might help her find a way to sabotage his attack.

"Oh by the way," Hasham said, "your precious little daughter, Mia, is just fine. My men are taking her into protective custody as we speak. I'll show you photos soon."

Nell stopped breathing.

ELEVEN

BEL AIR NORTH, MARYLAND

Amir Kareem focused his camera on the five-year-old blonde girl, Mia, playing in front of her grandmother's house with a younger neighbor boy.

Kareem sat in the driver's seat of a Maryland Gas and Electric van fifty yards down the street, skyping the video to Hasham Habib in the forest cabin.

"Where's the grandmother?" Hasham asked.

"Inside. But she keeps coming to the front door and checking on her granddaughter every few minutes."

"Where's the neighbor boy's mother?"

"A few feet away in her flower garden."

"When the boy goes home, grab the girl."

"Might be a while. No, wait - !"

"What?" Hasham said.

"The grandmother is taking the girl inside. The boy is walking back to his mother."

"Is Fadoul ready?"

"Yes."

"You're both wearing your MG&E uniforms?"

"Yes."

"Go now! Take the girl."

"What if the grandmother causes trouble?"

"Collateral damage."

TWELVE

After a few hours of restless sleep in the FBI lounges, Donovan, Drew Manning, Lindee, and Jacob met early the next morning in a conference room. Strong coffee and warm bagels welcomed them.

Donovan thought Lindee looked a little better this morning and hoped she'd remember something about Nell's abduction, something that might give them a solid lead.

"Lindee, you watched the two men force your sister into a white van."

She nodded.

"Can you try to visualize the van as it drove away?"

"Sure." She closed her eyes.

"Do you see the back of the van?"

"Yes . . ."

"Do you see the van's name?"

"No."

"What do you see?"

"The sun reflecting off the back window and something just above the left rear bumper. Something shiny and gold. It gleams in the sun."

"Gold letters?"

"No."

"Numbers?"

"No."

"A gold shape?"

"Yes."

"Shaped like what?"

She paused, blinked. "I don't know . . . shaped maybe like a . . . bowtie."

"A gold bowtie?"

"Yes."

Donovan had a thought. He sketched Chevrolet's somewhat bowtie-shaped logo and showed it to her.

"That's it!"

"Great, Lindee. Now, you said the last number on the license plate was a nine."

"Yes."

"As the van drives away, can you see the next number?"

Lindee closed her eyes. "Not well. It's curved at top . . . maybe an eight."

"Maybe we can find out later. You up for a short drive?"

She nodded.

THIRTEEN

"*There!*" Lindee said, pointing out the windshield.

Donovan didn't see what she was pointing at. "Where?"

"*LEATHER TRENDS.* The store Nell was looking into when the men took her . . . "

"Let's go inside," Donovan said, parking in a No-Parking zone and hanging his Government Permit on the mirror.

Earlier, when he'd suggested visiting the abduction scene, Lindee agreed. But now he worried the visit might trigger a painful flashback for her.

He learned that last year a man broke into Lindee's apartment, robbed her, beat her senseless and left her for dead. Nell found her and rushed her to the hospital where she was resuscitated twice. Back home, Lindee began a slow recovery and was still healing.

But Lindee was their best hope for some clue that led to Dr. Northam's abductors . . . and preventing what Donovan's gut now told him was an imminent attack on America. And based on

---

Dr. Northam's specific expertise . . . it would be an attack with a weapon of mass destruction. Why else would they abduct her?

The question was – how imminent was the attack?

They walked over to *LEATHER TRENDS*. Lindee stared at a spot in front of the store, then back at the street. She looked frightened as she pointed at the curb.

"That's where they pushed her into the van."

Donovan looked at the traffic. Horns honked. Airbrakes squealed. Trucks and cars roared away from the light. So much noise and activity, Nell could have been snatched without anyone noticing.

"Did the police interview all these shopkeepers?" Lindee asked.

"Yes. No one saw Nell get dragged into the van."

Donovan heard a car door shut behind him. He turned and saw two middle-aged men take suitcases from a SUV. They walked up to the *LEATHER TRENDS* door.

"Those might be the store owners. They were traveling yesterday," Donovan said. "Maybe their security camera saw something."

Lindee nodded.

"Excuse me, do you have a moment?" Donovan said.

"Sure," the taller man in his forties said, "Come on in. If you see something you like, just let me know."

"Actually, this is government business." Donovan flashed his CIA badge.

The man grew serious fast.

"Does your security camera face your display window and this sidewalk?"

"It shows the window and part of the sidewalk and curb. By the way, I'm Ted, and this is Randall, my partner."

"Nice to meet you both. This is Lindee Lindstrom. Her sister was abducted by two men as she looked in your store window."

"Good Lord!" Ted said.

Both men froze.

"We're so sorry," Randall said, adjusting horn-rimmed glasses.

"Police talked to your employee, Jennifer," Donovan said. "Jennifer said she saw someone fitting Nell's description looking in the window. But when your store phone rang, Jennifer turned around and answered it. When she turned back, Nell was gone. That's all Jennifer saw. She tried to get your security camera working for our agent, but it wouldn't work."

"It's hit and miss. But I'll try. We can also ask Jennifer if she remembers anything else."

Ted and Randall led them inside. Donovan breathed in the warm intoxicating scent of new leather. He saw a rainbow of stunning colors: beautiful purses, jackets, shoes, satchels, briefcases, luggage. Randall ushered them behind the counter to two security monitors.

Donovan suddenly stopped breathing as the scent of leather was overwhelmed by an odor he knew well.

The thick, coppery smell of *blood!*

"Oh my God!" Randall yelled from a back of the store.

Everyone turned toward him.

Ted hurried back.

Donovan and Lindee followed.

"Sweet Jesus, no . . .!" Ted whispered. *"Jennifer . . .!"*

Donovan looked down and saw a young woman in her early twenties, lying face down on floor, blood pooling around her right shoulder. He felt her neck, no pulse, but as he started to lift his fingers away, he detected something . . . a faint beat.

"She's *alive!* Call 911!"

Randall called as Ted grabbed some towels and placed them against the bleeding wound near her shoulder. "More towels," he said. Randall handed him a thick roll of paper towels.

Minutes later, an ambulance from nearby St. Luke's Hospital stopped in front. An EMS woman and man ran inside.

Donovan led them to the back room. The EMS woman checked Jennifer's vital signs.

"She's bled a lot!" she said. They lifted her onto the gurney, hurried her out into the ambulance and raced off.

Donovan called Agent Manning, explained what happened. Manning said he'd send his FBI CSI team over and coordinate with the NYPD.

Ted blinked moist eyes. "Jennifer is a wonderful person. An NYU senior. Handles the store when we travel."

"Has anything been stolen?" Donovan asked.

The two men scanned the back area, then the front.

"At first glance, no."

"This wasn't a robbery," Donovan said. "She was targeted. The men who grabbed Dr. Northam are responsible for this. I think they saw Jennifer on the phone. They feared she was calling the police and could identify them and their van."

He turned to Randall "Could we see the video facing the sidewalk?"

"Sure." Randall pushed a button on the video console. Snowy screen, followed by more snow. He fast-forwarded again. Snow . . . snow . . . snow . . .

"Someone deleted this video."

"What about the in-store video?"

He checked the other monitor and shook his head.

"Deleted."

"Do you have backups?"

"No, sorry." He shook his head. "Oh wait – maybe Jennifer saved it in the Cloud." He tapped in a security password, and seconds later, the video popped on showing the front window and part of the sidewalk.

Donovan eased the air from his lungs. "What time was your sister taken?"

"Around 1:20 in the afternoon."

Randall fast-forwarded to 1:18 and hit *Play*.

The video flickered, then showed the sidewalk, the curb and some street.

Donovan watched Nell Northam walk up and look in the window. Behind her, a red Malibu drove by, then a vegetable truck, two Yellow Cabs. No white vans. Seconds later, a Staples truck and a cab went by.

Nell then turned and said something to Lindee two stores down.

"That's when Nell told me she saw a Michael Kors purse she loved in here."

Donovan saw a flash of white fender. A van. It crawled to a stop behind her. He saw the gold Chevy logo on the wheels.

The van door slid open. Two men, one big, one small, stepped onto the sidewalk. The camera angle only showed them from the chest down. They walked calmly toward the store. Nell did not see them coming.

"Look," Ted said, "Jennifer's turning around to answer our store phone."

The two men walked up and grabbed Nell from behind. The big man put one hand over her mouth, the other arm around her waist. The short man stared in the store window at Jennifer on the phone. He looked alarmed that she was calling 911. Then he and the big man hurried Nell into the van and drove away. It was all over in ten seconds. The license plate was blocked by a bus.

Donovan said, "Can you make a copy of this?"

"I'll email you a copy now."

Donovan handed him his email address.

Lindee walked over to the window and looked at the store window.

Donovan walked over and saw something was bothering her. Her eyes filled with tears.

"You okay?"

She nodded. "Nell was standing outside and grabbed right there. Now Jennifer has been shot. It's just too much . . ."

"Look!" Randall said, pointing at the video. "I recognized something on the van's rear bumper."

He pushed *Play*. They watched the van pull away from the curb. He hit *SLOW-MO* and the van crept forward, frame by frame.

"See - that blurry yellow, red, blue, and white bumper sticker."

Donovan nodded. "I've seen that logo somewhere."

"I've seen it right here!" Randall said, reaching under the counter and pulling out a baseball hat with a NASCAR logo.

FOURTEEN

BEL AIR NORTH, MARYLAND

" *What?* You haven't grabbed the child yet?" Hasham shouted at Kareem over the phone.

Kareem froze, knowing Hasham hated excuses. "We tried. But the lady next door kept talking to the grandmother. Then the lady left, and these two Jehovah Witness guys walk up. They're still showing stuff to the grandmother."

"When they leave, take the girl! Fast!" Hasham said, hanging up.

Kareem exhaled, relieved Hasham didn't go ballistic as usual.

"What did Hasham say?" Fadoul, his partner, asked.

"He said when the Jehovah guys leave, we take the girl."

"Take her picture. I got the camera."

"No. Hasham wants her picture *and* the girl."

"Why?"

"More leverage with her mom, Doctor Northam."

Fadoul shook his head. "I don't like grabbing and scaring little kids."

"I don't like disobeying Hasham. People who do, disappear!"

Fadoul cursed and began fingering his Arab *misbahah* worry beads.

Kareem looked at Fadoul's uniform. "Button your shirt! We gotta look like *real* Maryland Gas and Electric guys."

Fadoul buttoned his shirt.

"Remember," Kareem said, "we tell the grandmother we're here to check the gas leak near her house."

"She'll say she don't smell no gas . . ."

"We say that's the problem! This gas doesn't have enough rotten-egg smell. It's real dangerous. We're here to fix it . . . prevent an explosion, save her life."

Fadoul frowned. "I hate waiting around. Why don't we just go tell the Jehovah guys to take off! Say we got a serious gas problem here!"

"Are you crazy? Let them see our faces. Testify against us later?"

Fadoul cursed, opened the window and spit out a gob of green khat, dribbling some down onto his shirt.

"Look!" Kareem said.

"What?"

"The Jehovah guys are leaving."

"Let's go."

Kareem and Fadoul flicked their Beretta safeties off, stepped from their Maryland Gas and Electric van, and walked toward the house.

* * *

Donovan marveled at Ginny Beauregard, an attractive young video wizard, as she magically enhanced the security tape from the LEATHER TRENDS store. They sat in an FBI's visual-tech center with Agent Manning, Lindee, and Jacob.

"Got 'em!" Ginny said. "The computer just nailed the words on the side of the Chevy van!"

"What are they?" Manning asked.

"*American Transit*," she said. "The computer also confirmed the NASCAR bumper sticker and that the last three license plate numbers are six-eight-nine."

"This helps a ton, Ginny. Thanks," Donovan said.

Manning grabbed his ringing phone, listened, and hung up. "We just eliminated twenty-two more white Chevy vans. Mostly plumbers, electricians, florists, painters, AC guys."

Donovan's phone rang and he saw it was a fellow CIA Agent, Lonnie Laker.

"What's up, Lonnie?" Donovan punched the speaker button.

"We're driving to Jacob Northam's mother's house to guard Nell's daughter. But Google shows her house is surrounded by thick forest in back."

Jacob Northam nodded. "The forest comes right to mom's back door."

"Perfect for breaking in unseen," Laker said.

"I'll send an FBI team over now!" Manning said.

"How far away are you from her house?"

"Maybe fifteen minutes. But we got a problem."

"What?

"Tractor trailer-car accident ahead on 95. Traffic is already backing up."

"Can you exit?"

"Yeah. In two miles."

"Drive down the shoulder!"

"I am."

"Drive faster!" Manning said, hanging up.

Donovan's phone rang instantly. A fellow CIA agent. He hit the speaker button.

"What's up Dirk?"

"Good lead maybe. A police officer in upstate New York saw a white Chevy van pull out of a rest area. Ten minutes later, he saw our bulletin. This sounds good, Donovan. He's on my line. I'm connecting you. Go ahead . . ."

"You there Officer?" Donovan asked.

"Yes."

"Were there three dark-skinned men in the van?"

"Yes."

"Woman in back?"

"Yep, slouched down."

"What was she wearing?"

Pause. "I saw a white blouse and something red around her neck. Maybe a scarf."

Lindee jumped to her feet. *"That's her!"*

"Did you see writing on the side of the van?"

"No. I only saw back of the van."

"Did you notice a sticker on the left rear bumper?"

"Yeah. A racing sticker. Maybe Holley or AC Delco. No wait – it was red, blue, white . . . like NASCAR I think."

Donovan's heart jackhammered. "Where'd you see the van?"

"Upstate New York. Between the towns of Gloversville and Mayfield. Near the Adirondack Park."

"Heading which direction?"

"Toward the Park."

"Alert all police in the area. We'll move additional agents there now," Manning said.

They hung up.

"This feels solid," Donovan said. "But there's a problem."

"What?" Jacob said.

"The Adirondack forest."

"Why?"

"It's *six million* square miles of trees."

"You could hide Rhode Island in there," Manning said.

FIFTEEN

Fifty feet beneath the Adirondack forest, Nell adjusted her HazMat suit as she hunched over the Meiji MT 6000 fluorescent microscope. The Meiji was state-of-the-art, like every piece of lab equipment surrounding her. Clearly, Hasham had vast financial backing.

Enough to acquire his massive amount of weaponized nerve agent . . . capable of killing hundreds of thousands of people in minutes.

The question was *how* would he deliver the deadly VX to his intended victims? *How* was the key. She had to find out.

"I assume you're dispersing VX by air?"

Hasham said nothing.

"Or VX in water?"

He shrugged.

"VX in food?"

Another shrug.

"How can I assist you if I don't know your delivery system?"

"Not your concern, Doctor. But perhaps later I'll share my ingeniously unique system with you."

"What's so unique about it?"

"Everything. It's unlike any delivery system ever considered for this weapon. No one at Aberdeen, or Fort Detrick, or any other government, would ever envision it. Not in their wildest dreams!" He puffed up with pride.

She sensed he wanted to brag more, but probably feared she might somehow find a way to tell authorities.

"Unlike *any* delivery system?" she said. "That's very hard to believe."

"Why?"

"Because *many* VX delivery systems have already been tested."

"Trust me. *Never,* ever, anything like this!"

Which terrified her, because he seemed to be telling the truth. So even if she found a way to tell authorities he was using VX gas – she couldn't tell them *how* he would attack with it . . .

. . . or *who* the victims would be . . .

. . . or *when* he would strike . . .

. . . or *where* . . .

But why, she wondered, would he use a new *untested* delivery system? It made no sense . . . unless he positively *knew* it would work . . . and *knew* the authorities would not expect it . . . and *knew* they couldn't stop it once he launched it.

All terrifying possibilities.

Or . . . was Hasham flat out lying to her? Would he use a proven, regular VX delivery system?

Two hours earlier, Hasham had forced her to start blending his mystery substance into the VX nerve gas, following his exacting mix ratios and tolerances. The blending required intense concentration and her specific experience.

Knowing the identity of the mystery substance might reveal how he'd attack.

But how could she warn authorities? The cabin's two doors were key-locked from the inside and the men carried all keys and phones in their pockets.

She watched him check her work every few seconds. How did he learn about her highly classified work at Aberdeen? That information only existed on Aberdeen's closed *InTRAnet,* an *Air-Gap* system physically separated from the Internet. Information about her work could not be obtained through the Internet.

But if a seventeen-year-old Ukrainian kid compromised fifty million Target credit cards, and someone cracked into Home Depot's and J.P. Morgan's customer bases, and North Korea cracked into Sony's internal systems, and Russian hackers broke into the Democratic party files, maybe someone circumvented Aberdeen's *Air-Gap* system and pulled her personal information from Human Resources files.

Or did someone at work betray her? She'd worked well with her co-workers. Minor disagreements on occasion. On the other hand, people told her she was far too trusting. Maybe she was. Three months ago, she told a colleague her idea for a more efficient process for producing an antidote. A week later, he presented some of her work as his. Fortunately, their supervisor knew it was her work and demoted the guy. Was he so angry he betrayed her to these terrorists?

She glanced at some file folders, as Hasham placed them on his lab bench. The file labels indicated biological agents and chemical weapons. Clearly, the man had solid scientific credentials. He was confident and relaxed in the lab, and obviously familiar with the weaponization of a wide range of lethal agents.

And his knowledge of weapon delivery systems and corresponding kill rates proved he'd worked extensively in biochemical and nerve agent weapon systems. His accent suggested schooling in England.

"How's the blending?" he said.

She had to stall him. "The blend consistency is not quite right. It's taking longer."

"You will finish by this evening."

"But it's - "

" - *this evening,* Doctor! By 8 p.m.*"

She had to slow the process, find some way to sabotage the blending process.

"I can't promise - "

"*I* can promise that your daughter Mia will fetch a handsome price from my rich sheik friend. He's seen her photo and is already quite smitten with her lovely blue eyes."

Nell's stomach churned.

"But I have no proof you have her."

He stared back.

"I want proof of life. I must see her. How else can I know?"

"You doubt me?"

"Yes! Until I see her!"

"You doubt she's in good hands?"

"I must *see* her!"

Grinning, he took out his iPhone and seconds later, she was looking at a video of Mia sitting on the couch in her mother-in-law's house. Mia looked terrified. Beside her, a masked man beside held a large curved knife.

Nell's eyes flooded with tears.

"As you can see, Doctor, she's in excellent hands. Not to worry."

Nell couldn't speak. She bent over the microscope. A tear spilled onto the lens, blurring her vision. She had to blend the weapon, but also stall a bit, claiming she didn't know why the blending process was proving so complicated.

Would Hasham believe her? Probably not. The problem was he was always close by, watching her, checking the blending process, learning how she did it. And he was smart enough to know when she was doing something incorrectly.

"This doesn't seem to be working right," she said. "Our blend equations are not - "

His dark eyes flashed anger.

"Make it right! Oh, by the way, I forgot to mention something."

She waited.

"The sheik is a very religious man. But also a very strict traditionalist. You know what that means . . .?"

She didn't want to know.

"It means Mia must be circumcised."

Nell's heart stopped.

"No big deal. Just your basic female genital surgery. After all, we can't have Mia seeking carnal pleasures with anyone but the sheik when she matures. You understand, of course."

Nell felt like she might pass out.

Mia would be gone forever . . . she would be circumcised, maybe with an old rusty knife and without anesthesia like millions of young girls worldwide are butchered each year, some only weeks old.

Perspiration ran down her face despite the air-conditioned bio suit.

Will I ever see my daughter again?

* * *

BEL AIR NORTH, MARYLAND

Special CIA Agent Lonnie Laker grew worried when he saw a Maryland Gas & Electric van in front of Nell Northam's mother-in-law's home. He pointed out the van to his partner, Agent Young.

"Check if MG&E has a service call at Mrs. Northam's house."

Agent Young phoned his MG&E contact, and moments later looked at Laker. "No gas or electric service on this street this week!"

Laker nodded. "Where's our FBI backup team?"

"Stuck in Route 1 traffic. Ten minutes away!"

"We can't wait!" Laker said.

"Agreed."

Both men checked their Glocks, and hurried quickly toward the house. Laker moved up the side drive, paused at a window and peeked between the blinds. He froze at what he saw.

An armed man in a MG&E uniform stood beside Mrs. Northam who looked panicked. The man was shooting iPhone video of something across the room.

Laker leaned left and saw little Mia tied to a chair. Her eyes were red from crying. Beside her, a guy held a large curved dagger. Mia looked terrified.

Is he about to behead her?

Laker considered shooting the man through the window, but feared the guy's dagger reflex could severely injure Mia. Laker and Young hurried to the rear of the house and saw a Dutch door. The top half was unhinged. Laker eased the top open, reached in, unlocked the door. They stepped into the empty kitchen, moved down a long hall and on a three count, burst into the living room.

"FBI! Hands up!" Laker shouted.

The shocked men spun around toward them. The guy beside Mrs. Northam started to raise his hands, then yanked out a gun.

Laker's bullets ripped into the guy's eye and neck. He slumped to the floor and did not move.

The man beside Mia threw his dagger at Agent Young – but missed as Young's shoulder crushed into his chest and slammed him down hard on the wood floor. The man gasped for breath as Young grabbed his gun and cuffed him.

"You're both safe now, Mrs. Northam," Laker said, untying her hands.

She hurried over and pulled Mia into her arms.

"Our agents will take you both to a secure location, ma'am."

Mrs. Northam nodded, looking stunned. She rocked Mia in her arms until Mia's sniffling quieted.

Laker leaned close to the cuffed man. "Guess what, asshole?"

The man said nothing.

"It's come-to-Allah-time."

SIXTEEN

Donovan grew more frustrated with each minute in the stuffy FBI conference room. He sat with Agent Manning, Lindee, and Jacob, waiting for word of the white van with three black-suited men and a woman, and "American Transit" on its door.

All reports of vans with the word "Transit" were automatically forwarded to the conference room. So far they'd eliminated thirteen "Transit" labeled white vans.

Manning's phone rang and he hit the speaker button. "White Chevy van," the caller said. "Three men wearing black, plus a woman in back. Word *Transit* on the door."

"What are the exact words?"

"*MASS Transit.*"

"Mass?"

"Yes."

"Who's inside?"

"Three priests and a nun."

Everyone smiled and relaxed a bit.

Manning's phone rang again and he hit speaker.

"White Chevy van near the Adirondacks, heading north on Highway 9. Three men and a woman."

Donovan hoped this was their best lead from earlier. "Where's Highway 9 go?"

"Up to Canada."

"Are Canadian customs alerted?"

"Yes."

"She can't enter Canada," Jacob said. "Her passport's at home."

"Good. Does the van have Transit signage or a NASCAR sticker?"

"Too far away to see."

"Stop and check the van anyway."

They hung up.

A young female FBI agent hurried into the room. When Donovan saw her face, he prepared himself for bad news.

"What's up, Ann?" Manning asked her.

She paused like she didn't want to tell him. "A white Chevy van near the Adirondacks Park. Three men and a woman inside . . ."

She took a deep breath.

"The van ran a stop sign. An oil tanker slammed into it."

"And . . .?"

"All passengers were pronounced dead at the scene."

SEVENTEEN

"When the blended weapon is ready, how will you test it?" Nell asked Hasham.

"Follow me."

He led her to a metal door at the end of the laboratory. He unlocked it and took her inside a large room. LED bulbs flooded the room with brilliant light. She smelled animals, then saw them trapped in cages: monkeys, cats, and farther back some puppies and two big golden labs. The puppies begged for attention and she reached in and petted them.

He led her to the golden labs who hurried over, wagging their tails.

"These two will tell us if your blended formula works tonight. Their weight is sufficient for human extrapolation testing."

"Please don't poison them. I promise it will work."

"You expect me to accept your word? An *infidel?*"

"Yes."

"Impossible!"

"But - "

"We'll test it on *them*!" He walked away.

She wanted to test it on *him!*

"But right now, you're going for a ride."

"What? Where?"

"It's a surprise."

She grew worried fast. Was it a Tony Soprano one-way ride? It made sense. Hasham now had virtually all her expertise incorporated into the weapon. He could probably finish up the last bit of blending tonight now that he'd seen how she did it. He didn't really need her any more.

Hasham led her upstairs. She saw Aarif walking toward her with a strip of cloth. He blindfolded her, led her outside, pushed her into the back of the van and sat beside her, engulfing her in his *eau de garlic*. Hasham and the driver sat in front. They drove at highway speed for about ten minutes then entered what sounded like a town. She heard a church bell and stop and go traffic.

They pulled into a garage, and the door thudded shut. "Stay in the car!" Hasham said to her, as he got out. Aarif stayed beside her.

Beneath her blindfold she saw two men start loading several large heavy metal boxes into a black Suburban. She wondered what was in the boxes?

After the boxes were loaded, Hasham got back in the van and they drove off. But she noticed the Suburban took a different road.

"Now where?" she asked Hasham.

"The cabin. You have work to finish."

"So why bring me here?"

"You know why."

She did know why. He feared she'd try to sabotage the weapon if they left her alone. And he was right. But how could she? She couldn't even get down to the underground laboratory without Hasham's thumbprint. Or he feared she'd try to escape. Again how?

The windows were nailed shut and covered with thick wire. The doors were double-locked.

Back at the cabin, Hasham returned her to the laboratory.

"Finish by eight!" he said.

"How will I know it's eight? You took my watch."

He frowned, walked over to a desk drawer, unlocked it, took out her watch, Jacob's anniversary gift, and handed it to her. She put the watch on and it felt wonderful, almost like being with Jacob.

As they continued working, her mind kept flashing to the photo of her daughter Mia beside a man with a long curved knife. Mia looked absolutely terrified. And where was Dorothy, her mother-in-law? Had they hurt her? Had they hurt her in front of Mia? Please no . . .

Nell took a deep breath and exhaled. How did it all come down to this? How did her happy normal life turn into this horrific nightmare?

Jacob had begged her to find safer work. *But no – I convinced him, and myself, that I was safe, even though I worked with deadly toxins. And because I brainwashed myself, I'm now in a situation where I'll very likely lose my life, along with thousands of innocent people.*

She pictured their safe, cozy home near Aberdeen . . . Mia and Jacob playing SpongeBob games on the living room carpet after dinner. Mia and Jacob. Her reasons for surviving.

But will I ever see them again? Highly unlikely. She'd seen Hasham and Aarif's faces. They'd make sure she never got the chance to identify them.

Mia would grow up without her. Without Jacob. Instead, she'd probably grow up with a sheik who'll circumcise her and worse.

Or maybe she wouldn't grow up. Maybe Mia's acute lymphoblastic leukemia that nearly ended her life three years ago would relapse. The blood cancer could likely relapse without careful monitoring at a top-notch cancer center . . . the kind not likely available in a desert where the sheik likely lived.

Mia's cancer, untreated, would kill her.

Nell leaned against the lab bench, feeling nauseated and defeated. She hated her choice: save her daughter - or help Hasham kill thousands of innocent people.

Then a solution crept into her mind.

A deadly solution.

EIGHTEEN

Donovan saw his assistant calling in and punched the speaker button.

"What's up?" Donovan asked.

"We just got an update on that white Chevy van that crashed near the Adirondacks, killing three men and a woman . . ."

The room hushed.

"Everyone was over eighty. Bingo group."

Sighs of relief flowed across the conference table followed by moments of sympathy for the deceased seniors.

His phone rang again. It was Agent Lonnie Laker calling in.

He punched the speaker button again.

"What's up Lonnie?"

"Close call at Mrs. Northam's house."

Jacob Northam jumped up. "Are my daughter and mom -?"

" - they're both fine. But two terrorists who entered her house are not. One's dead. The other's in custody."

"Who are they?" Donovan asked.

"The deceased is Fadoul Khalof. The other guy is Amir Kareem. We're interrogating Kareem now."

"Enhance him!" Donovan said. "Find out *how* and *when* the attack is coming. And where Nell is!"

"We're already enhancing him."

Donovan knew Agent Laker had spent years interrogating terrorists at CIA black sites in the Middle East. His enhanced interrogations had helped prevent explosions in a New York subway, a Brussels mall, an Amsterdam kosher restaurant, and two Catholic churches in Paris. Conservative estimates suggested his interrogations had saved hundreds, maybe thousands of lives.

Donovan had no qualms about using enhanced interrogation of a terrorist who had information about an imminent attack upon innocent people.

Donovan remembered the day years ago when he learned that lesson . . . the day he'd captured an Al Qaeda terrorist who knew where a major bomb would explode in Baghdad within the next five hours. The terrorist refused to talk. Donovan requested permission to use enhanced interrogation. His boss in DC denied permission, citing "serious negative congressional reaction and grave political ramifications." Donovan cited several innocent deaths and grave injuries if they didn't enhance him. But permission was denied again. Four hours later, the bomb exploded in a grade school near Baghdad's Green Zone, killing sixteen children, ages six to eleven, and four teachers. When Donovan returned to DC he tossed the sickening photos of the sixteen bloody mutilated children's bodies on his boss's desk, and said "these kids' deaths are on you!" Then he stormed out.

Donovan never forgave himself for not enhancing the terrorist.

These days, he didn't ask permission.

* * *

In the cold dark interrogation chamber, Agent Lonnie Laker got in Amir Kareem's face. Kareem's boxer shorts were already drenched from two waterboarding sessions. The air conditioning was cranked down to fifty-six and a fan blew icy air onto him.

Kareem was shivering, but not talking. He was obviously trained to tolerate waterboarding, like Sheik Mohammad, the 9-11 planner. Mohammad had endured one hundred eighty waterboarding sessions without talking. What finally made him talk? Seven straight days and nights without *sleep*. Sleep-deprived brains will talk.

And Sheik Mohammad talked, saving hundreds of lives.

But Lonnie Laker didn't have seven days and nights. He had hours. Minutes maybe. He needed answers now.

"I want a lawyer."

"No lawyer! You're an enemy combatant."

"I'm a student!"

"With a fake visa!"

Kareem said nothing.

"What are Dr. Northam's abductors planning? When are they attacking? How? Where?"

Kareem looked away.

"Where is Dr. Northam being held?"

Kareem's mouth bent in a sneer.

Laker wanted to smash his fist into it. Instead, he nodded to two fellow agents. They tilted Kareem's chair back so his head was lower than his feet. Blood rushed to his head.

Another agent placed the white towel over his face and began pouring water into the towel, slowly . . . then faster and faster.

Kareem's body fought the sense of drowning. He tried to twist his head, but the head strap locked it in place. His arms jerked against their leather straps. His carotid arteries bulged fat as computer cables.

Water spilled into his nose and mouth.

They lifted his chair back up.

"Talk Kareem!"

He hacked and sputtered, "I know . . . nothing . . ."

They tilted him back again and poured *much* more water . . . drenching his face, chest, stomach. His lizard brain screamed that he was drowning, but he was obviously trained to ignore the feeling. He bucked like a wild horse.

Laker hoped the man didn't pass out. Or worse, stroke out. Kareem had answers they needed now.

But clearly this approach was not working.

Laker stopped the session. Time to crank up the pressure.

"Okay, Kareem. New rules. Listen real close"

Kareem seemed to catch the hardness in his tone.

Laker leaned in inches from Kareem's eyes. "The new rules are simple. Talk . . . or your ISIS friends will learn the truth about your wife."

Kareem's eyes shot open. "What truth?"

"She's been giving the CIA important information about ISIS and Al Qaeda for a year."

"That's a *lie!*"

"Not if we prove it's true."

Kareem looked panicked.

"You know what happens then?"

Kareem said nothing.

"What happens then is that ISIS will grab your wife and two sons. Then sadly, they'll torture them to find out what she told the CIA. She'll deny it. But they won't believe her. And then she and your sons will likely be tortured and killed. You know it. I know it. Do I want to do this? Of course not. But you give me no other choice. Their deaths will be on you, Kareem! On *you*! Do you understand?"

Kareem looked terrified. "You won't do this . . ."

"I've done it before," Laker lied. "And I'll do it again. What's killing three of yours if you're killing thousands of ours?"

Kareem stared back, enraged.

"Then finally, Kareem, we'll set *you* free and tell ISIS that you told us everything. That you gave us names. Addresses. Then we'll tell them where to find you."

Kareem looked panicked.

"You would not do all this."

"I have and I will," he lied again. "So talk to me."

Kareem said nothing.

Laker nodded to his agents and said . . . *"Niagara Falls!"*

The agents dumped three consecutive buckets of ice water over Kareem's nose and mouth . . . heavy non-stop flowing water. Seconds later, Kareem coughed hard and vomited into a bucket.

"O. . .kay . . . Stop! . . . I . . . talk." He gasped for breath. "Must . . . rest . . . a minute."

They sat him upright.

"You've got three minutes to rest. Then you talk. If the sensors in this chair detect you're lying, your wife and family will be running for their lives. It's all up to you, Kareem. Understand?"

Kareem paused.

"Tafahhum, Kareem?"

Kareem looked surprised that Laker had used the Arabic word for understand.

"Yes. I understand."

An agent cuffed his hands in front and chained his ankles to the chair. Laker and the others left the room to let Kareem stew over what he'd say.

In an adjoining room, Agent Laker looked through a small window. Kareem sat shivering, dejected, his head in his hands, obviously pondering his fate.

Laker walked over to a desk, sat down and wrote three questions he'd ask Kareem.

When? . . . Where? . . . How?

NINETEEN

Nell Northam and Hasham left the underground laboratory, stepped on the elevator floor and headed back up to the cabin. She watched him dab his left nostril with another fresh linen handkerchief, one of many stored in each room of the cottage.

"Deviated septum?" she asked.

He paused, then nodded.

"I know a surgeon who can fix that."

"So do I."

"So why don't you - ?"

" - I don't want it fixed."

Puzzled by his answer, she asked, "Why not?"

He paused as though considering whether to bother responding.

"I received this injury from the US missile that killed my wife and daughter."

She paused. "I'm very sorry . . ."

"Too late."

She said nothing.

"The injury reminds me of their ultimate sacrifice."

She nodded.

"It also reminds me of my ultimate goal."

"What's that?"

"*Al-Thar!*"

"What's Al - ?"

"- *Revenge*! You know, like our successful 9/11 attack!"

The elevator clicked to a stop at the cabin level. They walked into the living room area where she saw Aarif cleaning an assault rifle that looked like the AK-47s she'd seen at Fort Detrick.

On the table beside him, she saw two handguns, a small automatic submachine gun, and two Uzi-like weapons. Aarif cleaned his guns often, and when done, locked them in a cabinet. His handgun never left his shoulder holster. He probably slept with it.

"Go to your room," Hasham said to her. "In one hour we'll continue our lab work."

Your lab work, she wanted to shout at him.

She walked into her room and sat on the cot. She knew Hasham brought her upstairs because he feared she'd try to find a way to sabotage the weapon. He was right. She *had* to try, because once the weapon was released, there was little anyone could do to prevent thousands of deaths.

Thump . . . Thump . . .

She realized someone just knocked on the cabin door.

My rescuers!

No . . . they wouldn't knock! They'd toss stun grenades and charge in!

She saw Hasham and Aarif draw their guns, stand up and stare at the door, clearly not expecting visitors. Aarif peeked through a window curtain, looking puzzled by what he saw. He waved Hasham over for a look.

Thump . . . softer.

Hasham walked over and looked out the window. His expression did not change.

"Help . . ." A man's voice . . . weak . . . in obvious pain.

Fingernails scraped the door.

Hasham nodded to Aarif.

Aarif holstered his gun, then opened the door.

A middle-aged man in an orange hunter's jacket stumbled inside holding his right arm. Nell saw his right hand was blue and red, and swollen twice as big as his left hand.

"Timber Rattler bit me. My phone's in my truck three miles back. Could you please call nine-one-one . . ."

"Sure," Hasham said, "Here, sit and rest. We'll call for help."

Aarif helped him into the chair.

Nell knew Hasham would not call nine-one-one.

The man's face was flushed, but he seemed fairly calm despite the injury.

Then he noticed Aarif's collection of assault weapons and guns. The man looked concerned by the guns, especially the AK-47 and Uzis.

Hasham and Aarif noticed him staring at the guns. Staring too long. Growing alarmed.

"Just close your eyes, relax, rest . . ." Hasham said. He nodded at Aarif.

Aarif stepped behind the man. Then he pulled the hunter's head back and slashed his neck from ear to ear with a curved dagger.

The man's eyes shot open as his severed arteries pumped streams of blood onto his orange jacket and the cabin floor.

Crushed with sadness, Nell collapsed back on her bed and wept for the poor man.

★ ★ ★

Agent Lonnie Laker sat at his desk preparing to question Amir Kareem in one minute.

Laker needed answers. Now. And he sensed Kareem had them. Like when and where and how the attack would come. But Laker needed a bit more leverage with the terrorist. He phoned a fellow agent.

"Monte, did you get photos of Kareem's wife and kids? I want Kareem to *see* we will involve them if he doesn't talk."

"They should be in your email in-box now."

"Great."

They hung up.

Laker heard a strange sound . . . coming from the interrogation room. Scraping sounds. Probably Kareem scooting his chair away from the fan blowing icy air on him. To check, Laker got up, walked down to the window and looked in.

Kareem had scooted his chair a few inches, and he was shivering.

As Laker started to turn away, he noticed Kareem moving his face down toward his bound hands. No way he could chew through his flex ties. Then Kareem started using his teeth to apparently scratch a forearm itch.

Laker soon realized Kareem was scratching *too hard.*

Kareem was *biting* into his skin . . . biting hard, sending blood down his forearm.

He's *digging* for something!

"*SHIT!*" Laker shouted as he and his assistant ran into the room and raced over to Kareem.

Laker's assistant, John, gripped Kareem's head, as Laker tried to pry open Kareem's mouth and dig out what was in there. But the man's jaw was locked tight.

Then Laker heard and felt a crack. Kareem had bitten down on the something hard, a capsule, breaking it, releasing its contents.

Laker watched as Kareem swallowed everything in his mouth, then closed his eyes.

Kareem began gasping, his body convulsed, his eyes rolled, his face went beet-red and frothy saliva spilled from his mouth and nose. He slumped over, eyes fixed, staring at nothing.

Two minutes later, the department nurse hurried into the room. She checked his vitals, then slowly looked up at Laker.

She shook her head. "He's gone . . ."

Laker whispered, "So are our chances of learning about the attack."

TWENTY

No news is bad news kept racing through Donovan's mind as he and the others sat waiting for an update on their best van lead. A van that vanished near the Adirondacks.

They'd also waited for news from Agent Lonnie Laker's interrogation of Kareem, the terrorist. The enhanced interrogation should have produced some information by now.

Donovan sipped his coffee, saw Laker calling in and pressed the speaker button.

"Did Kareem talk?" Donovan asked.

"No, he -"

" - *push him harder*!"

"He's dead."

"What?" Donovan felt like he'd been punched in the gut.

Agent Laker explained how Kareem bit into the cyanide capsule he'd gnawed out of his arm and died seconds later.

Donovan slumped in his chair. "Check his phone and Internet contacts. Get names!"

"We're already on it."

They hung up.

Donovan's fellow agent, Kate Kearns, hurried into the room, looking upbeat.

"What you got, Kate?"

"The right van, I think."

"Where?"

"State Route 30. Near the Adirondacks, around the Mayfield area. A truck driver heard our police BOLO. He saw a white Chevy van pass him with three dark-skinned guys. A woman in back. She wore something red around her neck."

"A *scarf?*" Lindee said.

"Maybe."

"Did he see American Transit on the side of the van?"

"No. He didn't see the sides."

"Any stickers on the rear bumper?"

"Yes. NASCAR!"

Donovan's pulse kicked up.

"When?"

"An hour ago."

"Gotta be the van!" Manning said.

"Dragnet that area and find it!" Donovan said.

"How far is Mayfield?" Jacob Northam asked.

"About one hundred and ninety miles," Manning said.

Donovan sensed what Jacob wanted to do. "I'm going up there!" Jacob said.

Donovan and Manning looked at each other.

"Jacob," Donovan said, "it's safer to let our FBI hostage rescue teams handle this. They're experts!"

"I agree. I just want to be in the area when you rescue Nell."

"Me, too," Lindee said.

Manning looked concerned. "Lindee, these jihadists kill people on sight!"

"But Nell rescued me last summer. She saved my life. Now it's my turn."

"But we can't justify taking you up there," Manning said.

"Sure you can," Lindee said.

Manning looked puzzled. "How?"

"It's simple. I'm the only one who actually *saw* the two men abduct her. I'm your only eyewitness. I can identify them."

Lindee's right, Donovan realized. And identifying them fast could save lives.

Donovan also realized that Jacob would probably drive Lindee up there anyway. They'd wander around. If this situation got dangerous fast, as it undoubtedly would, Lindee and Jacob on their own could get hurt, or worse. It might be safer to keep them close by - under FBI team protection – instead of worrying about them.

Donovan nodded at Manning.

"You'll have to follow our safety instructions," Manning said.

They both nodded.

The extra responsibility felt like bags of cement had dropped on Donovan's shoulders.

TWENTY ONE

SANA'A, YEMEN

Bassam Maahdi dripped like a leaky faucet as he hustled his sweaty three hundred thirty pounds through the 105-degree heat rolling past the Sana'a Mountains. He knew his fellow jihadists marveled that a man of his bulk could walk with such agility and sprightliness - and even more amazed he could walk past western intelligence agents without ever being detected. It was a learned talent. He was a very cautious man.

He scanned the crowded noisy souk and saw no one following him. The scent of *Ali's* delicious garlic-lamb stew wafted into his nostrils and even though he'd just gobbled down a six-course lunch, he signaled Ali for a two-kilo carton of stew to tide him over until dinner. He paid, grabbed the carton, and walked on.

A hundred feet later, he stepped inside his shop, *Halabi's Rare Religious Books,* near Old Sana'a University. The air conditioning felt like manna from Allah. He saw his clerk, Daood the Dwarf, stacking eighteenth-century Korans that swirled dust bunnies into the afternoon sunlight. Daood was his aunt's three-foot-six illegitimate son, and a nasty little cross-dressing pervert.

Maahdi walked through hanging red glass beads into a small room and descended the circular stairwell to his secret underground level. He placed his thumb on the wall panel, the door clicked open, and he entered his private inner sanctum, eighteen feet underground, safe from drones and US bunker-buster bombs, and Daood the Nosy Dwarf.

He grabbed his expensive *safe* phone, but still worried that the NSA's new technology could maybe listen in.

He also worried that the NSA paid too much attention to Yemen – and sometimes to *him*. Of course, with him they wasted time chasing his six aliases.

He dialed the only number the phone called.

"Hello . . .?" Hasham Habib answered, seven thousand miles away in the Adirondack cabin.

Maahdi remembered years ago transferring the money to build Hasham's sophisticated subterranean forest laboratory.

"Hello, Mr. Smith," Bassam said.

"Ah, Mr. Jones, you sound well?" Hasham said.

"Quite well, actually. Having a delicious lunch," Maahdi said, as he swallowed some lamb stew, sweat dripping from his chins.

"That's good to hear. How can I help you?"

"Just wondering how our medical supplies are coming along?"

"Everything's right on schedule," Hasham said.

"Excellent. So you'll deliver them to the assembly facility tomorrow?"

"Tonight actually."

"Even better. And is our assembly facility fully functional and prepared?"

"Fully functional and fully prepared."

"Well done. Where is it located?"

"Small town near the park."

"Well, our friends will be most pleased to hear all this," Maahdi said. "I'll be out of cellphone range for a few hours, so if anything comes up, let's use our favorite e-mail address."

"Of course," Hasham said.

"Good bye then, Mr. Smith."

"Good bye, Mr. Jones," Hasham said, hanging up.

Maahdi's sweat dripped onto his desk, despite the frigid air conditioning. He despised his rare genetic defect that caused his sweating. But fortunately, an American endocrinologist had just developed a new gene-replacement cure. Next week, Maahdi's men would abduct the talented doctor and fly him to Yemen to treat Maahdi.

* * *

Bobby Ameen Kamal, an NSA analyst, replayed the conversation he'd just listened to. It felt stilted, the words phony, like in code. The call was received somewhere in the northeastern United States and originated from Yemen.

Yemen. A big red flag.

Mr. Jones had said, "Let's use *our* favorite email address?"

Another red flag.

Our email address suggested both men used the same email draft folder to communicate with each other. One man accessed the folder, wrote his message in it, and logged out. Then, the other guy logged on to the same folder and read what the other wrote, answered him there, and logged out.

No email is ever *sent*. No email the NSA can intercept. Communicating without *sending* the communication.

To Bobby Kamal, their conversation seemed as suspicious as their names: Smith and Jones. Not with those Arab accents.

Kamal looked around at his colleagues at the National Security

Agency. Most hunched over their computer stations, working on large flat screens. The computers sifted through twenty *billion* messages and conversations each twenty-four hours, searching for keywords, those *trigger* words that red-flagged a potential threat to America. If someone researched bomb-making, explosives, bio-chemical weapons too many times . . . the NSA knew about it, and would put them on the Watch List, Suspect List, or No-Fly List.

Which put them on Bobby Kamal's enemy list.

Kamal felt honored to work for America . . . the country that saved his family when he was eight. Taliban assassins were en route to slaughter his entire family for the egregious crime of sending his sister to grade school. Four minutes before the assassins arrived, a CIA agent drove Bobby's family to the US Military Base near Kandahar. Today, his sister was a Baltimore obstetrician delivering babies into the world.

And Bobby was a senior NSA analyst, delivering terrorists into the hands of justice.

He looked around the NSA's sprawling underground campus in Fort Meade, Maryland. The Puzzle Factory. Eighteen acres of computers and sophisticated electronics helped NSA's fifty thousand employees analyze thousands of communications related to US national security, trying to keep America safe from attack, and protect federal government computer networks from cyber attacks.

So why didn't these two men speak Arabic, their obvious mother tongue? Kamal spoke fluent Arabic in addition to his native Pashto, English, and French. And what about their medicine? What does it treat? What's the brand name? Is it prescription or over-the-counter?

Kamal turned back to his computer and ran a more sophisticated trace on the Yemen-originated call. The NSA computers quickly identified both phones as untraceable burners.

Another red flag.

Phone-tracking specifics scrolled onto Bobby's screen: the Yemini call was bounced to Lima, Peru, to Antwerp, Belgium, and then to an upstate New York phone in the general area of Mayfield.

Bobby Kamal knew Mayfield was near the Adirondack Park, probably the "park" the men mentioned. His gut told him they were not delivering medical supplies. Worst case - they were delivering terrorism . . . possibly planning an attack.

Was it the same attack Donovan Rourke had just issued an alert for? Kamal knew Donovan; they worked together a few times. Kamal also knew Mayfield. He'd visited his uncle there. Kamal phoned the Mayfield mayor and spoke with her about the town's assembly facilities. Then he called Donovan Rourke.

"Hey, Donovan, Bobby Kamal."

"What's up, Bobby?"

"I intercepted a suspicious call from Yemen to someone near the town of Mayfield in upstate New York."

"Why suspicious?"

"Because they're talking about medicine that feels more like a weapon. They also talked about their assembly facility near Mayfield. Just one problem with that."

"What's that?"

"According to the Mayfield mayor, no assembly facilities like they described exist anywhere in the area any longer."

"Isn't Mayfield near the Adirondack Park?"

"Yes."

"So is the white van we're looking for."

TWENTY TWO

MAYFIELD, NEW YORK

Carmel Belle put down her pruning shears and watched the big white vehicle creep to a stop at *Fred's Food & Gas* across the road. Two men in dark suits got out. A large, muscular man began pumping gas, while a short man went inside and seemed to ask Fred something.

Fred shook his head. She wondered what Fred didn't know? Couldn't be directions? Fred knew every road and cow path from Manhattan to Montreal. But Fred was seventy-nine and his memory had slipped a bit.

The smaller man came back outside, shook his head to the big man, got in the big vehicle, and they drove off.

Who were those guys? They looked serious. Did Fred sign something he should not have? *I better go find out.*

Some people say I'm a busybody. Not true! She was just curious. And well, maybe a bit protective of Fred since his wife passed away six years ago.

Besides, she needed some milk and *Total* cereal.

Carmel put on a little lipstick, brushed her hair back the way Fred liked it, and headed outside. As she walked toward *Fred's* she wondered if one of these days Fred might ask her to the high school reunion.

She entered the store, jingling the doorbell, walked over and grabbed some milk and a box of *Total*.

"Hey Carmel, how you doing?"

"Fine, Fred. And you?"

"*Swamped!*"

"Doesn't look swamped!"

"Six customers in two hours. You're the seventh – and guess what?"

"What?"

"You're the best lookin' by far."

Carmel blushed.

"Freddie Thompson, you got smooth on your tongue!"

"Hey, I call 'em like I see 'em."

"What'd you call those fellas in suits just in here?"

"FBI!"

"You hittin' the sauce, Fred?"

"No ma'am. The fella showed me his genuine FBI ID with his photo."

"What'd he want?"

"Showed me pictures of a woman and a van. They're searching for the woman!"

"Why around here?"

"'Cuz a policeman saw a white Chevy van with a woman wearing a white blouse and a red scarf heading up thisaway. I told them I didn't see the van."

Carmel recalled seeing a few vans stop at Fred's and gas up.

"The woman in trouble?"

"Big trouble! The men grabbed her right off a New York street. World's gone nuts, Carmel!"

"That a true fact!"

She paid for the food and headed toward the door.

"Hey, Carmel?"

"Yeah?"

"I been wonderin' if you wanna go to the big event?"

"What big event?" she asked, hoping maybe.

"The Pig Wrestling Saturday!"

"Oh . . . " she said. *It's not the reunion, but what the hell . . .* "Well, sure Fred. I'm free this Saturday." *And,* she reminded herself, *most of the year.*

Back at her house, she decided to wear her new red blouse to the Pig Wrestling . . . which made her think of the red scarf worn by the poor woman in the van Fred mentioned.

Late yesterday, she watched a van pull up at Fred's. A big dark-looking guy got out and gassed up. The driver had his hoodie up. The other man stayed in the car. The men looked foreign. Seemed like there was a woman in back? She was sort of scrunched down. What was she wearing? Some kind of white blouse . . . and maybe something red, might have been a scarf.

But that van was *beige.*

Or was it beige because it picked up mud from the rainy roads . . . and because it was parked in the gas station shadows . . . and *because my cataracts are getting cloudier.*

She pictured the van driving away from Fred's. It turned up Harmon Road toward the Adirondack Park. As the van turned, sunlight flooded it and the van looked snow white.

TWENTY THREE

Strong crosswinds buffeted the FBI's Bell 430 Twin Engine helicopter as the pilot touched down at Fulton County Airport between Mayfield and Johnstown, New York.

Donovan, Drew Manning, Jacob, and Lindee stepped onto the runway and looked around. Donovan saw a large aircraft hanger, a terminal, and four Piper Cubs parked in a row on the tarmac. Nearby, the Fulton Water Tower loomed high over the airport and surrounding forest.

The chopper had saved them time. Enough time, Donovan hoped, to stop what his gut now told him, based on Dr. Nell Northam's expertise and everything else, was an attack on America with a weapon of mass destruction.

A weapon that NSA's Bobby Kamal told him was discussed between a man in Yemen . . . and a man in the Adirondack area. They talked about their so called "medicine" being assembled in a facility in this area, even though there were no medical assembly facilities near Mayfield.

Which happened to be the same area where their best Chevy van lead was last seen.

And minutes ago, DNI Director Madigan told him that the increasing volume of Internet chatter suggested an imminent attack by jihadist operatives somewhere in America. As a result, the White House and Homeland Security were likely to raise the attack threat level to *HIGH* at any time.

Donovan saw a black Ford Explorer and a black Suburban pull onto the runway and stop beside them.

Agent Manning waved to two FBI colleagues in the Explorer and turned to Donovan. "I'm going with my fellow agents to check out van sightings north of here. The sheriff has your vehicle here, Donovan."

The sheriff, a tall, trim man with a short Afro stepped out of the Suburban, introduced himself, and handed Donovan the keys.

"Tank's full," the sheriff said. "If you need backup or anything else, punch 99 on the dash phone. We'll come runnin'. Meanwhile, we're going to check out nearby towns."

"Thanks, Sheriff. We'll check the area near the park where our best lead was last seen."

The sheriff nodded. "There's an extra Glock in the glove compartment."

"Thanks."

The sheriff turned and left.

Donovan, Jacob, and Lindee piled into the Suburban and drove off.

As he drove, Donovan called Maccabee to see how her meeting with her obstetrician, Dr. Dubin, went. She didn't pick up. Probably still getting the test results at his office.

Or maybe she got bad news and didn't want to tell him.

The news that she could never become pregnant. He prayed she didn't get that news . . . and never would.

But right now he was not focused on bringing a new life into the world.

He was focused on saving lives.

Maybe thousands of lives.

TWENTY FOUR

Jacob Northam rode shotgun. Without a shotgun. Without any weapon. And it worried him.

He'd wanted to bring his Desert Storm Glock 19 from home, but knew he'd never get it past airport security with his carryon bag. The Glock had saved his life more than once. And his life, he sensed, might need saving again. Soon.

Now, as Donovan drove toward the Adirondack Park, Jacob grew more enraged at his wife's abductors. If he had a gun and saw them threatening Nell, he'd use it. He might even use it if she wasn't being threatened. So maybe it was better he didn't have a weapon until he cooled off.

In the back seat, Lindee worked on her iPhone GPS, checking roads around the park.

Jacob felt frustrated they still hadn't received further updates on their best lead – the NASCAR-stickered van with three men and a red-scarfed woman - in this area.

That must have been Nell. Why was she blindfolded? Has she been abused? Tortured?

What if she flat out refused to help? Nell could stonewall like General Jackson when she didn't want to do something.

Donovan braked hard as the semi tractor-trailer ahead slowed and turned down a side road.

"You think they're in the Adirondack forest?" Jacob asked Donovan.

"Probably."

"Why?"

"It's a huge place to hide."

"But how do you hide the kind of sophisticated chemical weapons laboratory she needs?" Jacob asked.

"Enough money can hide anything. And my sense is these guys have big money behind them."

Donovan's phone rang. He answered, listened, and hung up. "Agent Manning just dispatched an FBI helicopter to search for white vans around Mayfield. And another chopper for the Adirondack Park."

"Just one chopper for the nine thousand square mile Park?"

"Two more on the way."

"Still doesn't seem like enough."

"We'll soon have even more eyes in the sky."

"More choppers?"

"Nine drones."

"That helps," Jacob said, although deep down, he sensed Nell's chances were fading with each minute. She'd seen her abductors, worked with them, probably knew their names. If she tried to escape, they'd kill her. And once she finished their work, they'd kill her. How could they let her live?

But maybe she was stalling them. Maybe she was buying time. He had to keep hopeful. He'd loved Nell from the day they met. He couldn't even begin to think of life without her.

In Iraq, he'd lost two brothers-in-arms . . . *in* his arms. Felt their breathing go still, saw their eyes go dark. Somehow, he'd recovered from both deaths, although they still hurt. But this time, his fear for Nell was paralyzing him.

He grabbed his phone and called his mother to see how she and Mia were doing since the agents rescued them.

She answered on the first ring.

"Jacob . . ." She sounded greatly reassured to hear his voice.

"Hi mom, how are you and Mia?"

"Better now."

"Really?"

"Well, I'm still a little shook up."

"Understandable."

"And Mia?

"Better than me. She's playing video games. The FBI men brought us to this safe house."

"Good. Is Mia nearby?"

"Right here."

Jacob heard her hand the phone to Mia.

"Hi Daddy!"

Hearing her voice felt like Valium.

"What are you doing?"

"I'm playing *Angry Birds.* And guess what - I'm *winning!*"

"Good for you."

"When's mommy coming home?"

There it was: *the impossible question.*

Jacob's eyes filled. What could he tell her? What *should* he tell her? Something positive. Something that helped keep her hope alive. And his. "Maybe in a while, honey."

"Goodie, goodie!"

"I love you, Mia."

"I love you, too, daddy. And mommy, too. Tell mommy, okay?"

"Okay."

They hung up.

Jacob blinked away tears. He thought back over the eleven years they'd been married. Nell could never tell him about her top-secret work at Aberdeen Proving Ground. But he'd often overheard her on her safe phone, mentioning nerve agents and biological toxins. Deadly stuff. He told her he worried about her work. She promised she was safe and that she *loved* the job.

And he loved her. And if you love someone, you let them pursue their passion, even if on occasion it might be hazardous to them and the family. It had taken him a while to accept that. She said her lab environment was much safer than other laboratories. He hadn't been completely convinced, but he agreed.

But as it turned out – they were both wrong. The real danger was not *inside* her laboratory. The real danger was *outside* her laboratory.

Like the terrorists who grabbed her off the street.

TWENTY FIVE

Donovan saw another gas station ahead. He'd already checked out four stations near the Adirondacks where the white Chevy van had not stopped. He calculated that if the van left Manhattan with a full 31-gallon tank, it could have easily driven the 200 plus miles to the Adirondacks without stopping.

He pulled in at *Fred's Food & Gas,* a spotless station with the old time Mobil Gas sign with a red-winged flying horse. Everyone went inside, grabbed sandwiches, then walked over to the checkout counter.

An elderly man badged *FRED* brushed cookie crumbs off his bib overalls and smiled as he rang up their sales. Donovan flashed his CIA ID and Fred's eyes widened.

Donovan showed him Nell's photo. "Did you see this woman in a white Chevy van with three men?"

"I'll be damned! Two FBI fellas showed me the same dang pictures."

Donovan knew FBI agents had been in the area.

"Told 'em nope. Haven't seen any white vans."

"Do you have video surveillance?"

Fred shook his head. "Not much need. I know dang near everybody."

"Well, if you see her or the van, please call me immediately." He handed Fred his card.

"Glad to."

As they headed outside, Donovan looked across the street and saw an elderly woman working in her flower garden. Her purple dress was surrounded by purple lilacs, purple irises, and purple magnolias. She looked like a Gauguin painting, or one of those find-the-lady-in-the-picture puzzles.

Donovan noticed she was paying close attention to them. Maybe she paid close attention to everyone at *Fred's Food & Gas.* Maybe she saw the van.

"Let's talk to her," Donovan said.

They walked across the road to her garden. The silver-haired woman looked up and smiled.

"Lookin' for directions?" She placed a lilac branch in her basket.

"Looking for a vehicle, ma'am," Donovan said, showing her his ID badge.

"The white Chevy van?"

Donovan froze. "How'd you know about the van?"

"Fred told me. My name's Carmel Belle." The purple irises of her eyes matched the purple irises of her garden.

"We're looking for that van."

"Good, cuz I been thinkin' my eyes mighta tricked me."

"How's that, ma'am?"

"The van's color. See, I saw a van pull in at Fred's late yesterday. Big fella gassed up. The van looked kinda beige or tan to me. But it had picked up lotsa dirt and mud from the rain. Then when it drove away, the sun hit a clean fender, and I'll tell you what - that fender looked white. And that's a fact!"

"How many men in the van?" Donovan asked.

"Three."

"Can you describe them?"

"Dark-skinned fellas. Big bearded guy. Short thin fella. Driver stayed in the van."

Donovan felt his pulse ratchet up. "Was there a woman wearing a white blouse in back?"

"She was sorta scrunched down, maybe sleeping."

"Did she wear a red scarf?"

"Something red around her neck."

Donovan's hope soared.

"Any words on the side?"

"Yep. But too muddy to read."

"Any stickers on the back bumper?"

She closed her eyes. "A muddy sticker, but I saw blue, red, white under the mud."

NASCAR colors, Donovan realized.

"What about the driver?"

"He wore his black hoodie up."

Donovan's pulse raced. Beside him, he saw Jacob and Lindee grow very excited.

"Where'd the van go?" Jacob asked.

"Up there!" She pointed.

"Over that hill?"

"Nope. Turned right just before the hill. Onto Jackson Summit Road. That's where the sun hit the clean fender and it looked real white."

"Where does Jackson Summit Road go?"

"North a spell, then she splits off onto Tolmantown Road."

"Remember anything else, Ms. Belle?"

"Nope."

"Well thank you, ma'am. You've helped a lot. If you remember anything else, please call me immediately." Donovan handed her his card.

"Happy to."

They got back in the Suburban, and Donovan adjusted the Suburban's GPS Guidance map down so it showed smaller roads. They drove off and turned right onto Jackson Summit Road.

Donovan felt sure that Carmel Belle's muddy van - was *the* van. *But where did it go?*

He passed a silver Airstream RV and headed deeper into the massive Adirondack forest. Trees bent over the road like a cathedral dome. Thick gray clouds blocked the sun and darkened the forest. It smelled like rain was coming. There was no traffic, just a few narrow side roads with only small-car and motorbike tracks.

About five miles farther, he drove around a curve and saw three orange and white construction barrels blocking most of the road ahead. He looked for *Road Repair* signs and workers, but didn't see any. No *Detour* signs either.

He crawled to a stop at the barrels.

He saw just enough space to the left and started to steer around the cones.

POP!

A bullet slammed into his lower door panel.

POP!

Donovan watched his driver-side mirror shatter into pieces.

TWENTY SIX

Nell sensed Hasham behind her, sneaking up again, checking what she was doing, making sure she was finishing his blending, not sabotaging the weapon, not stalling.

She *was* stalling, looking for a way to weaken his weapon. Or derail his secret delivery system, whatever it was.

She rechecked her HazMat sleeves for holes. If she breathed just a few particles of what she was working with, she'd die in minutes. Sweat slid down her neck despite the air-conditioned suit.

She felt Hasham's small, piercing eyes watching her every move.

"You have thirty minutes to finish, Doctor," he said. "Then we'll test the final weapon."

"But I'm having difficulty achieving your exacting blend-consistency targets. I'm 1.9% short of your goal."

She showed him the results, hoping he didn't realize she'd tweaked them a bit.

He stared at the results, clearly not buying them.

"Fix this, or you'll be 1.9% short of saving your daughter's life."

Her knees buckled.

"By the way - look!" He showed her his iPad screen.

Nell's heart stopped when he showed her a photo of Mia surrounded by three masked men. Each held a long, curved knife, like the masked assassins who beheaded innocent captives. And Mia was no longer in her grandmother's house. She was in a strange room, but her face was still frozen in the same terrified expression as before.

"Complete the work, Doctor, or the sheik gets her."

Nell slumped against the lab bench and tried to calm herself. She felt helpless.

She had to fix the blend consistency. But helping Hasham was a death warrant for thousands of innocent men, women, and children. Could she help kill thousands to save her daughter? She felt like something was ripping her heart open. *My best choice is to finish this blend – learn how he's delivering the weapon, then somehow get word to the police.*

But getting word to the police seemed impossible.

Which left her with one last-resort - unleash VX here in the cabin. It will kill us all, but maybe stop Hasham's mass attack.

But even unleashing VX in the cabin seemed impossible. Only Hasham had access to the weaponized VX locked up in the lab. And he was with her every minute.

"Twenty-eight minutes and counting, Doctor."

She looked out through the lab window at Aarif. The huge man slathered gobs of hummus on some pita bread. He bit off a big chunk and chewed. But when he saw her, he stopped chewing and stared at her.

His vacant eyes said it all.

Aarif would be her executioner. It was only a matter of time.

Twenty-six minutes later, Nell handed Hasham her final blend-consistency report. It reached his target goal.

———

"Excellent," he said as he walked over to a VX container, unlocked it, and returned with a nose-drop bottle filled with the weapon.

"Test time!" Hasham said as he held the bottle up to the light. "It had better work, Doctor Northam."

"It will. But . . . "

"But what?"

"Its efficiency in the real world depends partly on *how* you will deliver it to your victims. But since you won't tell me how, I can't predict your ah . . . kill-rate . . . with any accuracy."

"But *I* can predict it. With amazing accuracy and precision."

"Precision is not possible with VX nerve gas!" she said. "Air dispersal, your most likely VX delivery, depends on too many environmental factors like wind, humidity, rain."

He smiled. "Oh, but precision *is* possible with my delivery."

"Based on what?"

"Based partly on top secret tests your own government conducted years ago."

She had no idea which tests he referred to. And how could he possibly know about such top secret US military tests? Clearly, someone at Aberdeen or an ex-employee told him. She couldn't think of anyone who'd betray their work. But then people could be bought or blackmailed.

"Follow me!" he said.

He led her down the hall toward the kennels where he'd shown her the beautiful Golden Labs.

She didn't want to watch this. "You don't need to kill the dogs. I promise that the blended VX will work."

"I don't accept promises from infidels."

"Please don't do this!"

"Okay . . . I won't."

Did he mean it?

He signaled for her follow him, a strange smile on his face.

They walked *past* the door to the dog kennels.

Where's he going? she wondered. They continued walking around the corner and down a long hall with a door at the end.

He unlocked the door and they entered what looked like a small windowless room. She saw a sink, mirror, toilet. A low-wattage bulb hung from the ceiling.

She heard something. Wheezing . . .

She turned and saw a withered, older man with a gray beard, lying on a cot, snoring. His scruffy soiled clothes and wrinkled face suggested he was a homeless man they'd grabbed off the street. Beside the cot lay several empty Four Roses bottles. The room smelled like whiskey and sweat.

The old man's eyes flickered open, then shut.

"You're not going to - ?

" – I am! A scientist always tests his product on the intended target."

"But this is *murder!*"

"*Au contraire.* It's mercy. Look at his pathetic condition."

"He's alive!"

"Not for long."

She hated what he was about to do.

"Maybe test a cat or . . . dog."

"My dogs are far too important."

He's going to kill this poor man. She felt dizzy.

"Please don't do this. I guarantee it will work. What would I gain by lying?"

"I must *see* it work."

Wearing gloves, Hasham took the nose-dropper containing the liquid, unscrewed the top, and drew some VX up into the dropper. He opened a small box and took out something she couldn't see.

Nell refused to watch. She walked out of the room into the hall, placed her face against the wall, closed her eyes, and prayed for the poor man. She blocked her ears, but soon heard his breathing become labored, then heard gasping and groaning. She pushed harder on her ears, but still heard him wheezing, rasping to breathe. Seconds later, she heard silence.

"Look! It works perfectly!"

She knew the poor man was dead, knew his pain had been horrific, knew blood would soon spill from his body . . . knew that thousands of people would soon die the same way.

Her eyes filled with tears. She looked at Hasham, hating the merciless bastard. If she had a gun, she'd have shot him between the eyes.

"You've done your job," Hasham said.

"*YOUR* job!" she shouted back at him. *My job,* she thought, *is stopping you!*

Hasham walked her back to the main lab. His phone rang and he answered it. He suddenly grew angry with the caller and started ranting and raving in loud Arabic, waving his arms. As he turned his back to her and continued his screaming tirade, she grabbed something from a nearby desk. He hung up two minutes later, still furious and mumbling in Arabic. Then he ushered her straight upstairs to the cabin.

"Return to your room. I shall come for you shortly."

She headed to her room, but left the door ajar a bit to see Hasham and Aarif through the crack. Aarif began speaking in Arabic, but Hasham quickly reminded him, "English in America."

Aarif nodded.

"Trucks on time?" Hasham said.

"Arrive tonight."

"Good."

"What about . . . ?" Aarif nodded toward her room.

Hasham glanced at her room and switched to whispered Arabic.

Nell didn't need a translator. They were discussing what they'd do with her now that Hasham had seen the blended weapon kill the old man. Two things were clear: First, he didn't need her any more - and second, he wouldn't risk her escaping.

Nell realized her husband's great fear had come true. Her job jeopardized her life. And Mia's. She had long argued that there was no way terrorists could discover the weapons she worked with. But they had.

As a result, I probably have minutes to live . . .

TWENTY SEVEN

Donovan, Jacob and Lindee sped away from the forest area where bullets ripped into their Suburban's lower door panel and blew off the side mirror. Donovan watched for any sign the bullets damaged the engine, but so far no warning lights, no steering troubles, no one following them.

And no follow-up sniper shots.

"Could those bullets have been from hunters?" Lindee said.

"Those bullets were hunting us!" Jacob said.

"Agreed. Hunting season starts next month," Donovan said.

Donovan phoned Agent Drew Manning.

"What's up?" Manning asked.

"A sniper shot a couple rounds into our Suburban."

"Everyone okay?"

"We're fine."

"So you're getting close to the white van."

"Yep."

"We'll head over your way any minute," Manning said.

They hung up.

"The shooter could be close behind us," Jacob said. "But too many tight curves keep blocking my view."

"Keep checking," Donovan said. All he saw was the thick, endless wall of evergreens, a few narrow pathways, and two-rut lanes. The higher they climbed, the thicker the forest. The sniper could be twenty feet away and they wouldn't see him . . . nor would they see a white van.

"Look - the Jackson Summit Reservoir's on the right," Jacob said.

Donovan looked and saw flashes of pristine blue water between the towering evergreens. A postcard-perfect view. It reminded him how stunningly beautiful and serene upstate New York was . . . just hours from stunningly noisy Manhattan, but also beautiful.

Ahead, Donovan saw a young redheaded boy pumping an old fat-tire Schwinn loaded with a fishing pole and a wicker basket. The boy looked like he had just stepped out of a Norman Rockwell painting. Donovan signaled him and the skinny teenager rolled to a stop. Donovan flashed his CIA badge and the kid grew anxious. His light blue eyes, surrounded by sunburned cheeks and freckles, stared hard at the badge. Donovan explained about the white van.

"Well, last evening I saw a white van when I was froggin' over at the reservoir. Three guys inside. Mighta been a woman in back."

"Were they dark-skinned?"

"Mighta been. Couldn't see 'em good."

"Where'd the van go?"

"Past the reservoir and then, well, who knows. Mighta stayed on Tolmantown. Mighta turned up one of the side roads."

Donovan nodded. "Have you seen anything else around here that seemed kinda strange? You know, out of place?"

The boy licked his lower lip. "I saw a couple gray mid-sized delivery trucks heading up a narrow dirt road off Tolmantown. That was kinda strange."

"Why?"

"Ain't but one cabin to deliver stuff at. It's way back at the end. Never seen anyone back there. I kinda wondered about those two trucks."

"Moonshiner's trucks maybe?"

"Nope."

"How do you know?"

"Daddy shut down the last still in these parts four years ago."

"Remember anything else about the delivery trucks?"

"Nope. But I remember something about that white van . . . cuz it's got something I'd like."

"What's that?"

"A NASCAR sticker on the back bumper."

TWENTY EIGHT

Nell heard tires crunching over gravel. She walked to her small window, looked out, and saw four gray medium-sized delivery trucks pulling up to the cabin. She heard more trucks behind them.

The drivers got out, embraced Hasham and Aarif, then unlocked the trucks. The drivers entered the cabin and began carrying out the large stainless steel canisters from the laboratory - the canisters containing the blended VX. The drivers secured the canisters onto metal racks inside the trucks.

Several minutes later, with all canisters loaded and locked in, the drivers walked over to Hasham.

Hasham handed the drivers some documents and showed them a map. He pointed to a location and said something to them.

Nell cupped her ear to the window to hear better.

"You know this route?" Hasham asked one of the drivers.

"*Na-am, na-am,*" the man said in Arabic.

"English only!" Hasham said.

"Yes, yes, we know route good. Four times we drive. No police. No problem."

"You know where to go?"

"Yes. We know where. No problem." The other drivers nodded.

"Then it is time." Hasham said.

He embraced each man, watched them get in their trucks and drive off.

"*Allah Akbar!*" he shouted after them.

Is this it? Nell wondered. *Are they attacking now? Are the trucks themselves Hasham's secret delivery system? It was possible.* The drivers could simply connect the VX canisters to the trucks' exhaust systems and disperse the deadly gas into the city streets of Manhattan . . . into the lungs of people walking past . . . into the ventilation systems of passing cars . . . into the air vents of office buildings and homes.

Or they could be suicide drivers - simply drive onto crowded city streets and detonate their VX-loaded trucks, dispersing VX throughout the city.

Or they might deliver the VX canisters to a new location . . . where the VX will be incorporated into the unique delivery system that Hasham bragged about.

Moments later, Hasham walked into her room. "You've completed my assignment. If my weapon works successfully in the . . . marketplace, Mr. Brown here will set you free."

She said nothing.

"If you try to inform the police, or have compromised the weapon, or rendered it less lethal, then, as I mentioned . . . very bad things will happen to pretty little Mia. Oh, by the way, here's her latest photo. It's my favorite!"

He held up an iPhone photo. She saw Mia in a different room. Behind her was a black wall banner with gold Arabic script. Mia wore a young girl's *hijab* gown. Over it she wore a vest. The vest was stuffed with explosives. Mia also wore the same frightened expression as before.

"But you promised you'd do nothing to her if I cooperated."

"Right."

"And I cooperated."

"True."

"And your test with the old homeless man proves the VX kills!"

"Yes. But the real proof will be our final delivery. If it goes well, we will release her."

"How will I know if your delivery goes well?"

"You will know."

"When? Today? Tomorrow? Next week?" She wanted to know when the attack would come.

Hasham paused as though deciding whether to tell her. "Listen to the radio in the next twenty-four hours."

She stared at him long and hard. "Will I live that long?"

Hasham blinked, then slowly smiled. "Of course."

His eyes shifted right, suggesting he'd lied.

"You've earned the honor to witness the fruit of your righteous work," he said.

"It's *your* work!"

"In the meantime, Doctor, you are cut off from the outside world. We've terminated Internet access here. We've removed all phones. We've surrounded you with a forest that has deadly timber rattlers. Ask the snake-bitten hunter who stumbled in here."

"I can't. Aarif murdered him."

Hasham shrugged. "Collateral damage. The man saw our illegal weapons. He would have told authorities."

She said nothing.

"I must leave for a bit, but don't worry. Aarif will guard you, right Aarif?"

Aarif paused, then nodded.

"Together you will celebrate our glorious victory on the radio."

Hasham and Aarif walked back out into the other room and sat down. Hasham whispered something to him. Aarif's small black eyes slowly shifted toward her room. So did Hasham's. They were talking about her.

Hasham said something in Arabic. Aarif nodded and repeated the words slowly, *Dafnuha fi ghaba?"*

Hasham nodded. *"Dafnuha fi ghaba!"*

Nell wrote down phonetically what they'd said, then walked over to the bookshelf in her room. She reached up and took down the small electronic Ectaco Translator she'd found yesterday. She turned the device on, repeated the words Hasham spoke - *Dafnuha fi ghaba* – and seconds later, the devise displayed the English translation:

Bury her in the forest.

TWENTY NINE

Donovan zigzagged along dirt ruts, following car and truck tracks and dodging chuckholes and fallen branches every few feet. A brisk wind filled the Suburban with the scent of fresh pine.

Beside him, Jacob searched the right side of the forest for the van. Lindee the left side. But spotting a white van or a gray truck was very difficult thanks to the thick wall of dense evergreens.

And spotting a sniper was impossible.

Donovan worried about Jacob and Lindee. Their hope seemed to fade a bit more with each minute. Their bloodshot eyes and thousand-yard stares suggested they were preparing themselves for the worst.

Donovan was too. The worst was very likely.

Still, he had to keep their hope alive. "How's Nell's general health?" he asked.

"Excellent," Jacob said. "She jogs, eats healthy."

"That will help her. So will her professional expertise. Her abductors need it. Maybe she can use it to negotiate with them, stall a bit. Slow them down long enough for us to find her."

Jacob and Lindee nodded, but looked less than convinced.

Ahead, Donovan saw a skinny old man in his eighties walking slow-mo, like a praying mantis. He wore a navy blue and gray New York Yankees tracksuit. Donovan drove along beside him and explained what they were looking for.

"Ain't seen no white van."

"Any strangers? Men with black hair and dark complexions?"

"Saw couple of dark-skinned strangers in a gray delivery truck. Next dirt road up."

"Maybe the same truck the redheaded boy saw," Lindee said.

Donovan nodded. "When did you see it?"

"Five-six hours ago. Turn left next trail up."

"Thanks," Donovan said as he drove ahead.

Minutes later, as Donovan turned left on the trail, his personal phone vibrated against his thigh. He saw Caller ID. Maccabee.

"Any luck?" she asked.

"Some progress."

"Good. Where are you now?"

"In the Adirondacks. How's it going down there?"

"Just heard back from Doctor Dubin."

"And . . .?"

Her long pause said bad news. Something was wrong. Donovan squeezed the steering wheel.

"Turns out the lab sent him the wrong test results for me. They switched my tests with some woman in Brooklyn. Mine come in later today. I'm visiting Doctor Dubin in a few hours."

"So your results may be better."

"Maybe . . . or maybe not." She sounded worried.

He paused. "Do you want me to come back?"

"Absolutely not! The president gave you this assignment. Don't worry. Really, I'm fine, Donovan."

"Whatever Dubin says, please call me. One way or another, Mac, we'll have a baby."

"God willing," she said.

Donovan hoped God was willing . . .

THIRTY

Kadar Khoury drove the white Chevy van on Highway 29 near Johnstown, heading back to forest cabin. Beside him, sat Hasham's weapons and munitions expert, Waazi the Whiner.

In the last five minutes, Waazi moaned that his hashish was too weak, his baba ganoush too mushy, and his three wives too fat.

Khoury only had one moan – Waazi smelled like roadkill.

Waazi let out a long sigh.

"*Now* what's your problem?" Khoury asked him.

"Hasham!"

"Why?"

"He wants to blow cabin up?"

"It's his cabin!"

"Why blow up?"

"I told you why. To destroy all evidence."

"I can destroy all evidence. No blow up. No fingerprints. Save cabin."

"Why save it?"

"So I can hunt and fish here."

"Waazi - you don't get it! Hasham wants the cabin and everything in it *completely* destroyed."

Waazi cursed and huffed like a kid denied candy.

Khoury said, "We do what Hasham said. First we set fire. Then explosives go off. You placed the explosives exactly in the cabin where Hasham said, right?"

"Right. Cabin go boom!" Waazi said.

"You're absolutely positive?"

"Yes! Yes! Remember - I am the explosive expert!" Waazi shouted, even though his glass eye and two-fingered right hand suggested otherwise.

"What about the woman scientist?" Waazi said.

"By now, Aarif has killed her. Hasham wants us to help Aarif bury her in forest several hundred yards from cabin."

"I have better idea."

"What?"

"Destroy body in explosion and fire."

Khoury shook his head. "Hasham wants no trace of her DNA in the cabin. *No trace!* Must bury her deep."

Waazi moaned, knowing he and Aarif would have to dig the woman's grave. Waazi clearly considered physical labor beneath his exalted status as a bomb maker.

"But my bad hand!" Waazi whined. He held up his two-finger hand and squeezed it like a lobster claw, suggesting it was a serious handicap for digging graves, even though Waazi could easily bench press two hundred thirty pounds.

Khoury said nothing.

"And Hasham won't know she blow up in cabin if we don't tell him."

"He would know."

"How?"

"I'd tell him."

Waazi cursed and looked out the window, pointed at something and mumbled a curse.

"Now, what's your problem?"

"Trees."

"Why?"

"America has too many. Yemen so few."

THIRTY ONE

Nell sat in the cabin living room watching Aarif rip meat off his kebob. He washed it down with red wine, forgetting the Koran commandment forbidding alcohol.

He also forgot the commandment forbidding murder. Like the thousands of innocent Americans he would soon help Hasham kill.

But to Aarif we are not innocent. We are infidels!

In his mind and Hasham's, we are guilty because we exist. Like Jews were guilty for existing in Hitler's malignant evil.

She watched a morsel of meat fall onto Aarif's beard. His tongue shot out and flicked it back in like a lizard. He strutted into the living room, sat down opposite her and started smoking his hashish pipe. She watched his facial muscles relax and his eyes soften as the cannabis and wine took hold.

Was he relaxing to kill her? She didn't think so. Psychopaths like him didn't need to relax to kill. The killing relaxed them.

She *had* to get him talking, build some kind of bond with him and gain time to avoid what he planned to do to her.

"You're Muslim, right?"

He looked offended that she might think otherwise.

"Of course!"

"But you're drinking alcohol."

He blinked like the Imam caught him boozing in the mosque.

"Do you know why I drink?"

"No?"

He took a defiant gulp of wine. "I drink so I can blend in, walk among you infidels unnoticed."

Anyone with nasal passages will notice you.

He walked over toward her. "I like wine now. I also like other western things."

"Really? Like what?" *Keep him talking . . .*

He paused as though considering whether he should answer her. After all, he didn't have to answer her since he considered her a mere woman with all the status of a floor mat.

Keep asking questions, she told herself, *praise his answers, admire his English, keep him talking.*

"Really I'd like to know. Name something you like here in America?"

His thick wine-red lips curled in a sneer.

"Some television shows."

"Really?"

He nodded and chugged more wine.

"Like Arab-entertainment programs? Egyptian soap operas?"

"A few."

"But what about *American* TV shows? Name just one you like?"

He paused. *"Smackdown Wrestling."*

Nell remembered reading how many Middle Easterners loved watching American pro wrestling. Arab women in particular enjoyed watching muscular men toss their firm butts around the ring.

"You like watching men wrestle?"

"No - not men!" He frowned like she'd cast aspersions on his manliness.

"Who do you watch?"

"Women!"

Another Muslim no-no: watching bikini-clad women flip their bodies around the ring.

"Is it *professional?*"

"Very professional."

"Which channel?"

"*The Fight Network.*"

"Who's your favorite wrestler?"

"Kitty Kelly. Strong. Tough."

"Is she pretty?"

"Very pretty . . . blonde hair . . . sexy."

His grin revealed green khat stuck between his remaining teeth. Then, slowly, his gaze slid down to her breasts.

"Sexy like *you!*" His beady eyes slid open.

She stopped breathing. Her plan to get him talking just backfired. He was looking at her as a woman.

He grabbed the wine bottle and poured her a glass. "Here – you drink now. Make you feel good."

"No thanks."

He leaned close to her. "*Drink NOW!*"

To slow him, she took the glass and sipped some.

"Good, huh. . .?"

"Ummm . . ."

He gulped down the rest of his wine, belched, then gazed at her body again.

"More wine you drink!"

She said nothing.

"*DRINK!*"

She saw it in his eyes.

Aarif would rape her, then kill her.

THIRTY TWO

Towering evergreens, red spruces and sugar maples. That's all Donovan had seen for the last few miles. Now they drove past chalk-white birch trees thick enough to hide the White House.

He saw nowhere for trucks to pick up or drop off anything. No cabins, huts, garages, barns, storage bins . . . and no white van. Just this narrow dirt road crowded by tall trees. He felt like he was driving through a shag carpet. Only one kind of vehicles made sense here: logging trucks.

Agent Manning called in.

"Any more sniper activity?" Manning asked.

"No. But what about the three white vans you're tracking?"

"In van one, the man was eighty-six, van two, the woman was a ponytailed man. Van three was Meals on Wheels. We're driving toward you. Where exactly are you now?"

"Somewhere on a dirt road off Tolmantown where both a delivery truck and a white van were seen heading toward a cabin at the end. This white van feels *solid*, Drew!"

"Good. Just leave your phone on. Our techies will lock onto your location."

"Will do."

Donovan drove around a curve as two fawns shot across the path and vanished into a thicket.

A minute later, he stopped at a fork in the trail. The fork didn't show up on the GPS map. He studied the two branches. Similar in width. Both had car and truck tread marks.

Which one?

He decided on the left trail and drove off. The car compass direction said northwest.

Several minutes later, the trail seemed to narrow a bit. Then, a half-mile farther, the trail narrowed more. Something felt wrong.

Did he take the wrong trail?

THIRTY THREE

"Drink *more wine* . . ." Aarif said, raising Nell's glass toward her mouth. "Wine good for you."

She eased the glass up to her lips and swallowed some. The alcohol hit her hard, thanks to not eating breakfast.

Suddenly, Aarif grabbed her arm, and pulled her toward a nearby sofa and started to pin her down, rape in his eyes!

"Stop! The Koran teaches a man must respect women!"

"*No!* Koran say woman must obey to the *man!*"

"Her *husband!* Not all men!" she said.

Aarif clearly didn't like an infidel lecturing him on Islam. He chugged his wine, then grabbed her blouse, ripped a top button off, and slid his greasy fingers over her face and neck.

She had to reach the bathroom!

He reached toward her again.

"Wait - I'm going to be sick! The wine . . .!" She jackknifed forward, fake-vomiting toward him.

He leaned back fast.

"The bathroom. I must use it *now* . . ." She placed her hand over her mouth, leaned forward, and fake-vomited toward him again, and almost did vomit.

He jerked back.

"The wine makes me sick. I need the bathroom . . . before you and I do . . ."

"Before we do what?"

"You know, before we do what you want to do . . ."

He arched his eyebrows, looking excited that she might actually accept his advances.

"Bathroom window nailed shut. Wire over window. No escape!"

"I know. I know . . ."

Aarif stared at her, still deciding.

She coughed again.

He nodded for her to go ahead.

Nell hurried into the hall, turned the corner, stepped into the bathroom and locked the door. She had seconds. He would listen for her trying to open the nailed window. She wouldn't even try.

She hacked hard a few times, turned the faucet on full blast, flushed the toilet, then picked up the toilet tank cover and set it on the sink. She snapped on her lab gloves, reached into the tank and took out the small sealed eyedropper bottle. It contained the remaining milliliters of VX that Hasham had used to kill the homeless man in the lab. After, Hasham set down the bottle, assuming it was empty, and answered the phone. He grew enraged at the caller. When he turned his back to her, she grabbed the bottle and minutes later, still angry, he hung up and took her upstairs, forgetting the bottle.

"You come out *now!*" Aarif pounded on the bathroom door. A thin door he could easily kick open.

"Still sick. Just a minute, *please!*"

She flushed the toilet again – and grabbed an *Inspire* jihadist magazine from a nearby rack and flipped it to an article on the

American president. She unscrewed the eyedropper bottle top and placed the remaining drops of liquid VX on the outer edges of the pages. She fanned the magazine pages until they were a bit dryer.

He pounded the door again, rattling its hinges.

"You come out now!"

"Okay, okay I'm coming."

She flushed the toilet, threw her gloves away, placed the eyedropper bottle back in the toilet tank and replaced the tank cover.

"I said NOW!"

He kicked the door open . . .

She walked out holding the *Inspire* magazine, very careful not to touch where she'd placed the VX.

Aarif saw her holding *Inspire* and he looked confused.

"What - you read Arabic?" he asked.

"No. But I really wanted to know what this article says about our President? Your English is so good. Could you please translate a little?"

He stared back. "Why?"

"Because I think you're right!"

"Right about what?"

"That we Americans need to understand Islam better."

He frowned like it wouldn't matter in her case.

"You speak with so little accent. You have a gift for languages, you know!"

He shrugged, but the compliment seemed to puff him up a bit.

She felt justified with what she planned to do. The man was going to rape and then kill her, as ordered by Hasham. Then he would *"Bury her in forest."* This magazine was her only self-defense. But would he grab the slightly damp section of the pages? Would he hold the pages long enough? Was there enough VX? He was a large man.

"This important article here," she said, offering him the magazine in a way that forced him to grip where the pages were damp with VX.

His sausage-sized fingers grabbed the VX area. She exhaled in relief.

"Magazine wet."

"I washed my hands."

He seemed to accept that. Then he looked down at the magazine article.

"What does this article say?" She pointed.

"Says your president helps Zionists pigs occupy Palestine. Says he *pretends* to care for Palestinians, but sends US soldiers to occupy other sacred Muslim lands. Says America causes deaths of thousands of Muslims."

His fingers still gripped the pages.

"But," she said, "America gives millions in aid to the Palestinians. Billions to Egypt. Each year."

"Says here you give *more* money to Israel!" This angered him and he seemed to squeeze the pages even tighter. Sweat beaded on his forehead.

"We give aid to help bring peace," she said.

"No . . . to bring Arabs to their knees!"

Aarif's neck and face grew darker. Was it anger, or the VX entering his bloodstream?

"Says Pentagon will grab Saudi oil fields. Keep all money!"

He cleared his throat and sniffled. Clear fluid drained from a nostril. He wiped it, coughed hard several times. His eyes were pink now. The VX was mixing with the moisture on his fingers and seeping into his bloodstream.

He coughed hard again. His face grew dark red. "Six new Arab babies born . . . for every non-Arab baby means Arabs rule America one day!"

"But you'll never see the day, asshole!" she whispered a little too loud.

"What you say . . . ?"

He coughed and glanced at the magazine, then his fingers, then seemed to realize she'd poisoned him.

He grabbed her blouse, ripping it a bit, and tried to push her down on the sofa. But she kicked him in the groin – buckling him over.

Then suddenly - the VX hit him like freight train - he grabbed his chest as VX shut down the nerve impulses regulating his breathing. His entire body went rigid and his eyes turned crimson. His left nostril bled. His face twisted with rage – but somehow he still lunged toward her.

But Nell jumped back. He missed her, fell and gashed his head open on the corner of a glass coffee table. Blood poured from the gash. His body shook in a violent seizure as he struggled to breathe. Chunks of meat, blood and green vomit erupted from his mouth.

He'd be dead in seconds.

She had to escape *now!* But first she had to find the flash drive Hasham always worked on.

She hurried over to his computer and checked the USB slot. Empty. Where'd he hide it? She checked the side drawers. Only printer paper and ink cartridges. Did he take the flash drive with him?

She reached under the desk and felt lumps of dried gum.

Then she saw the flash drive – taped to the far side of the printer. She pulled it off and put it in her pocket. Turning back, she nudged the desktop computer to the side a bit and saw another thumb-sized flash drive – hidden behind the screen.

Hidden because it's important!

She grabbed the flash drive and stuffed it in her pocket.

Then she heard something.

Tires crunching on gravel.

Glancing outside, she saw the white van driving up.

She ran over and saw Aarif's gun wasn't on him. She took the keys from his pocket. *Where's his cell phone?* Not on him. No time to look. She raced to the back door. Which key? She tried the large one. It didn't work. She tried the other four.

None worked.

Where's the hell's the key? Her head throbbed with every heartbeat.

Outside, the van doors opened . . . then slammed shut. Men mumbled . . .

Seconds later, she heard a key slide into the front door.

THIRTY FOUR

"I took the wrong damn trail!" Donovan said, as he stared at the rain-swollen, fast-flowing creek water blocking the Suburban.

The water looked at least fifty feet wide.

"The trail continues on the other side," Lindee said, pointing.

"But the tire tracks don't," Donovan said.

"Because this water's too damn deep," Jacob said.

"Agreed," Donovan said, as he spun the big Suburban around and raced back toward the fork in the trail. They'd lost time.

"How long back to the fork, and down the other trail to the cabin?" Donovan asked.

"I can't tell," Lindee said. "These small trials don't show up on my GPS map."

Minutes later, back at the fork, Donovan careened onto the other trail and drove toward what he hoped was the cabin at the trail's end. But he worried that the same waterway might block them again since it seemed to flow in that general direction.

He accelerated, but the deep mud holes kept bucking him to the side, preventing him from driving more than ten miles an hour.

A mile later, something glinted off his eye. Glass. He crept forward and saw a cabin window a hundred yards ahead. A row of large oak trees stood along the front of the cabin. He turned the car off and pointed.

"Light inside!" Jacob said.

"And behind the cabin is something *white!*" Donovan said.

"Where?" Jacob leaned to the side.

"Behind those bushes. A propane gas tank . . . or . . ."

"No – that curves like a van fender!" Jacob said.

"Look!" Lindee pointed down at the dirt trail. "Lots of fresh truck tracks heading *toward* the cabin."

Donovan grabbed the open line to Manning.

"Drew, *this* cabin looks like it!" What's your ETA here?"

"Six minutes maybe."

"When you get to the fork, go right."

"Roger that."

Donovan studied the old cabin. No visible movement inside or out.

"Let's go check the vehicle in back," Jacob said.

Donovan nodded, but didn't like risking Jacob's or Lindee's life, or approaching the cabin without backup. On the other hand, if Nell was inside, every second counted, and acting now might save her life . . . maybe even thousands of lives targeted for imminent death.

He suddenly worried that someone in the cabin might see a reflection from their black Suburban.

Donovan quietly reversed down the dirt road a few hundred feet and parked behind some dense bushes. He couldn't see the cabin and hoped no one inside saw the Suburban.

"You ever fire a Glock, Jacob?"

"Saved my life in Iraq a few times."

Donovan unlocked the glove compartment, reached in, and handed Jacob a holstered 9mm Glock 19.

Jacob flipped the safety off. And checked it out.

"Lindee, when we get out, please get in the driver's seat and lock the doors. If you see trouble, *text* me. Don't phone unless it's an emergency. Special Agent Manning's team should be here in a few minutes."

She nodded but looked nervous.

"Don't worry, we won't charge the cabin until Agent Manning's Rescue Team gets here!" Donovan said.

"Unless Nell's in danger," Jacob said.

"Agreed."

He and Jacob got out and stepped through the dense forest toward the cabin. The carpet of pine needles muted their footsteps.

Donovan worried a sniper had them in his crosshairs. He also worried about Jacob. Seeing Nell in trouble might overwhelm him, make him rush in and get shot.

Behind Donovan, leaves rustled. He spun around and saw a shadow move behind some trees fifty yards away. A sniper? He raised his gun, waited, looking for the reflection of a rifle, a face . . .

Suddenly a huge buck bolted from the trees and ran down a hill.

Donovan and Jacob approached the left side of the cabin. No movement in the window. No sound from inside. They circled left and saw more of the white vehicle. They moved a few feet closer.

A white Chevy van.

License ending in – *6 8 9!*

American Transit on the side.

NASCAR sticker on the rear bumper.

Donovan touched the van's hood. Warm. Driven in the last thirty minutes or so. The driver was in the cabin.

Jacob looked ready to bolt into the cabin any second.

Donovan heard something. A soft hiss . . . a strange crackling sound.

He looked in the window and saw orange-red reflections flickering in the darkness. Gray smoke seeped out under the front door. The cabin was on fire!

Jacob saw the flames and his eyes went wild. He raced toward the cabin door.

Donovan raced after him.

Suddenly, giant red flames blew out the windows and engulfed the entire cabin. Fire curled up around the eaves and roof.

But Jacob continued running toward the cabin. Donovan tried to stop him. If Nell was in there, both of them would be burned alive. Donovan grabbed his arm.

"*Stop!*"

"Nell's in there!"

Then it hit – Donovan and Jacob felt themselves flying backward in the burning air and fiery chunks of debris - as the cabin exploded.

THIRTY FIVE

Donovan spit dirt. Clumps of dirt. He lay face down on the ground, ears ringing, mind spinning, but arms and legs moving. Fifteen feet away, Jacob stumbled trying to stand up.

But they were alive. The wall of thick oak trees absorbed most of the explosive blast from the cabin.

Donovan spit more dirt and grass from his mouth and noticed his arm was bleeding, sliced by flying debris. His eyebrows felt hot. He touched them and realized they were burnt off.

Jacob looked shaken, but okay, except for a cut on his cheek. They stood up, shook off debris, and stared at what was left of the cabin – piles of smoldering rubble. The explosion had snuffed out most of the fire, leaving black smoke curling up from the cherry-red embers.

No one inside could have survived the blast.

Panicked, Jacob limped into the ruins and started searching for his wife. Donovan followed him. Lindee sprinted up the hill and joined them.

Step by step, they combed through the still smoking, charred rubble, kicking burnt logs aside, stumbling over chunks of blackened walls, terrified to look beneath large slabs of debris.

Where was Nell? Where was the van driver?

Donovan stepped over a smoldering log. A kitchen table had melted into a fat gray lump. The stench of burnt plastic stung his nostrils.

He looked for some hint that Nell had been here, some hint of a laboratory, but saw neither. Nor did he see any hint of how her abductors would attack. The explosion had undoubtedly destroyed all evidence of it.

On the other hand, no sign of a laboratory suggested they'd driven Nell to a lab. Maybe she was there now.

They heard something. Turning, they watched a blackened hand flop out from beneath a fallen roof beam.

They walked over and stared at the hand, afraid to lift the beam and see who lay beneath. Donovan leaned down and saw it was a *man's* hand. The man's thick blackened fingers were stuck to the charred pages of an Arab magazine. Donovan and Jacob kicked the red-hot roof beam aside and saw that the man's face was badly burned and his left ear was missing.

"That's the man who grabbed Nell in Manhattan," Lindee said, pointing to his missing ear.

Nearby, Donovan saw a chunk of collapsed roof propped up by something big. Human-body big. He, Jacob and Lindee stepped slowly toward it, again fearing the worst. Jacob stared at the burnt slab. Lindee closed her eyes.

Donovan reached down, lifted the chunk of roof to the side and saw a long sofa cushion beneath. Lindee leaned against Jacob in relief.

They searched for several more minutes, but found no clue Nell had been in the cabin.

"No hint of a laboratory . . ." Jacob said.

"Probably drove her to it," Donovan said.

Jacob nodded, looking a bit more hopeful.

Donovan saw something shiny. He hurried over, kicked some debris aside and picked up a silver buckle attached to a burnt leather strap.

"That's Nell's purse strap . . ." Lindee whispered. "And look – there's her purse." She picked it up and shook off the ashes.

Outside, two police sirens wound down.

Donovan saw Drew Manning jump out with his rescue team in blue FBI windbreakers. Behind them was a dark blue CSI van, two New York State police vehicles, and the sheriff's car.

Manning ran inside. "We heard the explosion. Everyone okay?"

"Everyone but him." Donovan pointed at the body. Donovan said. "Let's leave this cabin to your techs." He handed Nell's burnt purse to Manning who turned it over to an FBI tech team member.

Donovan, Jacob, and the others stared out at the surrounding forest. Thunder rumbled overhead and a light mist started falling.

Jacob turned and stared back at the thick stacks of cabin rubble. "She's beneath all this . . ." His eyes welled up.

"No. We would have found her by now," Donovan said, hoping he was right.

Donovan turned to Agent Manning. "Drew, have the choppers searching around this cabin area found anything?"

"No. The choppers were just grounded." He pointed at the fast-moving coal-black clouds. "Strong wind and storms coming."

THIRTY SIX

Nell ran for her life.
 For real!

She'd been running through the forest for nearly twenty minutes – chased by the two men who entered the cabin seconds after she finally unlocked the back door and raced into the woods.

The men obviously found Aarif's body, discovered her gone, saw her footprints outside, and ran after her.

And were still running after her, easily tracking her footprints in the damp soil.

Thunder rumbled as she ran around boulders and trees. Her flat shoes kept slipping in the slick grass and soil. She needed her Nikes. The men were maybe sixty seconds behind her.

But gaining.

Her heart pounded, but she couldn't seem to pull away from them, or get enough air into her lungs. And she was tiring. A tree branch ripped her lower lip and she tasted blood in her mouth.

Then - a muffled *thwack!*
A silenced gun!
Tree bark nicked her neck.
She sprinted harder.

Ahead, she saw a large outcrop of boulders that might shield her from gunfire for a few seconds. She ran around the boulders and saw another problem - the path ahead was long and straight - a one hundred yard shooting range. She had to get off the path fast.

She yanked out a crumpled tissue, ran up and dropped it on the path to make them maybe think she'd continued on it. Then she sprinted to the left, jumped behind dense holly bushes and waited, burying her breathing into her shoulder.

Seconds later, she watched the men run around the boulders, point to her tissue, mumble something, and continue running down the path.

She waited until they were out of sight, took a deep breath, then took off running another direction. But after a minute or so, she realized her path was twisting her back toward their path. Would she run into them? Should she turn back now?

Fifty yards later, some luck.

A semi-paved road.

She ran along the road's shoulder, hoping for a car.

No cars showed up.

But the two men did - one hundred fifty yards behind her. She started to duck back into the forest as one man fired his gun, kicking up dirt just feet from her.

She sprinted back across the road and disappeared into the thick forest, running downhill.

The men raced after her.

Lightning streaked across the sky. Light rain fell. The forest terrain sloped down and she gained speed. But so did the men, closing on her from the left.

She ran around some trees and froze at the edge of an eight-foot-deep drop-off. She looked down at large, jagged chunks of rain-slick slate, glistening black, looking sharp as razor blades.

She had no choice.

She jumped, landed on her feet, fell forward, bruised her left palm on the slate, sprang up, and ran on.

As she skirted another wall of boulders, she saw a sprawling blue lake at the bottom of the hill. The men shouted to each other, maybe planning to encircle her. She ran toward the lake looking for boaters, campers, fishermen.

She saw no people. Only one boat. Docked a half mile away on the opposite shore.

She looked behind her, couldn't see the two men, but heard them *gaining!* Seconds from shooting at her again.

It was only a matter of time before their bullets hit her - unless she did something totally unexpected.

But what? Nothing came to mind.

Then, glimpsing the lake, she had an idea. If it worked she might have a chance, if it didn't . . . game over.

She took a large stone and threw it down toward the lake. It missed. She grabbed a heavier rock and threw harder. It clacked off a stone and bounced into the water, making a loud splash.

One man shouted, suggesting he'd heard the splash. Both men ran down toward the water.

Now the hard part. She took a deep breath, turned around and started running back *up* the steep hill she'd just run down. Within seconds, she huffed like a marathoner. Her lungs burned, her legs turned to cement. But she refused to stop.

Two minutes later, she slowed to a jog, sucking in air. She heard the men far *below* her now, searching for her alongside the lake – going *away* from her. They'd taken the bait. But for how long? She continued jogging back up the steep muddy hill. Her shoes kept slipping and dropping her to her knees.

Moments later, she emerged onto the same road she'd crossed earlier.

Still no cars. She slow-jogged away, regaining her breath.

The men sounded like they were still down near the lake.

Soon, they'd realize she'd set them up with the lake splash. They'd head back up the hill and emerge onto the road. She had to find a place to hide first – because the rain made her footprints as trackable as Day-Glo.

Then she heard something.

She turned and saw a miracle!

An older Ford Taurus drove toward her. A silver-haired couple in front.

She stood in the middle of the road and waved her arms.

The Taurus stopped. She ran back to the passenger window.

The elderly woman stared with shock at her drenched, muddy clothes and bloody face. "My goodness, dear! What happened?"

"- two men are chasing me."

The frightened woman looked around. "Oh, good Lord! Hurry dear, get in!"

She jumped in the back seat and the car raced off. She looked back and didn't see the men.

"Thank you," Nell gasped.

"You're welcome, dear!" said the woman. "Where are the men?"

"Down near the water. Do you have a cell phone I could use? It's very important."

"Oh . . . gosh, we only have our house phone."

"Can you get me to a phone or the police fast. It's extremely important."

The silver haired driver with bushy black eyebrows turned and smiled at her. "I'm afraid we can't."

"Why?"

"We promised Hasham we'd bring you back."

THIRTY SEVEN

"Let's check out back," Donovan said, as he, Manning, Jacob, and Lindee trudged through charred, smoking rubble to the area behind the cabin.

The explosion had flipped the white van on its side and left the undercarriage and tires burning. Fearing a gas tank explosion, Donovan backed everyone away from the van and signaled the sheriff and his deputies. The deputies hurried over and extinguished the undercarriage fire in seconds.

Donovan searched for some hint that Nell had escaped the cabin, but saw none. He did see several man-sized shoeprints in the moist soil.

"What shoes was Nell wearing?" he asked.

"Black flats, slight heel," Lindee said.

"Size?"

"Nine."

"Here's something!" Lindee pointed.

They hurried over to her.

She picked up a necklace with a silver heart shaped charm.

"That's *Nell's!*" Jacob said, opening it.

Donovan saw a tiny picture of Nell, Jacob and Mia inside. Tears welled up in Jacob's eyes. Donovan could only imagine the pain the man felt.

"Look - her shoeprints!" Lindee shouted, pointing to a woman's shoe prints.

"They head into the forest," Jacob said.

"So do these!" Donovan said, pointing at two sets of large male prints. "And the space between these prints says the men were running . . . probably chasing her!"

Manning turned to his FBI team, "Dragnet the forest surrounding this cabin."

"We'll help," the sheriff said, nodding to his deputies.

Jacob stared at the men's footprints. "The two men will catch her."

"Not if she had a good lead," Donovan said. But then he noticed Nell's prints and the men's seemed equally fresh, suggesting they were made about the same time, suggesting Nell might not have a good lead, suggesting the men might have caught her.

Lighting exploded, bleaching the black sky white, and he realized that rain might wipe out any hope of tracking her footprints.

"*Agent Manning!*" an FBI agent shouted from the cabin. "Over here!"

Donovan feared the worst.

Jacob leading, everyone hurried over to the agent near a huge pile of cabin rubble.

Donovan was relieved to see no body. But was shocked to see a twelve-by-twelve foot section of floor that had somehow sunk below ground. He heard a motor running.

"What the hell's this?" Donovan asked.

"An industrial-size elevator platform for lowering heavy equipment below ground," Manning said. "Special Agent O'Keefe hotwired its touch pad somehow and got the elevator working. He's down there."

Moments later, Agent Jim O'Keefe's bushy red hair dusted with ashes, arose slowly from the elevator shaft like a ghost ascending from Dante's Inferno.

"What's down there, Jim?" Manning asked.

"Dr. Frankenstein's laboratory. In damned good shape despite the explosion."

"Bodies?"

"No . . ."

"What's the lab make?"

"The equipment suggests chemical and biological agents."

"Dogs too?" Manning asked as they all heard barking.

"Yeah. Noah's Ark's down there too," O'Keefe said. "Dogs, cats, monkeys. Get the humane society down here fast."

"Before that," Manning said, "get our FBI Techs down there to see what the hell the lab was making."

"And test the animals," Donovan said. "Find out what he's been testing on them."

THIRTY EIGHT

EAST BALTIMORE

Sexy Lexy slithered down her dance pole like a python.
What a BOD! Mason Schlumpf thought, sipping his dirty martini. *Marvelous curves!*

This was Lexy's first week in Baltimore's "classy" new topless club - *StarBUTTS*.

Lexy smiled at him and he smiled back. Then she laughed her cute little girl laugh. Schlumpf's wife, Inez, hadn't laughed since President Ford fell down the airplane steps. Inez was like Antarctica – ice at the bottom . . . Lexy's bottom was hot as a Corvette tailpipe.

StarBUTTS had only the best-looking girls, except for Meatflap, a three hundred pounder who snapped her pole last week, unleashing a splinter that lodged in the bartender's ass.

Schlumpf met Lexy a year ago after the Army dismissed him from Aberdeen Proving Ground. They claimed he'd stolen sensitive computer equipment, but never proved it. Nor could they unless they visited North Korea.

Then, a few weeks after his dismissal, he met the guy sitting across the table from him now. John Baker, whose real name he later learned was Wassif Shadid.

Shadid had asked him for some basic information about the military's work at Aberdeen and Fort Detrick. Simple stuff. Basic product information, like which biological and chemical agents were worked on. Background info, much already online.

And the information not online, Schlumpf could provide for a fee. He'd worked at both Fort Detrick and Aberdeen for twenty-seven years.

Shadid also wanted to know the names of certain lab scientists so "our company can possibly offer one a prestigious directorship in our renowned medical-pharmaceutical division in Dundee, Scotland."

Wassif Shadid then asked him, "So what is your fee for this information?"

"You're asking for very valuable information," Schlumpf had said, knowing Shadid couldn't obtain much of the data anywhere else. So he said . . . "Five hundred thousand dollars. Half up front. Half after I give you the names of scientists."

Shadid didn't blink. "Deal."

Music to a jobless man's ears.

So a week later, Shadid gave him $250,000, and Schlumpf handed Shadid important product information. A few weeks later, Schlumpf gave him the names of five scientists and a description of what each worked on. And tonight Shadid would hand him the final $250,000. The money had made Schlumpf's life much more pleasurable, like Sexy Lexy.

Shadid wore Ray-Ban sunglasses in the dark club and despite the air conditioning, he sweated like a steam pipe.

"Mr. Schlumpf, why must we meet in this cesspool?"

Schlumpf knew Shadid detested meeting in the strip club almost as much as Schlumpf enjoyed making the sanctimonious Muslim bastard reeking with lemony cologne, meet here.

"Because, Shadid, it's *safe* here. My former colleagues and your associates would never find us in a seedy place like this."

But also, Schlumpf thought, *because it's fun to see you squirm as you try not to look at the naked girls.*

"These harlots will burn in hell!"

"If Allah wishes," Schlumpf said.

Shadid bolted upright in his chair. "You *blaspheme!* You must never mention His name here!"

"Whoops! My bad, Shadid."

Shadid attacked his Diet Coke. Schlumpf sipped his martini.

"So, how is Doctor Nell, my former Aberdeen colleague doing?" Schlumpf asked.

"She is doing what we've requested. But if her product fails, she will face serious consequences."

"If it fails," Schlumpf said, "don't pay her."

"Not that simple."

"Why not?"

"Just because."

Schlumpf said nothing.

"If she fails, *you* will also face consequences."

"Me?" Schlumpf said, leaning back. "How the hell can you hold me responsible if *she* fails?"

"You recommended her."

"That's bullshit! I *suggested* six people. *Your* people evaluated them. *Your* people chose her! Not me! Remember?"

Shadid said nothing.

Mason Schlumpf gulped his martini down and signaled the waitress for another.

"Did you test her work?"

Shadid had refused to tell him what she worked on.

"Yes."

"And . . .?"

"It was successful."

"So what the fuck? Release her from her contract when she's finished. End of story."

"That's what we've told her."

"That's what you told *me!*"

Shadid shrugged, leaned back and sipped more Diet Coke.

Schlumpf now realized that Shadid had probably been lying all along. Lying was like breathing to these people. Which meant they might have forced Nell to make something illegal or even worse, *lethal*. Which meant they might harm her if she didn't do what they asked. And even if she did.

And then . . . they might come after me.

Schlumpf's armpits felt damp.

"Where's the rest of my fee?" Schlumpf demanded, gulping down his martini.

Shadid reached down, picked up a gleaming alligator-leather briefcase and handed it to him.

Schlumpf clicked it open, reached inside, and fanned the thick stacks of hundreds. After rough-counting the stacks, he was satisfied it was all there, and clicked the case shut.

"You must never mention our relationship to anyone," Shadid said. "Even after."

"After what?"

Shadid paused. "After our product is in the ah . . . marketplace."

"Which product?"

"You'll know soon enough. If you talk to anyone about it, then you will not like what happens to you and Ms. Sexy Lexy."

There it was. An all-out threat.

Schlumpf understood now. They were planning some kind of disaster and he'd unwittingly helped them. His throat was chalk-dry.

The waitress walked over, leaned forward, placed Schlumpf's martini on the table, and her bare breast on Shadid's shoulder.

Shadid turned beet-red. "Such godless depravity! Our business is completed, Mr. Schlumpf. Good bye." He stood and stormed out of the bar.

Schlumpf sat back and worried about Shadid's "product in the marketplace." What the hell was it? The more he thought about it, the more he felt the product might even be a serious weapon, maybe even mass destruction, an MWD. He grew terrified at what he'd unintentionally helped Shadid do. Tomorrow, he'd use a library computer to alert authorities anonymously.

Two martinis later, Schlumpf stood and stumbled out the rear exit of the bar and headed toward his new Jaguar. Hot, humid air swept in off the Baltimore harbor. He noticed the parking lot was much darker now that the big overhead light had burned out.

As he walked, he smelled lemony men's cologne.

He heard footsteps moving close behind him.

He started to turn - when a steel wire whipped around his neck and jerked back hard.

Schlumpf dropped the briefcase to get his fingers under the wire. But it was too tight. Warm blood slid down his neck onto his $250 monogrammed shirt. Blood spattered onto the fender of his shiny Jaguar.

He couldn't breathe! He was losing consciousness.

Another man picked up the briefcase. The man turned and faced him.

Shadid.

He walked up to Schlumpf, paused a moment, then plunged a long, curved dagger deep into Schlumpf's lower abdomen, ripped up and sideways hard.

The last thing Mason Schlumpf saw in life . . . was his intestines spilling out onto the parking lot.

THIRTY NINE

Hasham Habib felt proud as he waved the first gray delivery truck into the shipping dock of his assembly facility. Within two minutes, all trucks had parked inside. Hasham ordered the facility manager to close the shipping dock doors.

The drivers got out and walked over to Hasham. He embraced each man, then turned to the lead driver.

"Were you followed?"

"No."

"Unload the trucks and store the cargo."

Within minutes, the drivers had removed the heavy stainless steel canisters of blended VX from the cabin lab, placed them in large cabinets near the assembly area, then locked the cabinets.

Hasham was most pleased. Everything was going smoothly . . . just like his plans. He permitted himself a smile.

He walked around, rechecking all equipment. When he was certain everything was in order, he went to his office, locked the door and sat at his desk. He lit a long Cohiba, took a deep drag, and paused a moment to savor the cigar's robust aroma.

Time to update the moneyman.

Hasham unlocked a drawer, took out his burner phone, and punched in the only number it ever called. Seven thousand miles away in Yemen, Bassam Maahdi answered.

"Hello, Mr. Smith," Bassam Maahdi said.

"Hello to you, Mr. Jones," Hasham said. "How's your weather today?"

"Beautiful. And yours?"

Hasham saw the thick black rain clouds overhead, but said, "Sunny with blue skies."

"Excellent. I trust your medical supplies have arrived?"

"Yes. They just arrived at our distribution facility," Hasham said.

"Good. So tell me, how many ah . . . patients do you estimate will benefit from our medicine?"

Hasham looked at the computer screen and scrolled down to his estimated Phase One Kill-Rate total. "Approximately 270,000 in Phase One."

"And Phase Two?"

"Another 220,000."

"My, my - that's much better than I expected. Incredibly good news. We'll make medical . . . history."

"Indeed."

"When will they benefit from it?"

"Over the next forty-eight hours."

"More magnificent news."

"Quite."

"So . . . approximately a half million sick people will ah . . . be helped by our product."

"That is correct."

Long pause. "Congratulations, Mr. Smith."

"Thank you . . ." Hasham said.

———

"But tell me, do our, ah, competitors suspect our new medicine is coming?"

Hasham paused. "No. They have no idea at all."

"So they'll be surprised?"

"*Shocked* is the word."

"Shocked indeed! Excellent work, Mr. Smith. I will so inform our generous associates."

"Most kind of you, Mr. Jones."

Hasham wanted the generous associates well informed since their hands turned the money spigots.

Hasham and Maahdi hung up.

* * *

So did Bobby Kamal in Fort Meade, Maryland. He replayed their conversation. The Yemen phone number had again triggered a red-flag alert on his NSA monitoring system.

Kamal still wondered why these two obvious Arab-speakers spoke English.

And why use such obvious aliases – Smith and Jones - to discuss *medical* supplies? It made no sense.

And why no mention of the product's brand name, or which medical condition it treated, or whether it required a prescription or was an over-the-counter product, or where it would be sold, or which health plans accepted it, or what marketing or promotional activities were planned? Why no mention of these issues so critical to the success of any new medicine?

Maybe, Kamal suspected - *because their medicine is not medicine.*

And how could they be so certain nearly five hundred thousand patients would receive their medicine within two days? And how could the competition not know about the new product? The profit-rich drug companies paid enormous fees to corporate moles who told them exactly what their competitors were making. These same drug companies also paid huge bribes to FDA employees to reveal which drugs the FDA would and would not approve.

So what game are Smith and Jones really playing?

Counterfeit medicines? Sold on the Internet? Fake Avistan for cancer patients? Fake Exelon for Alzheimer's patients? Fake half-strength drugs cost less, but sometimes cost lives. Were Smith and Brown selling fake drugs to retirees who can't afford America's criminally high drug prices?

Possibly.

But Bobby Kamal's gut told him these two men were not exporting Yemen-manufactured medications to America. Yemen's exports were fish and produce.

Yemen's best-known exports came with two legs: jihadists. The capital, Sana'a, a city of two million, had the highest per capita concentration of Al Qaeda, ISIS, and Houthis jihadists in the world.

Kamal feared the worst. Based on the nearly 500,000 people these two men mentioned, they were very likely talking about a weapon of mass destruction . . . a WMD like a bio or chemical weapon maybe. Or God forbid, a suitcase nuke . . .

Kamal turned back to his computer and tried to zero in on Mr. Smith's location in New York. Two minutes later, he'd tracked his location to the area in or around the southeast corner of the Adirondack Park.

Mr. Smith had said his park weather was "sunny with blue skies," yet AccuWeather showed that the Adirondack Park area was socked in with thick rain clouds all day.

"Sunny with blue skies" probably meant, *"our plans are going well."*

To get a more precise location for Mr. Smith, Kamal tried a new phone tracking software developed by his tech-genius college buddy, Dave Cousineau. Fifteen minutes later, Dave's software fixed Mr. Smith's location within twelve miles of Mayfield.

FORTY

Behind the cabin, Donovan felt his phone vibrate in his pocket. He checked - it was Maccabee.

"How's it going?" she asked.

"Things are heating up," he said, touching his singed-off eyebrows. He didn't want to mention the cabin explosion, since she had enough to worry about. "Any luck with Doctor Dubin?"

"He just called back."

"I hope he got *your* test results this time?"

"He did." Her voice seemed tight.

"So . . .?"

She took a deep, slow breath, as though not wanting to tell him more. If she didn't want to tell him, he didn't want to hear.

"So . . . the results were not so good," she said.

He slumped against a tree.

"I have stage three endometriosis . . . bad enough to lower my chances for getting pregnant."

He felt his stomach sink.

"And he wants to check out a cyst on my ovary."

Donovan couldn't speak.

"He said the vast majority of cysts are benign."

Which means the rest are trouble, he sensed. "So I guess getting pregnant is . . ."

" . . . less likely. But he says new surgeries, plus laparoscopy and precise timing procedures increase the chances of getting pregnant."

"So we'll try those."

"We will."

"What time are you seeing Dr. Dubin?"

"In a couple of hours. I'll call later and let you know what he says."

"Okay. . ."

"Oh, by the way," she said, "I got a strange call a few minutes ago,"

"Strange?"

"Yeah. An air conditioning service guy called. He's coming over to fix a Freon leak from our AC unit. Apparently our pipe is dripping into the apartment below us."

Donovan went on full alert. "Mac – all the building's AC Freon units are in the basement. And the Freon won't be added for two more months!"

She said nothing.

"When's he coming over?"

"He said ". . . any minute now.""

"Mac - get out of the apartment now!"

"What?"

"Leave the apartment right now!"

"But - "

" - just grab your stuff and leave! Go to Mrs. Hansen's apartment on Three. She's always there."

"What's with the paranoia? What's going on?"

"This service guy is probably linked to the terrorists I'm chasing. They're targeting family members."

She said nothing.

"Please leave now and call me wherever you go."

"Hang on . . ."

"What?"

She put the phone down and he heard her talking to Johnny, the lobby guard, on the apartment's two-way phone.

"Johnny said the AC service man is heading up to see me."

"Leave the apartment *now!*"

FORTY ONE

Dr. Nell Northam's gray-haired rescuers in the Taurus turned out to be middle-aged jihadists working for Hasham.

After they removed their wigs, revealing black hair, the man flex-cuffed and blindfolded Nell and pushed her down in the back seat. The bulky woman sat beside her, gripping a small black handgun.

The man drove at normal highway speeds, making several turns. The woman kept saying, "Clear," telling the driver no one was following.

Soon, they drove into stop-and-go traffic. She heard horns, truck brakes, a church bell, a truck beeping as it backed up, town noises. The car stopped and a garage door rattled open. They drove in and the door thudded down behind them. The driver cut off her flex-cuffs, pulled her out of the back seat and removed her blindfold.

She was in an enormous garage.

She saw four of the big gray delivery trucks with VX canisters from the cabin. Were the canisters still in the trucks?

Nell sensed someone behind her. Turning, she saw Hasham a few feet away. He walked toward her, looking angry, and slapped her face hard. The blow knocked her back so hard her ear started ringing.

"That's for killing Aarif!"

"Because he tried to kill me - "

"You disobeyed me." His eyes were crazed.

"No - I helped you blend your weapon and it worked."

Hasham's face was crimson. He and a tall bearded man led her from the garage down a hall through a much larger room that looked like some kind of assembly area.

She wondered if this was where they would weaponize the blended VX into the secret delivery system Hasham bragged about.

But she saw none of the expected VX delivery paraphernalia. No air dispersal equipment. No water delivery devices or other dispersal methodologies. Hasham apparently told the truth when he bragged that his delivery was unique. And if it was unique, Homeland Security authorities would not be prepared to defend against it.

She looked out a window and saw a tall red brick warehouse next to an abandoned gray concrete-wall building. She was apparently in some kind of warehouse district. But where? Which town? The drive took maybe fifteen minutes from where they picked her up near the cabin. But where was the cabin? She had no idea.

Hasham and the bearded man marched her over to a twelve-by-fourteen-foot room, pushed her inside, and locked the door from the outside. She looked around. She was in a janitor's storage room. When they walked away, she tried the handle. It was locked in place. The door could only be unlocked from the outside.

She was trapped.

She looked around. Mops, brooms, big drums and vats filled with what looked like industrial cleaners.

She flipped the light switch. A bulb hanging from the ceiling gave off as much light as a birthday candle. She searched for a tool to use for self-defense. She found none. Just cleaning compounds, half empty paint cans, stir-sticks, and sandpaper. She looked up and saw faint daylight through a small glass-block window at the ceiling.

The window seemed too high to get up to . . . too hard to break without a tool . . . too small to crawl through.

Beside her, a flash of light caught her eye. The light spilled through a tiny slit in the wall's wood panels. She squinted through the slit and saw an office. Beyond the office, she saw floor-to-ceiling cabinets filled with the steel canisters of blended VX.

She heard Hasham speaking as he walked into the office.

Quickly, she reached up and turned off her light so he wouldn't see light through the slit. He sat at his desktop computer and opened it to what looked like an online Arab newspaper. Beyond him, she saw the large assembly area. She scanned the room for some hint of what the machines assembled. She saw no clue. Still, she sensed the assembly area held the secret to Hasham's unique VX delivery system. If so, she might find a way to thwart it.

But, she reminded herself - although Hasham said his system is unique, he might be lying. He might use a *proven* VX delivery system. The necessary delivery equipment might be stored in another part of the warehouse.

She flashed back to the Kurdish village of Halabja where Saddam Hussein's aircraft sprayed VX, sarin, and tabun gases onto the innocent villagers. She visited the village shrine years later and saw photos of the horrific massacre: five thousand men women and children killed, their bodies twisted in death, their mouths crusted with green bloody vomit.

She saw faces distorted in excruciating agony as their lungs screamed for air, and pain ripped through their bodies, and their hearts exploded, until mercifully death gave them peace.

She wept as she looked at the carnage. Mothers clutching their small children and infants, faces frozen in pain.

And soon she would weep for thousands of Americans who would die a similar death.

Unless she did something.

FORTY TWO

"Is Maccabee at home?" Donovan asked the CIA agent.

"No sir!"

"Did you check Mrs. Hansen's on Three?"

"Mrs. Hansen's in Savannah."

"Did the lobby guard see Maccabee leave?"

"No. He just came on duty."

"Check the lobby video."

"I did. It shows a service guy stepping onto the elevator and heading up about that time you talked to her. But we can't verify if he's the AC service guy or not."

"He probably is. He was heading up to her then. Check all building security cams."

"We're checking them now."

Donovan swallowed a dry throat. *And call me!*

"Yes sir."

They hung up.

Donovan phoned Maccabee again and was bounced into voice mail. He left another message asking her to call. His sixth call. He tried Doctor Dubin's office and learned she hadn't gone there.

Why isn't she returning my calls? She always answers within minutes. Where is she?

He directed two agents in Manhattan to check with her friends, and ask tenants if they saw her leave the building.

Donovan's mind was spinning with possibilities. All bad.

He took a deep breath and tried to calm himself as he pulled into *The Highwayman Tavern* north of Mayfield on Highway 30, a popular hangout for locals.

He hoped someone in the bar saw Nell or the white van. The lot was filled with pickups, four-wheel vehicles, and a 1962 green VW minivan in mint condition.

An FBI team had tracked Nell's footsteps through the forest to near the Jackson Summit Reservoir where rain washed them out. They found them again alongside a road, but then her steps simply vanished. A vehicle had obviously picked her up. Most likely her abductors, since she hadn't phoned 911, Jacob, or Lindee.

Worse case scenario, her abductors dumped her body in the forest.

Donovan, Agent Manning, Lindee, and Jacob went inside *The Highwayman Tavern*. The busy, two-story bar smelled like fried burgers, beer, and spicy nachos. Neon beer signs celebrated Utica Club, Saranac, and Stella Artois. Several customers celebrated a Yankee home run.

Farmers with sunburned faces and white foreheads chatted with men in suits and ties. Construction workers threw darts. An ancient Wurlitzer pumped out Springsteen's *Born in the USA*. Some guys looked like they were born in the bar - and never left.

Donovan preferred this kind of cozy saloon, hard to find in chichi, tony Manhattan. Everyone here probably knew everyone. And noticed strangers.

He introduced himself to the bartender whose frizzy silver hair looked like a Brillo pad. Donovan showed him his badge, a photo of Nell and the van, and explained.

The bartender squinted at the photo, shook his head. "Haven't seen her. But if she or the van's in these parts, one of these rummies might know." He nodded toward his customers. "Just ask 'em."

He handed Donovan a small microphone. Donovan tapped it and it popped like a firecracker.

The chatter quieted a bit.

"Pardon me folks, but we need your help. My name's Donovan Rourke. I'm with the federal government."

Silence.

"Please hold your fire until I finish."

Some chuckles and smiles.

"This is your basic CIA badge." He held it up.

The bar immediately got quiet. The CIA badge was a Mute button.

"We're searching for three men who are middle-eastern looking. They kidnapped a woman, Dr. Nell Northam. They were just seen in this general Park area in a white Chevy van."

Drew Manning and a police officer handed out copies of Nell's photo and the van.

"Has anyone seen her or the white van'?"

No one answered. Most shook their heads.

"They snatch her?" shouted a skinny older woman with blonde hair stacked up like a beehive.

"Yes. But these men are more than abductors."

"Rapists?" a young blonde waitress asked.

"Terrorists."

No one spoke. Someone unplugged *Born in the USA*.

Donovan didn't want to incite panic, but he had to level with them. "We think they're planning an attack."

"In itty bitty Mayfield?"

"Probably New York City."

Silence.

"So why're these bastards way up here?"

"They have a large underground laboratory in the Adirondack forest."

The customers looked stunned. Clearly, they had no idea a laboratory had been built there.

Donovan continued, "Anyone see anything or anyone out of place, out of the ordinary, anything strange in the area?"

A short guy with a beer belly pushing out his grass-stained Oshkosh overalls stood up. "Name's Maynard Trott." His cheeks gleamed like polished red apples.

"I seen a strange truck. Bearded dark-skinned fella driving."

"What kind of truck?"

"Delivery truck. Gray, mid-sized."

Maybe the same gray truck the boy on a Schwinn saw, Donovan thought.

"Why strange?"

Maynard Trott spit tobacco into a tin can. "'Cuz where it was at."

Trott walked over to the wall and pointed to a spot on the Fulton County map.

"This here dirt trail. Ain't but one place to deliver at. Cabin way at the end."

Donovan saw it was the same trail to the destroyed cabin they'd just left. "Was the truck heading toward the cabin?"

"Nope. Coming *out*. Turned left on Tolemantown."

"What was strange about it?"

"Side of the truck."

"Why strange?"

Maynard honked a nasty gob of chewing tobacco into a spittoon with the accuracy of a Marine sniper.

"Name on the side."

"What name?" Getting information from Maynard was like pulling stumps.

"Said *Zelda's Fresh Garden Flowers*."

———

"Delivering flowers maybe," Donovan said.

"Nope."

"Why not?"

"Ain't no *Zelda's Fresh Garden Flowers* store nowheres in the whole damn state of New York. And that's a true fact!"

"How the hell you know that, Maynard?" A fiftyish red-haired woman shouted.

"'Cuz a my new iPhone, Juwanna." He pulled it out of his bib overalls and proudly waved it around. "It tells me *Zelda's Fresh Garden Flowers* is somewheres else!"

"Where's it at?"

"El Paso, Texas. Three-thousand-mile flower delivery. Gotta be one of them secret boyfriends you always braggin' about, Juwanna."

Everyone laughed. Juwanna threw a stack of swizzle sticks at Maynard.

Donovan knew El Paso bordered Juarez, Mexico, a sometimes US entry location for jihadist terrorists posing as Mexicans.

"We'll put out a BOLO on the flower truck," Manning said.

"*Trucks!*" Maynard said.

Donovan grew more concerned. "How many?"

Maynard closed his eyes. "I seen four trucks, mighta been more. All had *Zelda's Fresh Garden Flowers* on the side. Four trucks from El Paso delivering flowers to a New York forest road whut ain't got but one cabin? Them flowers'd be all shriveled up and dead by the time they got here. Don't make a lick a sense to me!"

"To me either, Maynard," Donovan said, as he walked over to the map and placed his finger on the cabin road. "You're positive *this* is the road where you saw the trucks?"

"Yep!"

Donovan sensed the fleet of trucks were connected to the attack. Maybe the trucks would release the bio or chemical weapon through their exhaust systems on Manhattan streets.

Or maybe each truck would attack a different city.

———

Donovan heard Manning call in the description of Zelda's flower trucks.

"Anything else, Mr. Trott?"

"Nope."

Donovan thanked everyone and asked them to call him or 911 if they saw Nell Northam, the white Chevy van, or the flower trucks.

His phone rang, he listened a minute, hung up and turned to Manning, Jacob, and Lindee.

"That was my NSA contact, Bobby Kamal. He just listened into another conversation between a man in Yemen and a man in this area . . . a man within twelve miles of us."

"Did he get a name for the guy here?"

"No."

"The NSA is also picking up credible buzz about a major attack. And the buzz is growing louder. Bottom line - Washington, Homeland Security, the FBI and NSA, and now the White House, suspect an imminent attack."

"How imminent?" Manning asked.

"Probably within forty-eight hours. They're raising the terrorist alert level to *HIGH ALERT!* Maybe even to *SEVERE ALERT* - if we find out where, when, and how it's coming."

No one spoke.

"Are they still looking for Nell?" Jacob asked.

"Yes. Finding Nell is the key," Donovan said.

And finding Maccabee is the key to my family, he thought. He checked his calls-received and saw she still hadn't called or texted him. He dialed her number again. No answer.

He tried to leave a voice message, but the message box was full. Panic was scrambling his brain.

As Manning made a call, Donovan stared across the bar at an old friend of his: Jameson whiskey. He felt incredible pressure to chug some down. Jameson had often eased his panic and pain after his first wife, Emma, was murdered in Brussels because he wasn't there to protect her. The drinking grew worse until he hit bottom a few months later back in Manhattan. Finally, he got the rehab treatment he needed.

But now, once again, his wife was in danger - because of his job. Namely, protecting America. No small task. But how could he protect America if he couldn't even protect his wife?

With Maccabee in probable danger and her ovarian cyst fears, he should probably consider asking to be relieved from this assignment.

And looking at the bigger, long-term picture, he should probably consider reassessing his current appointment by the DNI and the President. The job threatened his life and the lives of Maccabee and Tish. What right did he have to endanger his family?

Sooner or later, he'd have to decide about the job.

FORTY THREE

Nell's throat felt raw from breathing the caustic cleaning-chemical fumes in the small, dank janitor's room. She stared at her only escape route - the steel door - still dead-bolted from the outside.

It was only a matter of time before the men unlocked it, dragged her out, and executed her. She'd seen their faces, knew their names, knew their weapon, knew Hasham wanted revenge for killing Aarif and for escaping the cabin.

He wouldn't risk her escaping again. If she told authorities about VX, Homeland Security would quickly distribute VX antidotes like Mestinon, or pyridostigmine bromide, to people in the most likely target areas, densely populated cities, probably Manhattan. If people received antidotes before being exposed, or just in time, they had a chance to live.

And *if* Hasham dispersed VX by air, authorities could curfew people to stay in their homes and offices, turn off ventilation systems, and seal their windows. Eventually, the winds would blow the nerve gas away, and when air levels tested safe, people could come outside.

And *if* Hasham dispersed by water, authorities might have time to turn off the water system and in time make water safe again.

It all depended on warning people.

And warning people depended first on warning authorities!

And that depended on *her*.

She heard men speaking Arabic walk into the next room, Hasham's office.

She bent down, looked through the slit in the paneling, and saw Hasham and two other workers. Beyond them, she noticed the steel VX containers were no longer in the cabinets. Where were they?

A tall bearded worker walked past the cabinets, and pulled down a large power lever on the wall. Instantly, motors rumbled to life and an assembly line belt began weaving through various machines and devices.

She heard glass jiggling, then saw small empty bottles rattle along the belt, shimmy around corners, clatter along a big curve.

What's going on?

The bottles reminded her of the original small Coca-Cola bottles. They passed under the nozzles that filled them with a chocolate milk-colored liquid.

The bottles jiggled closer to Nell, and slowly turned their bright yellow label around toward her.

She saw the label and stopped breathing.

The label read *ChocoYummy*. It pictured a smiling young girl and boy, about nine, with baseball caps.

NO . . .!

Please God . . . no!

They're putting VX in a chocolate drink for children!

One sip will kill a child in minutes.

She couldn't breathe.

Is that your strategy, Hasham? Kill our kids and you destroy our families. Destroy our families and you destroy our country. Destroy our country and your jihadist fanatics grab control of it.

Her eyes filled as she envisioned Mia drinking *ChocoYummy* and dying in excruciating pain. Nell's heart slammed into her throat. She broke out in a cold sweat.

Somehow she *had* to warn the authorities.

She stared at the locked door. Again, she searched the room from corner to corner, ceiling to floor, and found no tools to pry up the hinges.

Then an idea hit her. Maybe deadly, but maybe her only hope.

Quickly, she studied the list of contents on the cleaning product vats, looking for certain ingredients with which she might be able to create a small chemical explosive with enough power to blast off the door lock. She'd have to wait until the men left tonight.

But what if they don't leave . . . what if they'd decide to kill her before tonight?

She couldn't wait. She had to do it now and try to escape in the confusion of the explosion.

Assuming the explosion didn't kill her.

She searched each container, each cleaning drum, each list of ingredients. Amazingly, the main ingredient, hydrochloric acid, was not listed in any of the cleaning compounds. Nor were other essential compounds like toilet bowl cleaner, ammonium nitrate, and pool sanitizer chemicals. Did Hasham anticipate she might create an explosive and remove the necessary compounds from the room? Possibly. Her hope sank.

Bottom line: She had nothing to make a small chemical explosive.

She was trapped in this room.

Until they eliminated her.

* * *

"Where'd I hear this guy's voice?" Bobby Kamal wondered.

He sat at his desk in NSA headquarters. He was using voice recognition software, comparing the taped voice of Mr. Jones in Yemen – with the voice patterns of known Yemeni jihadists and terrorists. So far no match.

But somewhere within the last two years, Kamal knew he'd heard the soft, buttery voice of Mr. Jones. He grew more frustrated with each failed comparison.

He tried some new outspoken radicals like Abda Yusef, Saffa Khoury, Baba Azzim, Fawzy Hassan. No match.

Bobby Kamal began comparing Mr. Jones's voice to his second tier candidates - radicalized mullahs, intellectuals and vocal supporters of jihadists, ISIS, Hezbollah, and Al Qaeda.

No match.

He compared Jones to the three most rabid anti-American Yemini professors of Middle Eastern history.

No luck.

He decided to try a man who'd dropped off the NSA radar two years ago. Bassam Maahdi. An MD, with a PhD in chemistry from Beirut University and a PhD in microbiology from the University of Florida. He played Maahdi's voice.

Four soft, buttery words later . . . Bobby Kamal stood up.

Gotcha!

Bassam Maahdi is Mr. Jones. Voice Recognition registered a *97.4% match!*

Maahdi was very bad news. Born in southern Lebanon to a middle class family. When he was nine, his parents were killed in an Israeli air raid on his father's illegal weapons warehouse. Then he was raised by his jihadist uncle who intensified Maahdi's hatred of the West. Became an MD, but continued funding jihadists. He regularly received millions from an unidentified Saudi sheik, who used *hawala,* the hand-to-hand paperless transfer of massive amounts of cash between brokers. No banks, no paper trails. Just cash, hand to hand. Impossible to track.

But Bassam Maahdi himself was easy to track. At five-foot-four, three hundred thirty pounds, he looked like the Michelin Man in an Arab robe.

The question was - why did Maahdi speak English in obvious coded language to another Arab in upstate New York? These guys were not talking baba ganoush recipes. Nor were they talking medicine, as they claimed.

Most likely they were discussing something to do with Maahdi's expertise in chemistry and biology. Which suggested they might be talking about a chemical or biological weapon disguised as a new medicine.

Enough medicine for roughly a half million Americans they said . . . medicine located just a few hours from New York City's eight million people.

Bobby Kamal had a sinking feeling in his gut. The tiny hairs on his neck rose. He briefed his boss, then called Special Agent Donovan Rourke. Murphy's Law ruled.

Rourke's message box was full.

FORTY FOUR

Nell squinted through the slit in the wall, watching full bottles of *ChocoYummy* jiggle along the conveyor belts. The bottles were deposited in cases and loaded onto trucks that she heard drive off and return again and pick up more cases to deliver.

Clearly, the *ChocoYummy* bottles contained the deadly VX toxin. How many bottles? Based on the number jiggling past per minute, she estimated many thousands.

Liquid death.

Kids' deaths.

She saw Hasham watching the bottles jiggle past him. He looked quite pleased.

He walked over and pulled out a bottle. He studied its label, checked the yellow cap, and nodded approval to a worker. He checked a case of bottles. Another nod. Then he strolled over to a large printing machine. The printer was churning out something she couldn't see, probably related to *ChocoYummy*. Maybe coupons, discounts, direct mail, buy-one-get-one-free deals.

What kid could resist FREE? What mother?

Nell flashed back to another free drink . . . psycho James Jones' special *Flavor-Aid*. He ordered his followers – mothers, fathers, children, and babies – to sip his cyanide-laced drink. They drank. They died. Authorities found nine hundred corpses bloating in the blistering jungle sun, including three hundred children and infants.

ChocoYummy is Hasham's deadly drink.

She heard more trucks drive up outside. Through the wall slit, she saw a delivery bay door roll up. Men rolled more cases of *ChocoYummy* outside. She heard them being loaded onto the trucks.

A driver walked into Hasham's office carrying a five-foot long, flimsy magnetic sticker.

"I just took the last flower signs off the sides of the trucks," the driver said. He showed it to Hasham:

ZELDA'S FRESH GARDEN FLOWERS

"Off *all* trucks?"

"Yes."

Hasham nodded, reached into a large drawer and took out another package.

"Time to attach these new signs to sides of each truck."

Nell watched Hasham unfurl a new fifteen-foot magnetic sticker. She squinted through the slit and read:

ASK MOMMY FOR CHOCOYUMMY

Nell slumped against the wall. There it was! Hasham was going to kill thousands of kids with – *ChocoYummy* - his unique delivery system.

She felt like she might vomit. She banged on her door and begged the tall guard to let her go to the bathroom. He finally unlocked the door, grabbed her arm and walked her down to the small filthy restroom. She stepped inside, shut the door, bent over the broken, stained toilet, but couldn't vomit. It figured. She hadn't eaten since last night. She leaned against the wall and tried to calm herself, but it didn't work.

She heard noise outside. She looked out the small, nailed-shut window and saw Hasham lead the drivers over beneath some shade trees. The men stood in a line beside two large white bathtub-sized basins filled with what looked like water. Clean white towels sat stacked on the table. He gestured for the men to approach the basins.

The drivers walked up to the basins, whispered to themselves, and stripped to their underwear. Each man began to pour water over his hands three times. Then over his face three times, then over his arms, torso and feet, three times. Each man rinsed his mouth with water three times.

They did not speak. They lifted their eyes and arms toward the heavens. Their lips moved in silent prayer.

Nell understood.

She was witnessing a Muslim purification ceremony. They were cleansing themselves, preparing for their likely sacrificial death.

They are preparing to die.

The attack is imminent . . .

FORTY FIVE

Hasham strolled around his *ChocoYummy* factory. It had served his purpose well over the last six years. The years of searching for the right location to build a subterranean laboratory within striking distance of New York City, and searching for the right kind of assembly plant nearby, and the right mystery substance to blend with the VX, and the right reformulation of the blend mix to make it more lethal.

And of course, the years of identifying the right Aberdeen scientist to help him with the delicate blending process - all his years of channeling his rage into his jihad . . .

. . . would all pay off in hours.

He watched his men stack more cases of *ChocoYummy* onto the trucks and double-lock the doors.

He smiled at the truck *Ask Mommy for ChocoYummy* signage.

Then he walked inside to where Izzat was working on his iPad.

"What's a new product without advertising, Izzat?"

Izzat smiled. "Unknown . . .?"

"And unsold!" Hasham said. "Watch this!"

Hasham inserted a DVD into the large screen television. On the screen, Hasham's new commercial popped on.

He watched as . . .

> . . . *a young blond boy and girl, around nine,*
> *skip down the street and hurry into a small*
> *neighborhood grocery store. They ask for*
> *ChocoYummy. The smiling grocer hands*
> *them each a bottle. They twist off the top,*
> *chug some down and lick chocolate off their*
> *lips and grin into camera. Chocolate drips*
> *down the boy's chin and the girl giggles.*
>
> *Then the ChocoYummy logo pops on, the*
> *announcer says . . .*
>
> *"ChocoYummy . . . is fresh whole milk*
> *with lots of yummy organic nutrients. So ask*
> *your mummy for ChocoYummy . . . cuz it's so*
> *good in your tummy!"*

"Perfect," Izzat said.

"Agreed," Hasham said as he walked into his office and shut the door. He took out his safe phone and dialed. Time to tell Bassam Maahdi in Yemen the good news.

"Ah . . . Mr. Smith, so nice to hear from you," Maahdi said in Yemen. "How are things?"

"Just fine, Mr. Jones. And there?"

"All is well. Tell me, is our medicine on its way to market?"

"Yes."

"Wonderful. And will it be delivered to our patients on schedule?" Maahdi asked.

"Yes."

"And you will tidy up the assembly facility?"

"A most thorough cleaning indeed. Just minutes from now."

"Most reassuring, Mr. Smith."

"So we'll talk *after* the product's in the marketplace," Hasham said.

"Yes. After!" Maahdi said.

They hung up.

He looked around the plant and smiled. *My global jihad begins here now.* France and England in a few months. Tel Aviv in ten months. The world will learn . . .

Hasham smiled. He was filled with an overpowering sense of fulfillment, unlike anything he'd ever felt. Just one last task. Destroy the bottling plant.

And Dr. Nell Northam with it.

He and Izzat walked over to one of the drivers near the bottling assembly line.

"It's cleanup time," Hasham said.

Izzat and his assistant followed Hasham over where they grabbed five-gallon cans and began splashing gasoline onto the floor. They poured some on the rolls of paper near the printers, some near the bottling machines, garage loading area, and the corners of the building. They spilled more onto some flammable lubricants near the small machinery and computers.

Everything would be destroyed.

Hasham would have preferred to use his favorite explosive: TATP, triacetone triperoxide. TATP was his weapon of choice for his suicide bombers in Europe and Israel. Wearing their vests, they pushed their TATP detonators with such unwavering bravery and devotion. He was especially proud when they blew themselves up during Ramadan to earn greater rewards in heaven. Such devotion!

But traces of TATP found here would shout *terrorism*. Which would bring in the techs from FBI and Homeland Security. Hasham did not want expert FBI techs investigating the bottling plant fire. They might get very lucky and stumble upon his most important secret from the plant, a critical secret he did not want discovered.

Hasham wanted *local* firemen - bumpkins - investigating the fire.

The firemen would declare that gasoline caused the fire. They'd conclude the fire was set for the insurance money and suspect the factory owner. But the factory owner, one Felix Frampton, they'd learn had been deceased for twenty-six years.

By the time they realize I borrowed Mr. Frampton's identity, I'll be six thousand miles away in a country with a non-extradition treaty with America.

Hasham walked over and splashed an entire can of gasoline near the janitor closet door where Dr. Nell Northam was locked up. The fire would seep into her room and cause the chemical compound vats to burn and likely explode.

It was unfortunate to sacrifice someone with her expertise. *She's a brilliant scientist who could have created powerful weapons for our cause. But a cause she would never accept because she's infected with infidel thinking.*

And now she knows too much. She certainly read some of my files in the lab when I was busy. Critical files that detail extremely important future plans. And she can identify me.

It's simple. She must be terminated.

He looked toward the janitor room again. Should he feel guilty that Dr. Nell Northam would never see her husband and daughter again? *Of course not!*

Did she, or any Americans, ever feel guilt for killing his wife and daughter?

"An eye for an eye, Doctor!" he whispered at her door.

The word - *eye* - jolted him, as always. He flashed back to the last time he looked into his wife Leyla's eyes . . . flat and opaque as life drained from them. Minutes earlier, they'd been bright and luminous and brimming with life. But that night even the full moon couldn't animate them as she lay on the ground, bleeding to death.

Just minutes earlier, they'd been sipping tea in their Tikrit home.

He'd said, "Leyla, I'm going down to Abdul's for a few minutes."

"You're planning another attack, aren't you?"

"We're always planning." She worried too much and he wanted to calm her concerns. "But we plan very carefully, Leyla. Then we act."

"You mean *attack*. And the attacks always beget attacks."

He shrugged, knowing how she wanted him to cease all his jihadist activities.

"Leyla, you have nothing to fear."

But that night, he couldn't have been more wrong.

She had everything to fear.

He'd stepped outside and walked down toward Abdul's. He noticed the evening sky had turned dark amber. He smelled jasmine. The full moon lit the heat waves shimmering off the desert sands. A breeze swayed the palm tree fronds. A beautiful night.

A few steps later, he heard a unique whistling overhead. He recognized the sound, knew it was too late. Knew he was a dead man. Looked up and saw the missile streaking toward the bomb-makers' house next to his. Saw the explosion, felt his body blown over a car and dropped onto the street where a speeding truck missed his head by inches.

His nose was broken and bleeding. He spit blood and sand. A bloody bone stuck out of his forearm. Struggling, he managed to hobble back toward his home. But it wasn't there. Only rubble . . . and body parts.

He knelt down beside the dismembered bodies of his wife and daughter. His beautiful young daughter, Adara, lay dead, still gripping her mother's severed arm. He buried his head into Leyla's blood-drenched body, wept, swore revenge, and passed out.

He awakened in a hospital two days later.

Why am I still alive?

Only one reason made sense.

Allah wants me to punish those who did this to my family and the others.

He persuaded a wealthy Saudi benefactor to help the injured victims of the drone attack that killed his wife and daughter, and nine others, including two widows and their children. But after six months of helping victims, Hasham decided it was time for *payback*.

It was time for *Al Thar - revenge*.

FORTY SIX

Nell heard nothing for several minutes. No machines humming, no bottles rattling, no printers clacking, no computers beeping, no trucks coming or going.

And no men talking.

Only silence.

Hasham and his men had shut down the bottling operations and left for the night. Had they left her alone? She doubted it. Hasham had to have a night watchman walking around. A very silent watchman.

She heard a noisy truck drive down the alley behind her, spewing gasoline fumes in its wake.

She had no tools to unhinge the door. Just screws, nails, bolts, paint. She saw a small stepladder and a longer ladder, some boxes of printer paper. She had no chemicals to make an explosive.

She heard a pigeon cooing above her.

She looked up and saw the bird's silhouette through the small glass-block window near the ceiling. The bird's shape was clearly defined, suggesting the glass might be thinner than she thought.

Could she break the glass?

Could she even get up to it?

And if she got up to it, she had no tool to break the glass.

But if she somehow did manage to break the glass, could she squeeze through? The window looked too small.

Or was it?

She held a broom handle up and measured the window to be maybe fourteen inches high and twenty-four inches wide.

Could she crawl through? She was thin, one hundred eighteen, five-nine. Maybe with twisting, she could squeeze through. But even if she couldn't, she could stick her head through and shout for help.

It was her only hope.

But the ladder didn't look long enough. She carried the rickety wooden ladder over and leaned it against the wall. If she stood on the top rung, she might reach up to the window.

But how could she break the glass blocks?

Again, she rummaged through the room for something to break glass. She found nothing. Frustrated, she spun around too fast and tripped over a heavy box of printer paper, dragging it a few inches. Beneath the box, she saw the tip of a tool. She moved the box, grabbed the big rusty wrench.

Maybe seven pounds.

Maybe heavy enough.

Gripping the wrench, she started climbing the ladder. On the third rung, it wobbled so much she almost toppled over.

Slowly, rung by rung, she climbed the rickety ladder to just beneath the window.

She reached up and tapped the wrench against a glass block. The glass sounded thicker than it looked. If she could just break out the window and signal someone.

She smelled gasoline again. Another smelly truck probably drove down the alley.

She swung the heavy wrench against the glass hard and the wrench bounced back, nearly flying from her hands.

But it left a small crack in the glass.

She swung again and split the crack wider. She swung still harder and punched a bigger hole. Bits of sealant crumbled out between the glass blocks. Her next swing shattered the glass enough to see outside through a one inch hole. Fresh air whooshed onto her face and felt wonderful.

She listened for anyone responding to the broken glass. No one did. Maybe there wasn't a night watchman.

But she now smelled serious *smoke*. Not truck exhaust. Not Hasham's cigar smoke, but smoke from a fire, maybe from trash burning in the alley.

Or . . . maybe . . . *burning inside this building . . .*

She turned and saw smoke seeping under the door.

My God! The building's on fire!

Why didn't the fire alarm she saw go off? Did Hasham disable it? Did he set fire to the building to destroy everything – including me?

She bashed another glass block, but only a small chunk fell out.

She heard fire crackling right outside her door. Black smoke seeped through the slit in the wall. The smoke and the fire would soon fill her room . . . and then engulf the chemical cleaning drums . . . build pressure inside them, cause them to catch fire and possibly explode.

She slammed the wrench hard against the last three glass blocks, knocking one partly out. Smoke curled up the ladder into her lungs. She coughed hard and nearly fell off.

Fire crept toward the chemical drums – but even closer to the paint cans. Paint, she knew, could catch fire and explode.

Should she go down and move the paint cans - or keep trying to break the glass blocks?

She attacked the glass blocks with a vengeance, swinging again and again, knocking out one more glass block.

But the fire was now inches from the paint cans. She hurried back down the ladder, carried the paint cans to the corner farthest from the fire and threw a tarp over them.

She climbed back up the ladder and swung the pipe wrench at the last glass block. A slight crack. She swung again. No change. The smoke stung her nostrils.

She saw fire creep onto the tarp covering the paint cans. She'd have to risk it.

She swung harder and split the glass a bit more. Another swing knocked out a big chunk. Another knocked the rest of the glass block into the alley. She stuck her head outside, sucked in the cool fresh air and looked for someone.

She saw no one.

"HELP!"

No response.

"HELP!"

No response.

Somehow she had to lift herself - up and *over* - the sharp shards of glass sticking up from the lower sill - and then out through the skinny window. The alley was nine feet below. If she crawled through head first and dropped, she'd break her neck.

Legs first. No other way.

But how? How could she possibly get her legs up to the window without falling back down into the flames?

She had to try.

She lifted her heel up to the sill, but it slid off. She tried again, wobbling the ladder so much she almost fell down into the flames.

Teetering on the last rung, she managed to lift her right calf onto the windowsill. Sharp glass dug into her leg. Panicked, she gripped the upper windowsill, and tried to lift her other foot up into the window. Impossible!

She couldn't lift it without falling back.

Flames crept up her ladder. Smoke filled her lungs.

She suddenly felt very weak, couldn't breathe, couldn't see, couldn't think . . .

She was losing it . . .

She was not going to make it . . .

She was going to pass out . . .

She was going to fall and die in these flames . . .

Praying for strength, she threw her head back and gasped for air . . .

 . . . *and saw it!*

On the ceiling. Hidden in the smoke.

A long plumbing pipe. Right above her head.

She grabbed the pipe like a gymnast and pulled her other leg up and through the window, cutting her thigh a bit.

Pulling with both hands, she lifted her butt onto the windowsill, and tried to catch her breath.

Still clutching the pipe hard, she eased her butt and legs out the window as sharp glass cut into her lower back.

She let go of the pipe to drop into the alley.

She did not drop.

She wriggled hard.

She did not drop.

Her blouse had snagged on some protruding glass at the base of the windowsill frame. She tried to shake loose, but couldn't.

She was hanging half in the window, half out . . .

The flames reached the top of the ladder, inches from her hair.

She shook harder, nothing. She twisted right, left, right. Dropped an inch.

Panicked, she jerked and spun like a mad woman, tearing her blouse and . . . finally ripping loose and dropping into the alley below, landing on her feet and hands. Slowly, she stood up, took several deep breaths and looked around. Saw no one.

She staggered down the alley and leaned against a building to catch her breath. She sucked in delicious fresh air. Then she heard a car engine.

Behind her.

She spun around and saw a big black Lincoln drive into the alley, its lights blinding her.

FORTY SEVEN

"I saw her!" said Abu in the black Lincoln Continental. "By that red brick building."

"Impossible! She's locked in her *room!*" said Bashar, the driver.

"Not anymore!" Abu pointed to her broken window.

Bashar saw it, then sped down the alley.

★ ★ ★

As the Lincoln raced toward her, Nell ducked back into the narrow space between two buildings. She hid behind a garbage dumpster and waited.

The Lincoln stopped between the buildings, the space too narrow to drive down. The two men looked in her direction, but didn't appear to see her. Maybe they thought she ran out the other end. She held her breath.

The Lincoln sped on down the alley.

She paused, then walked back to the alley and peeked to see if the car kept going. Mistake.

Blinding headlights raced toward her.

Nell ran down the alley and ducked into an even narrower passageway between two large buildings. The Lincoln sped past the passageway, careened around the corner, and raced back to head her off at the other end.

Sensing their plan, Nell ran back the into the alley, turned down the first side street, and sprinted like hell. One hundred yards farther, she ducked behind some hedges beside a house, lay down flat, and rubbed dirt on her face to hide the glare of sweat. And waited . . .

Moments later, the Lincoln screeched around the corner, then crept down the street toward her. As it drew closer, she recognized the driver and tall bearded passenger from the bottling plant.

The Lincoln stopped. The driver turned on an LED spotlight. The brilliant beam lit up the other side of the street, checking between houses, behind trees, beneath parked cars.

Then the beam crossed the street to her side.

The light crept toward her hedge, reflecting on the grass just five yards from her . . . then four . . . three. If she moved, they'd see her. The light froze two yards from her face.

Did they see her face? Were they aiming a gun at her now?

Five seconds, ten . . .

Why hasn't the light moved?

Because they're aiming at me.

Finally, the light inched past her hedge, past the house, past the house next door, and moved slowly down the street. When she no longer saw the Lincoln's red tail lights, she finally breathed again.

Maybe they were waiting for her to reveal herself. If she stepped out now, the spotlight might light her up.

She waited two minutes, raised her head, and looked down the street. She saw no car headlights, no brake lights, heard no car engines. She crawled from the hedge, brushed some dirt off, and walked in the shadows toward the corner, looking for anyone who could help. The street was empty.

Warm blood skidded down her back. Her cuts were mostly small. But it felt like tiny slivers of glass might be stuck in some places. She brushed dirt from her clothes. In a store window, she saw her reflection: she was a *Walking Dead* escapee.

She moved along the darker side of the street, watching for the black Lincoln, and searching for an open store. A 7-Eleven, gas station, CVS, a bar, some place with a phone. Any place with a light on. Every store was dark.

Ahead, a pickup stacked with hay bales drove down a cross street before she could signal the driver.

She turned the corner and saw *lights* - a Mobil station. A hundred yards ahead.

She had to get there without being noticed.

Clinging to the shadows, she hurried down the street and over to the station. She stepped inside, heard the doorbell ring, and realized the store's lights lit her up like an Oscar winner. She ducked behind a magazine rack.

The skinny young attendant's thick dark eyebrows shot up when he saw her mud-smeared face and bloody blouse. He checked the door, obviously expecting her attacker to burst in.

His nametag said *Mustafa*.

"You are hurt, ma'am?" Strong foreign accent.

"Yes, a bit. Please hide me and call 911!"

"Hide you . . .?" He looked outside to see whether her attacker was there. Then he gestured for her to follow him quickly.

"Please to come!"

Should she trust a man named 'Mustafa' after what she'd been through? But he seemed genuinely concerned, helped her immediately, and hadn't signaled anyone outside.

Or had he?

Mustafa led her into a back room and gave her some antiseptic cream, Band-Aids, and paper towels to clean herself at a sink.

"Thank you, very much.

"I call 911 now!" he said.

"Thank you."

Mustafa tapped 911, explained her injuries, listened a bit, and hung up.

"Police will come. But they're all at a truck-car accident out on Route 30. Said it take a while to get here."

"May I use your phone?"

"Sure." He handed it to her. "Sorry, not much power left."

She couldn't remember Lindee's cell phone number. She dialed Jacob's number and he answered on the first ring.

"Jacob, it's - !"

"- *NELL!*" Jacob shouted, *"Nell's on the phone!"*

She heard people cheering and clapping.

"Where are you?" he asked. The phone signal started cutting in and out.

She asked the station attendant and he told her.

She told Jacob who immediately put her through to a man named Donovan Rourke.

"Doctor Northam, thank God you're free."

"But two men in a Lincoln are chasing me."

"Hide somewhere in the gas station. The FBI or the police will pick you up as soon as possible."

"Okay." The phone faded, came back a bit, flickered.

"Are your abductors attacking in the US?"

"Yes. . ."

The phone started cutting out. She looked at the power bars and saw the last one flickering.

"They're using a - !"

" - can't hear you – Using what?"

The line died. The power bars emptied.

She called out to the attendant, "Do you have a land-line phone?"

"No. Just my cell. Charger's at home. Sorry."

"Do you have a computer with Internet access?"

"No. Just our company's InTRAnet network. Not connected to the Internet."

She tried the phone again. Dead.

That's when she heard the explosion – coming from the direction of the bottling plant. She and Mustafa ran to the window and looked outside.

Massive plumes of purple-red fire and smoke soared into the night sky above the plant. The fire and the explosion had destroyed the plant.

Tires squealed into the gas station. She turned and saw the black Lincoln skid to a stop near the door.

Did they see me?

FORTY EIGHT

"Those two men are chasing me!" Nell ducked behind a shelf.
"Please to come! Better hide place." Mustafa said.

He hurried her back to an area with shelves, file cabinets and large cardboard boxes in the corner. He lifted the boxes to the side and pointed down to a cabinet with a half door that came up to her waist.

"Please to get inside. I push boxes in front."

The station doorbell *DINGED*.

"They come inside! Please to hurry!"

She bent down and crawled into the small space crammed with plumbing pipes, electrical wires, dust, and cobwebs. Something crawled into her hair and wriggled its way down to her scalp. She slapped it and the crawling seemed to stop.

She heard Mustafa slide the large cardboard boxes in front of her half-door, then hurry to the front of the station, where it sounded like the men were walking around, obviously looking for her.

"Did a tall woman, brown hair, thirty-five come in here?" Loud, thick accent.

"No woman."

"What is this?" another male voice.

"What?" Mustapha said.

"On floor!"

"Is *wet blood!*" the other man said. "Is more blood there.*"

"Oh that - I cut my arm with box opener," Mustafa said.

"You have no bandage."

"More fresh blood *here*! Where *woman* with bloody shirt*?*"

"What woman?"

"Show us back room now!"

"But sir -!"

She heard footsteps come toward her.

"Sir - customers not allowed in back!"

"Show me woman!"

She heard scuffling, someone throwing a punch. Mustafa moaned. Then the men walked back to the storage room next to her area and started opening cabinets and closets.

"Look – more *fresh blood*! Where woman?" The men spoke in rapid Arabic.

Mustafa said nothing.

"Ayn hy?" Where is she?"

"Ayn hy?"

She heard someone throw a punch. Then a groan. It sounded like Mustapha fell down.

"Tell us *now!*"

She heard what sounded like the metallic click of a gun.

"Okay okay! Stop! Don't shoot!" Mustapha said. "I tell you! She crazy lady! Come in here all bleeding. I don't know why? She's all bloody. Dirty on face! Dirty on cloths. Crazy woman! You drive in, she run away! Run out that back door!"

"Why no blood near back door?"

"She run crazy fast!"

The men said nothing for several seconds.

"Blood near this room with big boxes. We search in here now!"

"No. Just boxes!" Mustapha said. "She run out!"

Nell heard them step into *her* room. They began moving boxes. They would find her half-door and then her . . . in seconds . . .

Then she heard something.

Overhead.

Thump thump thump - the rhythmic clip of a helicopter. And then, she heard distant sirens getting louder. Fire engines for the warehouse fire? Police cars for her?

The two men mumbled in Arabic, then appeared to run back to the station entrance. The doorbell *DINGED*. Seconds later, she heard tires squeal out of the station.

She exhaled as the chopper and sirens grew louder.

Mustafa hurried back to her hiding place.

"Okay now. Men drive away." He pushed aside the boxes.

She opened the small door and Mustafa helped her out of the cramped space.

"Thank you, Mustafa. You saved my life." She wiped blood off his lips where they'd hit him.

He nodded and pulled a dead long-legged spider from her hair.

Three FBI-jacketed agents and a police officer ran into the storage room.

"What happened here?" a tall agent said.

"Two men were trying to kill me," Nell said.

"Where are they?"

"In a big black Lincoln that raced out of the station thirty seconds ago."

"Lincoln on security video. I show you," Mustafa said, pointing to the monitor.

The FBI agent nodded and turned to her. "Are you Doctor Nell Northam?"

She nodded as tears filled her eyes.

FORTY NINE

MAYFIELD

Hasham's rage burned like molten lava. He squeezed his hands into tight angry fists.

He hated incompetence, especially from his people. Like the two bumbling morons in front of him: Abu and Bashar. They'd just confessed to colossal incompetence – they'd allowed an unarmed woman, Nell Northam, to escape from a double-locked room in the bottling plant while it was on fire. How could this happen?

He hurled his cup of tea against the wall of the rental house. The cup shattered and plastered the wall with black tea leaves.

Abu and Bashar cowered in their chairs.

"Her steel door was bolted shut! Who left the door unlocked?"

"She broke the window and crawled out!" Abu said.

"Liar! It was too small! If you don't find her, you know what our leaders will demand of you?"

They said nothing.

"Your worthless lives! *Find her!*" Hasham threw his pen at them.

Abu and Bashar ducked and raced from the room.

Fighting to control his rage, Hasham grabbed his gold hookah pipe. He puffed hard, filling his lungs with the rich, soothing hashish. Within seconds, the cannabis calmed him, and he reminded himself that he still controlled everything.

Nell Northam's escape changed nothing. She could not possibly stop his attack. For a simple reason. She did not know *how* he would attack with the VX . . . because she'd been locked in the janitor's room and had no chance to see *how*.

Bottom line: the authorities could not stop his attack.

Even if they employed all the predictable protective measures against a VX attack – they would not save one life. Because the only protective measures they knew – were useless against his ingenious delivery system. They wouldn't see it coming, so to speak. And when it got there, it would be too late. Game over, as the Americans say.

Should he tell Bassam Maahdi in Yemen about Dr. Northam's escape? Absolutely not. Bassam always overreacted at the slightest setback. He might even cancel the attack. He'd canceled them before.

Not this time, Bassam. This time I will attack even if you cancel. This is my attack.

Of course, if you cancel, and I go ahead and attack, you'll order an assassin to terminate me. But . . . maybe before you give that order, you yourself might just expire.

Short, fat Bassam Maahdi was morbidly obese. Thanks to gobbling down kilos of cholesterol-rich lamb stew and baba ganoush each day . . . and getting less exercise than a boulder – the perfect lifestyle for a fatal heart attack.

Hasham knew a Yemeni cardiologist who'd be delighted to arrange a fatal lamb-stew-baba-ganoush heart attack.

FIFTY

Donovan counted the seconds until Dr. Nell Northam arrived at the command center in the Holiday Inn a few miles from Mayfield. Donovan, Manning, Jacob and Lindee sat around a large conference table, waiting . . .

At least Dr. Nell Northam was in safe hands, he knew.

Maccabee, his wife, was not, he feared.

Donovan still couldn't reach her and she still hadn't called him. And he hadn't learned whether she'd escaped their apartment before the fake air conditioning man got to her. Agents were looking for her and the fake AC guy without success. Donovan had left her several call-me-now messages. But no response. She was not in the apartment. She was not in the building. She must have been abducted, or worse. He was sick with worry.

Manning turned to Donovan.

"Police just found the two men who chased Dr. Northam to the Mobil station."

"They talking?"

"Nope. Both committed suicide in their Lincoln."

Donovan shook his head in frustration. "Search their phone records, contacts, homes, friends."

"We are."

"These suicides prove the magnitude of this attack!" Manning said.

Donovan nodded and grabbed his ringing phone.

"Rourke . . ."

"Hi," Maccabee said.

Donovan almost dropped his phone. His body seemed to melt.

"Guess you've tried to phone me," Maccabee said.

"Jesus, Mac! I've been calling and calling but – "

" - I couldn't call you. Your warning spooked me so much, I ran from our apartment without my phone."

"Oh . . ."

"When Mrs. Hansen on Three wasn't home, I grabbed a taxi to Jane's. But Jane wasn't home either. So I walked around looking for a public phone booth. Guess what? There are none! I'm at Jane's now, using her phone."

"Stay there. I'm sending agents to pick you up now and take you to my office. Tish is already there. My assistant Mamie is watching her. You'll both be safe there."

"You had Tish picked up early?"

"Had to. Didn't know where you were."

"I understand."

"Let's talk later."

They hung up.

Donovan exhaled like a punctured tire. Maccabee was safe. Mia was safe.

But thousands of people were about to die.

"Everything okay at home?" asked Denny Cage, a Homeland Security agent sitting beside him.

"It is now, Denny." Donovan had worked with Agent Cage, a Homeland Security Agent for years. The smart forty-year-old had thick blond hair and light blue eyes. Tinted glasses hung on a silver chain around his neck. Cigarette ashes dotted his scuffed Hush Puppies.

The door swung open again.

Donovan watched three agents escort Dr. Nell Northam into the conference room. Her bloodstained muddy blouse, bruised cheek, and slight limp told them what they already knew: it was a miracle she was alive.

Everyone applauded as Jacob ran over and hugged his wife. Then Lindee hugged her. Donovan felt like hugging her. She was their only hope for answers.

"Where's Mia?" Nell asked Jacob, her eyes wide.

"With mom. She's fine," Jacob said. "A government plane is flying them up here a little later."

Nell slumped back into Jacob's arms, tears flowing.

"They're attacking with a nerve agent," Nell said, still clutching Jacob.

"Which one?" Agent Cage asked.

"*VX!*"

"Aw . . . Jesus!" Cage slumped back in his chair, looking defeated.

"Fully weaponized?" Donovan asked.

"Yes. But the VX is blended with another substance."

"Which one?"

"I don't know. They kept it secret."

"Are they ready to attack?" Donovan asked.

"Yes."

"When?"

"Anytime now. Within twenty-four hours."

Donovan felt like he'd been tasered.

Silence filled the room.

"Where are they attacking?" Donovan asked.

"I tried to find out, but couldn't. The leader, a man named Hasham Habib, refused to tell me. But he bragged that that his delivery system was unlike any VX delivery system ever used . . . unlike anything our experts would ever consider or anticipate."

"You believe him?"

She paused and looked at him. "Unfortunately, I do."

"Why?"

"Because he's a brilliant, creative bio-chemical weapons scientist."

Donovan's hope sank. "Tell us what you know."

"First off all, Hasham's trucks picked up steel canisters containing VX from the underground lab at the forest cabin. The trucks delivered them to a nearby assembly plant."

"What did the plant assemble?"

"*ChocoYummy.*"

"Did you say . . . *Choco . . . yummy?*" Manning asked.

"Yes." Nell closed her eyes as though she didn't want to continue.

"What's *ChocoYummy?*"

Another pause.

"A drink for children . . ."

They let out a collective gasp.

Donovan asked, "Are you saying this *ChocoYummy* . . . contains the VX?"

"Yes."

Donovan felt blood drain from his face. He couldn't speak.

"I'll kill the bastard!" Cage hissed, his face crimson.

"I saw the bottling machines deposit the chocolate colored liquid into small Coca Cola sized bottles at the assembly plant. The bottle label had a smiling young boy and girl, about nine. It's clearly aimed at children. They filled thousands and thousands of *ChocoYummy* bottles with the chocolate drink, then loaded the cases onto trucks that drove off and kept coming back for more. Again and again."

Donovan cringed as he imagined Tish drinking the poison.

"The signage on the trucks says *Ask Mummy for ChocoYummy.*"

Agent Cage, red-faced, cursed.

"Did you see any other possible delivery system in the bottling plant or cabin?" Donovan asked.

"No. And I looked."

"Any hint of air or water delivery?" Cage asked.

"None."

No one spoke for seconds.

"So any kid who drinks it - " Donovan said.

" - will die in minutes. Painfully," Nell said. "So will any adults."

"The weapon is probably already in stores," Donovan said, his heart slamming against his chest. "Get the warning out *now!*"

Several agents grabbed their phones and made calls.

"So," Manning said, "they set fire to the plant to eliminate evidence of their secret delivery system."

Nell nodded. "And me!"

They stared at her.

"I was locked in a janitor's closet, but escaped through a small window minutes before the plant exploded."

Jacob reached over and held her hand.

Nell said, "At the plant, have your people check *ChocoYummy* bottle fragments for VX. Make sure they wear HazMat suits! The air should test positive for VX. The explosion probably spread the VX. We need to clear a one-mile area around the plant. Keep people in homes. Shut windows tight. Turn off ventilations systems until we can give the all-clear announcement."

Agent Manning gave the order over his phone. "Our Homeland Security MobileLab trailer is three minutes from the plant. They'll test *ChocoYummy* bottle fragments."

"Did Hasham mention target cities?" Donovan asked.

"No. But I grabbed two flash drives that might tell us." She took them from her pocket. "I took them from Hasham's computer office. This blue one was taped to the printer. The red drive was hidden under the computer."

Manning handled the flash drives like they were ten-carat diamonds. He gave them to an assistant who ran them back to three IT specialists set up in the corner.

"Anything else at the factory?" Donovan asked.

"Just the bottling machines, his office computers, a large screen television, and some printers."

"What'd they print?"

She shrugged. "I couldn't see. I assumed sales materials for *ChocoYummy*. Coupons, posters, free offers. More incentives for kids to buy it.*"

"Who are the men who abducted you?" Donovan asked.

"The boss is Hasham Habib. Short, thin, a highly skilled biochemist with extensive experience in bioweapons and chemical nerve agents. The other man, a big aggressive man, the muscle man, is Aarif . . . or rather was . . ."

"Was?"

Everyone stared at her.

Nell paused. "After the VX weapon was made and tested, Hasham ordered Aarif to kill me. When Hasham left the cabin, Aarif tried to sexually assault me first!" She looked at Jacob and closed her eyes.

"He forced me to drink wine . . . then . . . he tried to attack me. I told him I was feeling sick and needed the bathroom. In the bathroom, I removed a small bottle of VX I'd hidden in the toilet tank. I spread some VX liquid on an Arab magazine. I came back out and asked him to translate something in the magazine. He grabbed the magazine pages where I'd placed the VX and began translating the article. He read for about thirty seconds then tried to attack me again, ripped my blouse. But by then the VX had entered his blood stream. He suddenly clutched his chest, and collapsed. Thirty seconds later he was dead."

"From *touching* the magazine?" Donovan asked.

"Yes ... touching the *VX* on the magazine."

Everyone stared at her.

"Self defense," Manning said.

"Agreed," Donovan said.

Agent Cage hung up his phone. "We've collected several pieces of *ChocoYummy* bottles at the plant. The MobileLab should have test results in minutes."

Donovan needed them in *seconds!*

"We're also warning beverage distributors and identifying any retailers who might stock *ChocoYummy.*"

"The FDA will issue a *ChocoYummy* warning to retailers nationally," Drew Manning said.

"Let's pray *ChocoYummy* isn't already on store shelves," Donovan said, fearing it probably was.

His phone rang. He answered, listened and felt his heart pound like a jackhammer. He hung up. "A large fleet of *Ask Mummy for ChocoYummy* trucks drove over the George Washington Bridge into Manhattan."

"When?" Manning asked.

"*Yesterday* morning about ten."

FIFTY ONE

Near the Westchester Wastewater Treatment plant in Yonkers, Hasham strolled through his sprawling garage, admiring his fleet of immaculate delivery trucks. His Swords of Allah . . . his Avenging Angels . . . smiting the enemy at this very moment.

Even after several *ChocoYummy* deliveries, the trucks glimmered like precious gems beneath the LED lights.

Hasham walked over to a driver standing at a truck's rear door. "Unlock it."

The skinny, bearded driver unlocked it and rolled up the truck's door.

Hasham reached inside and examined a sample. Perfect. Irresistible. Desirable.

He nodded to the driver who rolled the door back down and locked it, then got in and drove off with the other trucks to make more deliveries.

Hasham returned to his office, sat at his desktop computer and opened a file. He scrolled through the pages, double-checking documents he'd checked many times. Everything was accurate, right on schedule, unstoppable. His burner phone rang in the desk drawer.

Bassam Maahdi calling from Yemen.

Why call me now? We agreed no calls until after the attack.

Hasham picked up. "Mr. Jones. Your call surprises me."

"I imagine so, Mr. Smith. But you see, *I'm* also surprised."

"Why is that?"

"I hear that our talented lady doctor has left us," Maahdi whispered.

Who told Maahdi she escaped? Only four people knew and none would dare speak directly to Maahdi. *Perhaps my police informant has loose lips. If so, I'll close them.*

"It's not a problem, Mr. Jones."

"It's not?"

"No. You see, the good doctor has already served our purposes quite well."

"But still . . . perhaps we should consider postponing."

"*Au contraire!* Postponing gives our competition more time to discover our plan."

"Yes, but. . ."

"No need to postpone, Mr. Jones. Trust me on this. Everything is ready to go. We will deliver our medicine on time. Nothing can stop us."

"But the doctor knows so much. She may reveal our secret formula to our . . . competitors!"

"She can't." Hasham said.

"Why not?"

"She doesn't know our secret formula." Hasham grew concerned that even though they spoke on safe phones, the NSA might somehow be listening.

"And more importantly, she does not know our secret distribution strategy."

"Distribution strategy . . .?" Maahdi sounded confused as usual.

"*How* we'll deliver our . . . medicine."

"But she might guess how."

"Never."

"Or our competitors might help her figure it out!"

"Not in a hundred years."

He heard Bassam breathing hard, probably squeezing his fat knuckles white on the phone.

"You seem so sure."

"I am absolutely sure." Hasham had explained this to Maahdi several times before. "Our product's delivery is simply too unique, too far-fetched, and too improbable for them to ever consider."

Maahdi breathed out. "I trust you are correct in all this, Mr. Smith."

"I am absolutely correct, Mr. Jones!"

Maahdi cleared his throat, sounding like he had chunks of lamb stew stuck in it. *Maybe he'll choke to death.*

"As you know," Maahdi said, "our friends have invested enormous amounts of money in the laboratory and the . . . medicine itself. They expect excellent results!"

"They will get them."

"But if they don't, well, you know how they react when they are dissatisfied."

Hasham knew a death threat when he heard one. "Everything will be a huge success, Mr. Jones. You have my word!"

"I certainly hope so."

They hung up.

Hasham felt a tightening in his chest. If Maahdi called back and ordered him to cancel his attack, Hasham would attack anyway. He'd invested too much of himself, too much personal passion into this attack.

The door opened, and Faisal, Hasham's assistant, nodded to him.

Hasham walked outside and ran his hand over the logo - *Ask Mummy for ChocoYummy* - on the side of one of the large trucks.

Such a tempting phrase.

He nodded at the drivers.

They started their trucks and drove off, delivering more jihad to Manhattan.

FIFTY TWO

Donovan hurried into the small conference room where everyone stared at phones . . . waiting for the test results on the *ChocoYummy* bottle fragments.

Waiting . . . while Hasham attacked.

Donovan's phone rang: Mamie, his assistant, calling from his Manhattan office. She only called if it was urgent.

"Donovan, a man on my line says he knows how the attack will happen."

"Who is he?"

"He won't say. But he'll only talk to you. He says it's very important!"

"You believe him?"

"He has an accent. And he mentioned Doctor Nell Northam's name."

"Put him on."

The phone connection clicked on, then he heard silence for several seconds, then . . .

"Is this Agent Donovan Rourke?" Strong accent.

"Yes."

The caller whispered, "There's a new children's drink . . . *ChocoYummy*. If kids drink it, they will die."

"Who is this?"

The line went dead.

"Trace this call!"

Manning nodded to his tech guy. A minute later, the tech guy shook his head. "Throwaway phone routed from Paris to Brussels to your office."

"But it confirms *ChocoYummy,* Agent Cage said. "Someone's betraying Hasham."

"But it may be too late," Manning said, reading a text message. "*ChocoYummy* delivery trucks were seen in several more New York City neighborhoods *yesterday* and again today."

"Assume bottles are on store shelves now," Donovan said. "Keep warning retailers to remove them."

"We are," Cage said. "But some retailers may have missed the warnings. Bottles may have been bought."

Manning lowered his head. "Kids will see the bright Day-Glo yellow *ChocoYummy* labels. They'll grab the coupons, buy bottles, twist the top and drink it . . . "

"*SHIT!*" Agent Cage said, reading a text message on his phone.

"What?" Donovan asked.

"*ChocoYummy* TV commercials. They've been running on kids programs and the Disney Channel for the last four days."

"Yank them!" Donovan said.

"We're trying. But there are 326 kids' shows on cable TV. We're trying to identify which are running *ChocoYummy* ads."

"What about media warnings?"

Manning nodded. "*ChocoYummy* warnings should be going out in minutes."

Agent Cage closed his phone. "We have confirmation that thousands of bottles of *ChocoYummy* were stocked on store shelves yesterday afternoon and today."

"Which stores?" Donovan asked.

"Mostly small mom and pop stores in the Bronx, Brooklyn, Queens, Manhattan, Hoboken, East Elizabeth, Bayonne . . . maybe upstate New York and Connecticut," Manning said.

"What about the big chain stores - Target and Kmart, Kroger, Safeway?" Donovan asked.

"Not on shelves yet. Their central office committees require several weeks to assess, evaluate and approve new product placement in stores," Manning said.

"What about school cafeterias?" Donovan asked.

"We're warning schools. No *ChocoYummy* deliveries so far," Cage said.

"Vending machines?"

Cage shook his head. "No vending companies stock it!"

Nell Northam said, "Are hospitals reporting cases of sudden-onset respiratory failure that led to immediate death?"

"Not yet," Cage said. "But we're canvassing hospitals every ten minutes."

Donovan knew it was just a matter of time. His worst-case scenario was steamrolling ahead right in front of his eyes. Nell Northam said *ChocoYummy* would kill. The mysterious phone informant confirmed *ChocoYummy* would kill. *ChocoYummy* was in stores. Bottles had been bought. Kids would drink it. Kids would die. Some kids may have already died. Families would be devastated. It was only a matter of time. Hasham was winning.

Manning answered his phone, listened to the caller, hung up, then stared at the floor.

"An eight year old girl in Brooklyn just died. Medical Examiner hasn't ruled cause of death yet. But . . ."

Donovan felt his heart stop.

" . . . fifteen minutes ago, she drank *ChocoYummy*."

FIFTY THREE

Donovan heard Nell Northam talking on Skype to her daughter Mia in Washington Airport. Nell looked relieved as she told Mia that a CIA aircraft would soon fly her to New York. Mia was safe. His daughter Tish was safe.

But Donovan knew that thousands of young daughters and sons were about to die.

Agent Manning said, "We've alerted all schools in New Jersey, Connecticut, Rhode Island, Delaware, Connecticut, and Massachusetts. Teachers will warn students. But many kids saw the *ChocoYummy* TV commercials. Many planned to buy it!"

Donovan feared many *had* bought it. Now everything depended on warning kids and parents fast enough.

Agent Cage slammed his phone on the table and stared ahead, his face like a death mask.

"A ten year old girl in Queens drank *ChocoYummy*. She just died."

The air went out of the room.

"Also," Cage continued, looking at the floor, "two nine year old twin boys in Hoboken drank *ChocoYummy* and died minutes later."

Manning's assistant handed him a note. He read it, "A forty-two-year-old man drank *ChocoYummy* and died in three minutes."

It's fucking happening, Donovan thought. He tried to catch his breath. Sweat beaded his forehead. His heart pounded. Hasham was killing kids and adults. *And if I get the chance, I'll force-feed him ChocoYummy!*

Manning hung up his phone. "A seven-year-old girl drank *ChocoYummy*. Her mom just rushed her to Mount Sinai Emergency."

"*When* did she drink it?" Nell asked.

Manning asked, then faced Nell with a puzzled look. "Four hours ago."

Nell's eyes shot open. "Are you sure?"

"Yes."

"How much did she drink?"

Manning asked.

They waited in silence.

"She drank the whole bottle, plus most of another one."

Nell's eyes shot open. "That's not possible! Something's not right. She should have died within minutes."

"Well, she's alive."

"Did she vomit immediately after drinking it?"

"No."

Nell closed her eyes. "What are her symptoms?"

"None."

"How's her breathing?"

"Normal."

"Fever?"

"None."

"She does not have VX poisoning."

Manning shook his head, struggling to make sense of it.

Donovan turned to the large screen television as it flashed a *Special News Bulletin.* CNN's Wolf Blitzer broke into political news . . .

> *"We have Breaking News . . . The FDA and Homeland Security have issued an urgent emergency medical alert regarding a choco-late drink for children called ChocoYummy. The CDC verifies that ChocoYummy con-tains a deadly nerve agent that causes im-mediate death to anyone who drinks it, both children and adults. If you've purchased ChocoYummy, do not open or drink the liquid. Call 911. The police will pick up the bottles. If you've bought ChocoYummy, call 911. And above all . . . do not drink Choco-Yummy!*

Donovan's assistant walked in and handed him a note. His gut twisted. Despite his trembling hand, he read it aloud.

"A seven year old boy in Brooklyn sipped some *ChocoYummy.* Two minutes later he was dead."

FIFTY FOUR

Manning walked into the conference room. "Two ex-NFL linemen drank bottles of *ChocoYummy* and dropped dead minutes later."

Donovan swallowed a dry throat. "Where'd they buy the bottles?"

"A mom and pop store in the Bronx."

Donovan's phone rang. He punched the speaker button.

"A woman in Queens says thirteen kids at her daughter's birthday party all drank *ChocoYummy!*"

Please God, no! Donovan closed his eyes, unsure how much more he could stomach. Everyone slumped in their chairs and waited . . .

"All thirteen kids are fine!"

"*What . . .?*" Donovan whispered.

"They're all outside running around, playing tag. *All thirteen kids are running and playing!*"

No one spoke.

"When did they drink *ChocoYummy?*" Nell asked.

"About three hours ago."

Everyone stared at the phone as though they'd misheard. "That's simply not possible!" Nell stood and paced beside the table.

No one spoke.

"Is she *positive* it was *ChocoYummy?*" Nell asked.

"Yes. She's looking at the empty bottles!"

"Test those bottles fast!" Nell said to Manning.

"Do some people have a delayed reaction to VX?" Donovan asked.

"No. VX's reaction is *immediate*. For all!"

"Can some people tolerate VX better?"

"Maybe for a minute or so. It depends on the dosage they drank, and their individual health. Real healthy people might last minutes longer. But VX kills everyone. No exceptions."

"What if they've taken antidotes?" Donovan asked.

"If anyone takes atropine sulfate and pralidoxime chloride before exposure, or within maybe thirty minutes after, they have a chance."

"Did some of the bottles receive much less VX?"

Nell closed her eyes. "No. Not from what I saw. Each bottle received the exact same amount of *ChocoYummy* from the assembly line depositing funnels. And my tests proved that *each* steel container held the exact same VX consistency. Hasham insisted on it. His tests confirmed consistency."

Agent Cage's phone rang. He listened, hung up, then faced Donovan with a stunned expression.

"We just learned that a large number of kids drank *ChocoYummy* with *no* adverse reactions. Absolutely *none!* The kids are all fine."

The room went silent.

"What the hell is going on?" Donovan said, looking at Nell Northam.

Everyone turned toward her.

Nell shook her head, looking more confused than anyone.

Agent Manning grabbed his ringing phone, answered, then hung up, looking confused.

"Just got the test results on the *ChocoYummy* bottle fragments at the plant."

Everyone leaned forward.

"*Seven* bottle fragments had traces of VX on them. *Forty-nine* bottle fragments had *no* trace of VX."

Nell Northam looked stunned. "Are you positive?"

"Yes."

"What's in the *ChocoYummy* with no VX?" Nell asked.

"Chocolate flavoring, milk, cream, sodium, sugar, and water."

The facts just didn't fit.

Donovan watched Nell's face turn sheet-white. Like everyone, she looked bewildered and shocked by the contradictory test results.

"Could Hasham have made a batch of non-VX *ChocoYummy* without telling you?" Donovan asked.

Nell shook her head. "No. I would have known. But he must have had some kind of a VX cut-off switch on the assembly line."

Donovan nodded. "But why? Why would he make some bottles of *ChocoYummy* with no VX?"

Nell shrugged. "It makes no sense."

Donovan agreed. He stood and walked alongside the table, trying to make sense of what was happening.

Nell said, "Hasham was too organized, too compulsive about details. Far too precise to allow an inconsistency of this magnitude."

Donovan stopped walking. "So, maybe . . . just maybe, his inconsistency was not a slip up. Maybe it was intentional."

Nell frowned. "You're saying he *intended* to put VX in only *some* bottles?"

"Yes."

"But why would he do that?"

"I don't know." Donovan thought about that a while. Nothing made sense. And then . . . something sort of clicked . . . a crazy possibility occurred to him . . . and it terrified him.

"Maybe one thing *does* makes sense," Donovan said.

Everyone stared at him.

He thought about what he was about to suggest, then turned and looked at Nell and said, "Maybe he's . . . misleading us."

No one spoke. Confused faces stared at him.

"Maybe *ChocoYummy* is misdirection . . ." he said.

Nell stared hard at Donovan, blinked, seemed to sense what he was suggesting, and then she nodded.

"He intentionally *directed* us to concentrate on *ChocoYummy!*" Donovan said.

"But the man phoned and warned you about *ChocoYummy,*" Agent Cage said.

"More *misdirection* maybe," Donovan said. "To make us concentrate everything we have on *ChocoYummy*. Hasham put VX in some bottles so we were forced to assign all police, all FBI, and all Homeland resources on *ChocoYummy,* while he – "

" – launches his *primary VX attack!*" Nell said.

"His *real* attack!" Manning said.

Donovan nodded.

FIFTY FIVE

"So what the hell's his *real* VX attack?" Cage asked.

All eyes locked on Nell.

"I have no idea," she said.

"Did Hasham pay special attention to anything else in the bottling plant?" Donovan asked.

She closed her eyes for several moments. "Not really."

"What'd he do most of the time?"

"Worked at his computer, scrolling through what looked like Arab newspapers and documents."

"What kind of documents?"

"Text. But too far away for me to see."

"Anything else?"

She looked out the window. "Well, his assistants spent time adjusting the bottling assembly line. And some time at the printing machines."

"Did Hasham pay special attention to the printers?"

"Not special. But a few times he walked over and looked at what they were printing."

Donovan wondered why Hasham bothered to check the printing.

"What were they printing?"

"I couldn't see the printed material through the wall slit. I assumed it was promotional items for *ChocoYummy*. Maybe coupons, sales flyers, store signs, labels, stuff like that."

Donovan nodded, stood and paced. "You said Hasham bragged about his super new unique delivery system."

"Yes, he did."

"What if he was lying to you? What if it isn't new and unique?"

Nell said nothing.

"Maybe he said "new and unique" to mislead you? What if he's using a *known* VX delivery system?"

She frowned and shook her head. "I saw no equipment for a known VX delivery system. And he seemed proud of *his* unique delivery. His eyes lit up when he talked about it. My instinct said he was telling the truth. And let's face it - *ChocoYummy* is a totally unique way to deliver VX."

"It is," Donovan said, "But again, why would he put VX in only some of the bottles?"

She shrugged.

No one answered.

"Let's assume," Donovan said, "that he used *ChocoYummy* as his unique delivery system to *divert* us . . . waste our time and effort on it. So he can launch his real attack . . . maybe using a *proven* delivery system."

Nell paused, then nodded. "It's possible. And he has a range of proven delivery options."

"What's his most likely and dependable VX delivery system?" Donovan said.

"Air," Nell said. "Dispersing VX in aerosol form."

"What's that depend on?"

"Weather and wind mostly."

"Would he use aircraft?" Donovan said.

"Probably. Just one ton of VX released in aerosol form from an aircraft could kill hundreds of thousands of people in a crowded urban area if the wind and weather conditions are right."

"How much VX is needed to kill one person?"

Nell pointed to the tiny eraser on her pencil. "This much."

No one spoke.

"What are Manhattan's wind conditions now?" Donovan asked.

Agent Cage checked his laptop. "Clear skies. Three-mile-per-hour winds. Today and tomorrow. Perfect for air dispersal."

"But airspace over Manhattan is highly restricted," Manning said.

"So's White House airspace, but those asshole drones keep sneaking through," Cage said.

"Could drones disperse VX?" Manning asked Nell.

"A fleet of coordinated VX droves could devastate a city."

Donovan felt his stomach churn. "Maybe drone dispersal is his secret delivery system."

He turned to Agent Cage. "Denny, have Homeland try to somehow ground or curfew *all drones* in the Tri-State metropolitan area - all boroughs - until further notice. Also have *all* airports in New England and the mid-Atlantic states start inspecting *all* commercial and private aircraft cargo before takeoff. Especially those with flight plans in or out of LaGuardia, Kennedy, and Newark. Have rural airports check crop dusters before they fly today and tomorrow. And check Goodyear or any other blimps flying over stadiums filled with fans."

Agent Cage repeated the orders into his phone.

"What other air dispersal options does Hasham have?" Donovan asked Nell.

"His trucks driving through crowded city streets."

"How's that work?"

"Simple. The VX canisters are connected to the truck's exhaust systems. The driver flips a switch and the VX is released out through the truck's tailpipes. The exhaust looks like normal truck exhaust. Cars draw it in, people on streets breathe it in . . ."

"But wouldn't the truck driver breathe it and die?" Donovan said.

"Not if his driver compartment is sealed air-tight."

"They might be suicide drivers," Manning said. "Three of Hasham's guys have already wasted themselves for his jihad."

"What about city trucks spraying for Zika and whatever?" Cage said.

"Examine them before they go out!" Donovan said.

"What other options does Hasham have?"

"Water," Nell said. "VX could be placed in the city water system. People wake up tomorrow, brush their teeth, make coffee, drink it . . . game over."

"But our water treatment plants are well protected against terrorist attack," Cage said.

"Maybe not from *inside* attack," Donovan said. "Remember - jihadists lied to get jobs in airports. They can lie their way into jobs at water plants. Or into nuclear plants for that matter."

The word "nuclear" caused some nervous coughs.

"Anything is possible," Nell said.

Donovan watched a nearby printer kick out some pages. It reminded him that Hasham kept checking the printed materials at the plant. Why?

"How many printing machines did you see?"

"I saw four. Could have been more."

"Four seems like a lot."

She nodded.

"What type?" Manning asked.

"The four were large commercial-size printing machines. I also remember a couple of smaller desktop printers."

"Why so many big commercial printers? Donovan asked.

Nell shrugged. "I saw Hasham walk over and check the big printers a few times. Maybe more. Also, one man brought paper samples to Hasham to look at from time to time. They spoke Arabic, so I don't know what was said. But now that I think about it, Hasham seemed very interested in the texture of the paper. He kept rubbing the paper between his fingers."

"Why would Hasham be so concerned about the texture of a *ChocoYummy* coupon or sales flyer?" Donovan asked.

No one answered.

Donovan asked, "Was he wearing gloves at the printing machines?"

Nell closed her eyes. "Yes. So were all the others, but - "

" - but what?"

"I assumed they wore gloves to keep the printer ink off their hands."

Suddenly, Donovan had a thought. "Or maybe, just maybe, they wanted to keep something else off their hands – like *VX!*

Everyone stared at him like he misspoke. He looked at Nell and saw something ignite in her eyes.

Agent Manning said, "Wait a minute - are you suggesting *VX is in the paper?*"

"Is that possible?" Donovan asked Nell.

All eyes locked on her.

She picked up a piece of paper, rubbed it between her fingers and stared at it a moment. "Yes, it *is* possible!"

Nell spun around to Manning. "Ask Agent Kim to test scraps of the printer paper near the printers for VX *immediately!"*

Manning speed-dialed Kim on speakerphone.

"Kim – check all printer paper scraps for VX!"

"What paper? she said. "It looks like the explosion and fire burned it all up!"

FIFTY SIX

"Good work, Pepe," Kadar Khoury said to the muscular, tattooed Hispanic lifting the last heavy case onto the new Learjet 31-A at the small airport near Toms River, New Jersey.

Kadar was relieved to work with Pepe, instead of Waazi the Whiner. Waazi would have whined how his poor two-fingered hand couldn't lift the cases.

Pepe lifted them with ease and had jumped at the chance to earn some extra cash. And he never complained. This was the third Learjet he loaded, each with five identical cases. The first two jets took off at five this morning.

"Cargo is secure," Pepe said, as he locked the cargo door and faced Kadar.

"Excellent," Kadar said. He peeled off five crisp one hundred dollar bills and handed them to Pepe.

"Thanks, *amigo*." Pepe stuffed the hundreds into the pocket of his royal blue airport maintenance uniform. "This money means new bowling shirts for our *Tom's River Tomcats.*"

"Glad to help."

"You mind if I ask you something?" Pepe said.

"Ask away?"

"Why you wearin' that fake beard? Too many girlfriends chasin' ya, right?" Pepe chuckled.

"Yeah!" Kadar smiled but grew uneasy, his disguise blown. "How'd you know it was fake?"

"Your beard moves kinda sideways when you turn."

"Oh. The beard hides my burn scars. Don't want to scare all those pretty women and little kids."

"I hear ya."

Kadar signaled the pilot to depart. He and Pepe watched the sleek white jet race down the runway and soar up into thick gray clouds, like the two earlier jets.

"Your cases are very heavy, man. What's in 'em?"

"Just company stuff."

"The same company stuff we shipped on the two jets flying to Chicago, Detroit, Los Angeles, Miami, Atlanta, and San Francisco?"

"Exact same stuff."

Kadar didn't like that Pepe remembered all the cities and that he noticed his fake beard, and that he asked a lot of questions.

"You know, I coulda fitted all them boxes in one of your jets. Woulda saved your company a buncha money."

"True. But management said it was very important that the contents reach all cities on the same day."

"How's come?"

Kadar shrugged. "Who knows? Probably a legal thing. Management doesn't tell me anything."

"Mine don't tell me jack shit neither!"

Kadar grew more concerned with Pepe's inquisition. Kadar's phone rang and he saw Hasham on caller ID. He walked over behind some large crates, making sure Pepe couldn't hear, and took the call.

"All boxes left yet?" Hasham asked.

"Yes. The third Learjet just took off. Ahead of time."

———

"Good. Any problems?"

Kadar switched to Arabic. "No, but the maintenance guy is asking too many questions."

"You wore a disguise, right?"

"Yeah, but he noticed my beard was fake. He's nosy. I could give him a few more hundred to keep him quiet."

"Do it. Then . . . keep him quiet for good."

Kadar paused, not comfortable with eliminating Pepe. He kind of liked the guy.

But not eliminating Pepe could result in getting himself eliminated . . .

"Then take back the money," Hasham said. "I'll give you another five thousand for handling him. You can keep it all."

"Okay." Kadar hung up and looked around. He and Pepe were still alone in the hanger. Lucky break.

He took out a syringe from his briefcase and concealed it in the palm of his hand. He walked up behind Pepe who sat reading the newspaper sports section."

"Who's pitching against the Yankees tomorrow?" Kadar asked him, looking over his shoulder.

"New guy for the Tigers. Emmett Vincent," Pepe said, leaning down to read the small print. "Guy's an ace! 100-mile-per-hour fastball! Curve ball that looks like it drops off a table."

"Sounds terrific!" Kadar said, as he plunged the syringe into the back of Pepe's neck. The young man jerked, then froze as though he'd been stung by a bee. He struggled a moment, then stiffened and slowly slumped to the floor.

Potassium cyanide was already shutting down his brain and heart . . . and, of course, his life.

"Nothing personal, Pepe."

FIFTY SEVEN

The door banged open.

Donovan watched an FBI agent rush into the room and hand Manning a note.

Manning read it and his fingers began to shake. "Aww . . . Jesus!"

Everyone stared at him.

"*All* paper scraps near the printers are highly saturated with *VX*!"

Donovan stopped breathing.

So that was it.

"*Paper!* That's Hasham's secret VX delivery system!" Nell Northam said, clearly stunned.

No one spoke.

Nell asked, "Did the lab identify the secret substance he blended into the VX?"

Manning ran his finger down the note.

"Yes! It's something called . . . D M S O."

"*DMSO?*" Nell asked, looking shocked.

"Yes."

"Are they absolutely certain?"

"They ran the test twice. It's DMSO."

Donovan had no idea what DMSO was, and wondered why it shocked Nell. "What's DMSO?"

She stared out the window. "It's a pharmaceutical. Many consider it a wonder drug for arthritis."

"What the hell does arthritis have to do with VX nerve gas?" Donovan asked.

No one answered.

"Why is it a wonder drug?" Manning asked her.

"Because it relieves arthritis pain quicker," Nell said.

Donovan still didn't get it. "But if his goal is to kill people with painful VX - why combine it with this DMSO pain-reliever?"

Nell shook her head. "I'm not sure." She began pacing alongside the conference table.

"I don't buy it!" Cage said. "Hasham decides to give people pain relief as he kills them? Doesn't sound like him."

"Doesn't make sense either," Nell said, walking around the table.

"What might make sense?" Donovan asked her.

She shook her head. Then she walked to the window, looked outside for a few seconds, then suddenly faced them with a very worried expression.

"Maybe one thing does."

Everyone waited.

"He doesn't want DMSO for its pain relief. He wants DMSO's speed. Its *faster* absorption into human skin. I just remembered something. Many years ago VX-DMSO was tested on animal skin. The VX-DMSO was absorbed through the skin and into the bloodstream *twice* as fast as VX alone."

"But we're talking *paper*," Donovan said. "Are you suggesting that just holding the paper laced with VX-DMSO in your fingers can be deadly?"

Nell paused. "Yes."

"But paper is . . . *dry!*"

"Our hands are not. They have a small amount of moisture. Some people have more moisture. Hasham's obviously formulated this VX-DMSO blend so that the normal moisture in your fingers, or maybe even less than normal moisture, is enough to activate the VX-DMSO in the paper. And he might have used special, tailor-made cellulose paper with a very high moisture content. Once VX-DMSO in the paper is activated, your skin will absorb VX *faster* into your blood, and by then, well, it's . . . too late."

No one spoke.

Donovan stood up and paced. "So how does he get the VX-DMSO paper in contact with so many people?"

No one answered.

"And how does he get them to hold the paper *long enough?*" Donovan said.

Again, silence.

"Maybe free offers?" Manning said. "Giveaways, handouts at malls, free gift cards and valuable vacation vouchers?"

"Possible," Donovan said.

"Newspapers maybe?" Cage said. "People hold newspapers in their hands a long time. Maybe he somehow laces VX into newspapers."

Manning shook his head. "Major newspapers generally buy their massive rolls of paper well before they print on it. I'm thinking the VX would probably degrade in long-term paper storage conditions. But I'll check it out."

Donovan nodded.

Agent Cage said, "Maybe he targets customers at specific stores like Macy's, Walmart, Target. Leaves 50% off coupons and coupon books."

"I just remembered," Nell said. "Hasham said his delivery system could reach people with *accuracy*. He was very proud of his accuracy and *precision*."

"He *bragged* about reaching individuals with *precision,* right?" Donovan said.

"Right. On a couple of occasions,"

Donovan wondered how precise? He stood, walked over to the conference room window and looked out at the Adirondack Forest. Thick dark clouds swept over the trees. Turning back, he walked alongside the conference table and noticed a Holiday Inn envelope addressed to a customer. He picked the envelope up and showed it to the group.

"The US Mail is very precise."

"It's also reliable, fast and cheap!" Manning added.

"I saw some envelopes near the printing machines," Nell said, growing excited.

"What size?" Donovan asked.

"That size. Regular size. White. The size bills come in."

Donovan turned to Manning. "Have Agent Kim search for pieces of the envelope and the contents and try to fit them together fast. Get a return address. And get some idea of what's inside."

Manning phoned the request to Agent Kim.

"So let's say," Donovan continued, "you get one of those envelopes in the mail and open it. You take out the VX-laced letter or whatever's inside. You hold it in your hands. You read it. How long do you have to hold it before the VX enters your blood?"

"Depends on the moisture in your hands."

"What's your rough estimate?"

Nell paused. "Based on normal moisture in your hands, I'm thinking maybe thirty to forty-five seconds before you absorb some VX. If you're fingers are normally moist, or sweating, or damp - maybe ten to twenty seconds."

Silence.

Donovan couldn't believe how fast it entered the body. "So the question is - how can Hasham make absolutely sure you'll take the envelope, open it and hold what's inside? How can he make sure you don't toss the envelope out as junk mail?"

No one answered.

"I toss my junk mail out in seconds," Nell said.

"Me too," Donovan said, "So it can't look like junk mail."

Heads nodded.

"And how can he make sure you hold the envelope's contents *long* enough?" Donovan said.

Again, no one answered.

"You're sure the envelope was this size? A regular, 9 by 4 inch envelope?" Agent Cage asked. He held up a regular white envelope.

"Yes. And it had a window for a name and address."

"Maybe the names and addresses are on the two flash drives you took," Donovan said. "Maybe Hasham spent time on his computer buying specific target lists. Maybe groups of people he wants to kill. Group lists give him accuracy! Precision."

Manning nodded. "Groups he blames, like US soldiers who fought against Muslims in Iraq and Iran. Or certain ethnicities like blacks, Christians, Jews, government personnel and politicians, you name it. He hates them all! Lists let him target people . . . give him the precision and accuracy he bragged about."

"Check if Hasham's purchased any lists," Donovan said.

"And check the flash drives," Manning said, turning toward his tech team in the corner. "Any luck on the two drives?"

"Still password-blocked! But Bobby Kamal at NSA is helping."

Donovan said, "Let's assume for a moment that Hasham's mailing out VX-DMSO letters in those bill-sized envelopes to hundreds of thousands of homes. Bobby Kamal heard Hasham tell Maahdi in Yemen that their so-called medicine would reach 260,000 people in Phase One, and then 220,000 more in Phase Two. So . . . roughly a half million people . . . are potential victims!"

Donovan felt like steel bands were squeezing his chest.

"The US postal system delivers . . . 660 *million* pieces of mail – each day!" Manning said. "And New York City is the largest mailing hub in this area."

"Check with the Postmaster General," Donovan said. "See if any Manhattan postal workers have died today from serious respiratory problems."

Manning gave the order.

"Whatever Hasham is mailing," Donovan said, "it has to make the person *want* to open it. It has to look very *important*. It has to look *valuable* to the person."

"Or maybe *legal*," Manning said. "A lawsuit notification. Legal process papers. Important stuff. You'd *have* to open it." Heads nodded.

"What else would make people open it right away?" Donovan asked. "And make them hold the contents in their hands long enough?"

"Cash," Cage said. "But postal workers might see the cash in he envelope, take it out and die."

"I don't think he's after postal workers," Donovan said. "He's *targeting* individuals. *Selecting* them. The letters are probably addressed to his *selected* victims."

"The *promise* of money would make people open it right away," Manning said.

"A *serious* promise of money. The *assurance* of guaranteed money," Donovan said. "Not some one-in-a-million-chance sweepstakes contest."

Heads nodded.

"We need to know who sent the letter. The mailer's name and address are critical," Donovan said.

"Agent Kim is collecting and piecing scraps together now," Drew Manning said.

Donovan nodded. "Alert the Post Offices and the Postmaster General. We may need to stop mail delivery in New York City and the northeast. Maybe even nationwide."

FIFTY EIGHT

FBI tech supervisor, Anne T. Kim, and her team crunched over rubble and broken *ChocoYummy* glass, searching for scraps of paper and envelopes to fit together.

But so far they'd found only tiny soot-smeared bits of paper. Too small and fragile to fit together. Still, her three assistants bent over a large table, trying to puzzle-fit the scraps into something readable.

"Remember," Kim said, "All we need is the return address. Or a few words on the envelope. The contents would be best. Or even pieces of the contents."

She noticed some paper scraps were light green and beige, vaguely familiar shades. But she couldn't recall where she'd seen them.

"Kim, over here!" an assistant said, pointing to something on the puzzle-fitting table.

Kim walked over.

"I've just fit together what might be the last postal digits of the return address."

"What are they?" Kim asked.

"The city name ends in *IA*. The zip code ends in *18*."

"Run them through the computer to determine location," Kim said.

A minute later, the assistant hurried over to her.

"The computer gives us a 92% certainty that it's - PENNSYLVAN*IA*, 191*18*. That's northwest Philadelphia. The Chestnut Hill area."

Donovan said, "Find companies or direct mailers in that zip code that might send out hundreds of thousands of letters."

Manning asked an assistant.

"Any more pieces of the envelope?"

"Just tiny bits. But no *words*."

Agent Kim walked back into the rubble. Breathing in her Hazmat suit tired her. But the air outside her suit very likely contained VX particles, which is why she'd ordered a one-mile evacuation of the streets around the factory and curfewed residents in their homes with windows shut and air ventilators turned off until Homeland declared it safe to come outside. Her team wore HazMat suits, walking down streets like alien invaders. Residents got the message.

Perspiration beaded on her lips. She'd die for some cool fresh outside air. She'd also die from it.

As she walked toward the charred printers, her boot nudged a small metal filing cabinet to the side. She looked down and saw the corner of an envelope beneath the cabinet. She lifted the cabinet to the side and stared at what lay beneath.

She couldn't believe it. She blinked to be sure.

She was looking at a complete envelope with the contents.

The return address and envelope were smeared with soot and ashes, but the envelope looked in good shape - and its contents appeared untouched.

She brushed ashes off the envelope, saw the return address, and her heart stopped. She reread the return address and the addressee window and blinked.

———

"Naneun nae nun-eul mid-eul su eobs-eo!" she whispered in Korean. *"This can't be what it is!"*

Wearing her gloves, she used an Exacto knife to ease open the envelope flap. Then she took her tweezers and pulled out the contents. When she saw the contents, she let rip with another long Korean curse.

Gripping the envelope, she ran outside and headed toward her lead technician, Deek Jenkins.

"Whatcha got?" he asked.

"The Holy Grail!"

"You mean *Holy Shit!*"

"Test the envelope and contents for VX-DMSO!"

Deek took them, ran into the MobileLab and jackknifed his six-foot-eight frame over his sophisticated testing equipment.

As she waited, Kim paced back and forth, fearful of what he would confirm . . . because she was certain of what he'd confirm. Thank God for the MobileLab she thought. A few years ago, she would have to drive the envelope to the nearest lab and wait hours, maybe even a day for the lab results.

Waited - while people died!

The MobileLab's on-site analysis was a godsend. It confirmed the presence of biological or chemical toxins in real time – fast! And fast saved lives.

Deek Jenkins tugged Kim's sleeve.

She turned and faced him.

His eyes shouted the results.

✱ ✱ ✱

Donovan heard Manning's iPhone ring on the conference room table. Manning hit a button that projected his phone's Skype video onto a large-screen wall monitor. They saw Agent Kim in the MobileLab.

"We found a complete envelope and its contents," Kim said. "Both are in good shape."

"Terrific!" Donovan said, leaning forward to see better.

"The envelope is addressed to Mr. Ernest T. Smythe in the Bronx. The outside of the envelope does *not* contain VX or DMSO."

Thank God postal workers won't die from touching them, Donovan thought.

"However, the envelope's contents are *saturated* with high levels of VX and DMSO."

No one spoke.

"What do the envelope and contents look like?" Donovan asked.

"Watch your screen."

Everyone watched.

Agent Ann T. Kim held up the envelope to the camera, but her hand trembled so much, Donovan couldn't read the return address. He squinted. Finally, she steadied the envelope using both hands.

Donovan read it and froze. "Awww . . . Jesus . . .!"

Gasps filled the room.

"Is that what I think it is?" Manning asked.

"Yes! You're looking at a Federal IRS envelope. And inside is an IRS tax refund check."

Silence.

She took out the check and accompanying letter.

"We reviewed and changed your 2011-2015 Form 1040s to match our record of your estimated payments, credits applied from other tax years, and payments received with an extension to file. As a result you are due this refund of $4,850."

"This refund check for $4,850 is for Mr. Ernest T. Smythe. The check itself and its accompanying letter are heavily saturated with VX-DMSO."

Agent Kim continued, "I assure you, this envelope, letter and check, look and feel, absolutely authentic. *Everyone* will see 'Pay to the order of.' They'll see their name in the envelope window. They'll rip open the envelope, read the letter. And they'll grab the check!"

And celebrate, Donovan knew, by holding it in their excited fingers as if their life depended on it . . .

When in fact their death did.

———

FIFTY NINE

Donovan, Manning, and Agent Cage raced up 23rd Street in a big FBI Suburban. Donovan watched their escort vehicles, two NYPD police cars, as they cornered onto Eighth Avenue. Their blaring siren and flashing lights forced traffic to the curbs like a snowplow. They were heading toward the James Farley Post Office in mid-town Manhattan.

"Death by IRS check!" Donovan said. "Hasham's *real* attack all along."

Manning nodded, looking angrier by the minute. "But we *had* to commit resources to *ChocoYummy*. Kids drinking it were dying!"

"And some may still be dying from it if they haven't heard our warnings," Cage said. "And if stores still haven't cleared it off shelves!"

Donovan couldn't stop himself from imagining the cruel, painful IRS-check deaths. A man looks at the IRS envelope, sees his name in the window, rips the envelope open. He takes out the check and letter, grips them in his excited fingers for several seconds, afraid to let go as he admires his unexpected windfall. Then he rereads both. Maybe hands them to his wife. She grabs it to make sure they aren't hallucinating. Their hearts beat faster. Their fingers moisten faster, the moisture pulls the VX-DMSO out of the paper into their skin and then into their blood stream faster!

Donovan watched them drive past a funeral motorcade. *An omen of deaths to come . . .*

"The question is - where are the IRS checks now?" Cage said.

"Assume they're in the postal system," Donovan said.

"But *where* in the system*?"* Manning said. "If we're lucky, still in post offices sorting rooms."

"Or in mailbags being delivered?" Cage said.

"Or in homes being ripped open," Manning said.

"Or in hands being gripped with joy," Donovan said.

The driver stopped in front of the mammoth gray stone James Farley post office building. Built in 1912. The structure occupied an entire block, eight full acres, and its row of massive pillars dwarfed many Federal buildings in Washington DC.

They got out, ran up the steps, then along the row of gigantic pillars and through the entrance. Inside, Donovan saw a tall, hulking man waving them over.

"That's Postmaster Burrell Jefferson. Good guy," Manning said.

Manning introduced everyone.

Jefferson was fifty something, six-five, two-fifty, with a short Afro. He had massive shoulders, one of which sloped lower, probably from lugging too many heavy mailbags for too many years. His beige sweater had tan leather elbow patches.

Jefferson hurried them into a large mail-sorting room.

Donovan saw and heard thousands of letters chugging along conveyors, moving into sorting machines that spit them into long conveyor belts that somehow knew when to re-spit specific letters into specific plastic bins. Machines clicked and hummed through the room. Many workers wore earplugs or MP3 players.

He saw at least forty workers: processors, sorters, clerks, and others sifting through stacks of mail and boxes at long tables. Some workers pushed large canvas carts stuffed with parcel packages. He felt relieved to see many employees wearing gloves. Some wore facemasks.

Jefferson hit a buzzer loud as a prison alarm.

"Heads up people!" Jefferson shouted in a deep baritone. Someone turned off most machines and the room quieted. The workers turned and looked at him with concern.

"We've got a serious threat in our system!"

The room grew graveyard still.

"A *deadly* threat!" Burrell Jefferson gestured to Donovan. "This federal agent will explain."

Donovan saw frightened faces turn and stare at him. He understood their fear. Anthrax-laced letters killed fellow postal workers and others just one week after 9/11. And deadly letter bombs were a constant threat. Each day workers worried if the letters and packages in their hands could kill them. They worked in a combat zone against cowardly, unseen enemies.

Donovan thought postal workers should get combat pay.

"Here's what we're talking about."

Wearing gloves, Donovan opened a large baggie, took the IRS check from the bottling plant and held it up for them to see.

"This authentic-looking IRS check, and thousands like it, are now in the mail, we believe. Maybe even in this post office. They contain a deadly nerve agent – VX. It can kill people in a few minutes. The letters are in the typical 9-by-4 inch white IRS envelope. On the outside of the envelope you'll see this logo - *Department of the Treasury, Internal Revenue Service* and a Philadelphia address. There's a see-through window for the addressee's name next to large print *USA*. Inside the window, you see - *Pay to* . . . and a recipient's name . . . on a light green and yellowish brown IRS check . . . identical to the genuine IRS refund checks."

More murmurs.

"We estimate around two hundred sixty thousand of these deadly checks are possibly already in the US postal system. Another two hundred twenty thousand may be put in the system later today."

Several workers gasped.

"As you can see, the check looks genuine."

All eyes riveted on the check.

"But here's the bad news - just *holding* this fake IRS check, or holding the letter inside in your bare hands, can kill you!"

Many workers gasped and stepped back.

"Just holding?" someone shouted.

"Yes. Holding it in your bare fingers."

Silence.

Several people put gloves on.

"What if we touch the outside of the *envelope*?" a young woman asked.

"We've found no trace of VX on the *outside* of the envelope. But the *inside* of the envelope has probably absorbed VX from the check and the letter . . . and therefore the inside of the envelope should be considered deadly! But to be safe - if you've touched any part of an IRS envelope, wash your hands immediately!"

"What proof do you have the *outside* of the envelope is safe?" a young worker said.

"Our lab test confirmed it's safe."

"Just *one* test?"

Donovan paused and stared at him. "Also . . . no postal workers have died from VX poisoning today."

They stood in stunned silence.

"But wait," a woman shouted, "we've been delivering IRS refund checks over the last seven weeks. I got mine and deposited it."

"So did I," someone said.

"Those checks were *genuine*. And the vast majority of IRS checks in the mail now are genuine. The terrorists timed their IRS checks . . . to coincide with the mailing of many genuine IRS refund checks."

"I just saw a new batch of IRS checks over here!" a skinny young worker said, rushing to a shelf stacked with envelopes.

"Put your gloves on Lenny!" Postmaster Jefferson shouted.

Lenny snapped on a pair of gloves.

Donovan, Manning, and Jefferson hurried over as Lenny pointed to the envelope.

Wearing gloves, Donovan picked up the envelope. It looked identical to the bottling plant envelope. So did the IRS return address.

DEPARTMENT OF THE TREASURY
FINANCIAL MANAGEMENT SERVCE
REGIONAL FINANCIAL CENTER
P.O.BOX 51320
PHILIDELPHIA, PENNSYLVANIA 19118

Donovan adjusted his facemask and carefully opened the new IRS envelope. He looked at the color-gradient-green-to-yellowish-to-beige treasury check inside for $3,760 to be paid to Mr. Neil M. McCall of Brooklyn, New York.

"Let's talk to Mr. McCall," Donovan said to Manning.

Manning got McCall's number, phoned him, spoke a bit, and hung up.

"Neil M. McCall received his IRS refund check for $1,020 dollars two weeks ago and deposited it."

Donovan nodded. "So . . . this IRS check is *fake!* It could have killed Mr. McCall." Donovan placed the check and envelope in a large sealed baggie.

No one breathed.

"Here's another big batch of IRS checks!" said an attractive young redhead, pointing down at a stack of envelopes beside her.

"Careful Deanna!" Postmaster Jefferson said. "Let's keep away from *all* IRS checks, people! In fact, process no more IRS checks until further notice!"

"Hang on," a tall, bearded man said. "I processed some of this batch of IRS letters *yesterday!*"

Donovan's worst fear. Some IRS checks were delivered. They were now in homes. They were now being opened.

Postmaster Jefferson's phone rang. He listened a moment and hung up.

"The US Postmaster General says the President is close to issuing an Executive Order stopping further delivery of all IRS checks today and tomorrow - nationally! We'll run computer-tracking software to see if we can determine how many of these IRS letters have gone out from the Manhattan and surrounding post offices. And which zip codes are targeted. But it may be too late to stop delivery."

"In the meantime, people wear your gloves and facemasks as you prepare to leave for the day. Check your email tonight to see if we're open or closed tomorrow."

Most workers grabbed masks and gloves and put them on.

Donovan heard a man coughing violently in the back of the room.

Everyone spun around and stared at him.

"LaMar . . . ?" the Postmaster asked, looking terrified.

"Sorry, Chief . . . the damn coffee."

SIXTY

Two floors below the post office sorting room, Bodie T. Burlip, a mail processor, sat in the comfort of the air conditioning maintenance room, his private man cave. He scoffed at Postmaster Jefferson's latest "Warning Meeting" and didn't go. *Another dumbass waste of time.*

In his hideaway, Bodie T. was safe from pushy bosses and even pushier ex-wives filing bogus spousal abuse claims against him. Minor stuff.

Here, he could relax and enjoy the sweet new gift in his pocket. Minutes ago, while sorting envelopes, he saw an IRS envelope to *Dottie Rae Smith.*

In his well-practiced move, he curled the envelope in his palm, then slid it up his sleeve, unnoticed by fellow workers. Poor old Dottie Rae had been pushing up daisies for nine months and she sure as hell didn't need the money. Bodie sure as hell did. Two nasty ex-wives were trying to skin him alive for child support.

He took out the envelope, opened it and removed the check. His eyes shot open when he saw the big beautiful $3,870 *US Treasury Refund Check* for Dottie Rae Smith.

"Holy shit! Dottie Rae – you are truly my Sugar Momma!"

And when he added this fat IRS check to Dottie Rae's monthly social security checks that kept coming since no one ever reported the old gal had croaked, well, Dottie Rae was the gift that kept on giving. Bless her stone-cold heart!

Bodie gave her IRS check a big wet kiss, pulled out his pocket flask and chugged down some well-earned Jim Beam. Then he licked his lips.

He endorsed the check with Dottie's signature and signed it over to himself. He'd deposit it later, then go have fun at the new strip club, *Bottoms Up.* He deserved to enjoy some bottoms for all the crap he put up with.

He wiped his runny nose on his sleeve. *Allergy season's starting early*, he realized.

Then his lips felt started tingling, and seconds later, stinging . . . stinging so much he started sweating. He chugged down more bourbon. He wiped his runny nose again and saw *blood!*

What the fuck. . .?

His entire body started perspiring heavily, drenching his new shirt, even though the air-conditioned room was cold enough to hang meat.

What's going on . . . with "Jesus - I'm sweatin' like a nigger at a lynching.

He felt sharp pain squeeze his lungs. He tried to take a deep breath, but couldn't. Something was shoving hot needles into his chest.

He couldn't breathe. Couldn't move. Couldn't figure out what the fuck was happening. Couldn't believe the *pain!*

Suddenly, it felt like a lead anvil landed on his chest.

He collapsed to the floor, his lungs exploding, his mind spinning, his body convulsing, his nose bleeding, his vision fading.

Bodie T. Burlip knew he wouldn't be cashing in Dottie Rae's IRS check . . .

. . . he knew *he* was cashing in.

SIXTY ONE

"Bad news," Manning's young blonde assistant said, running into the small alcove near the post office sorting room. She looked like she'd just watched a train wreck.

What now? Donovan wondered. He sat with Manning, Cage, and Postmaster Jefferson.

"Hasham has disabled major Internet servers in his targeted zip codes," she said.

"How the hell -?" Donovan said.

" - explosive devices damaged server transmitters and transformers. Also a cyber-security breach is causing electrical power-grid problems. The companies are repairing them, but it will take time."

Donovan felt his gut churn. "Which servers?"

"He's partially disabled the majors, Comcast, AOL, and the Dish. And other servers are reporting problems. The pictures are pixelating in and out. No sound."

Donovan was so angry he could barely breathe. "So what's the bottom line?"

"No cable warnings are being telecast about the IRS VX checks!"

Donovan thumped the table with his fist. "Blast warnings on all radio and other media. Also have Verizon, AT&T, T-Mobile, Sprint, and others send out robo-call warnings to cellphones and landline phones in the targeted zip codes."

"On it," Agent Cage said.

Donovan stood and paced beside the table. "Drive loudspeaker vehicles blasting warnings through city streets. Ask newspapers to print special editions with 100-point headlines. Hell, get small aircraft flying around cities with long banners warning about IRS checks."

Manning's phone rang - Agent Kim calling from the bottling plant. What's up, Kim?"

"He mailed IRS checks to more zip codes: upstate New York zips, Newark, East Elizabeth, Paramus, all over New Jersey and Connecticut."

"Why just *those* areas?" Manning asked.

"He probably wants one-day delivery range," Donovan said. "He gets checks into people's hands before they hear media warnings."

"Which they won't now hear, thanks to the disabled servers," Manning added.

Donovan nodded as his phone rang. It was Audie Millener in the CIA's anti-terrorism unit. Donovan hit his speakerphone.

"Just learned that Hasham's attacking nationwide."

Donovan's stomach twisted tighter. "Which states?"

"Michigan, Illinois, California, Ohio, Kentucky, Georgia, Maryland, also Florida. Still checking. Maybe *all* states."

"At least we have an extra day to stop delivery in those states," Donovan said.

"We don't. The IRS checks are already in the postal systems in those states."

"How the -?"

" - Hasham chartered three jets. They flew the IRS checks to those cities from a small airport in Toms River, New Jersey. As we speak, post offices in Los Angeles, Detroit, Cleveland, Indianapolis, Louisville, Nashville, Baltimore, Atlanta, and many other cities report checks are in process of being delivered."

"The bastard's always a step ahead of us," Donovan said. "Start the warnings in those states - before Hasham shuts down cable TV and Internet servers there. Blast all available media. Warn people on Facebook, YouTube, Twitter, Tweet, whatever! And all social media. Scare people!"

"*Scare* them?" Cage said.

"Scared beats dead."

SIXTY TWO

After a warm, soothing shower, Nell dried off and looked at herself in the mirror. She counted sixteen cuts, nicks, and scratches. She was a stigmata. Phone the Pope! Sainthood within weeks!

Crawling over the jagged window glass had sliced and diced her back and legs. She cleaned the cuts with antibacterial ointment and bandaged some. Then she dried her hair, dressed, and walked into the kitchen where Lindee was loading her dishwasher.

"Jacob just called," Lindee said. "He's at LaGuardia waiting to pick up his mom and Mia. They're flying in from Baltimore."

"Which airline?"

"CIA plane. Better security."

Nell couldn't wait. She'd hug Mia and maybe never let go. Just hours ago, Nell had feared Hasham would give Mia to a pedophile sheik for life. Now her sweet beautiful daughter would soon be in her arms, safe.

But other children were not safe. Some were still dying from drinking Hasham's *ChocoYummy* . . . and some might still die if *ChocoYummy* is still on some store shelves.

And his VX-laced IRS checks were in the mail, in homes, in hands being opened. Killing people. Hasham Habib was winning. And it sickened her that she'd been forced to help the monster.

The apartment landline phone rang.

"Can you grab that?" Lindee said from the kitchen.

"Sure . . . hello?"

"Hi, Nell," Donovan Rourke said. "Feeling better?"

"Much better, Donovan. Thanks to a shower and some Advil."

"Need stronger pain meds?"

"No. Advil's working."

"Good. Just got word that Mia's flight from Baltimore is weather-delayed. She should land in another hour or so. Jacob will wait at LaGuardia for her and his mother."

"Good. Any luck with the flash drives?"

"One drive gave us more mailing zip codes. The other flash drive is more difficult. But NSA thinks they can crack it eventually."

"Let's hope." She felt frustrated that she hadn't found a way to stop the attack. But at least the flash drives might reveal something that prevents Hasham's future attacks.

"One more thing, Nell."

"What's that?"

"We believe Hasham is very worried that you took his flash drives. He's also very worried about what you saw and read in his lab files."

"He should be. I glanced into some files that appeared to involve deadly weapons and horrific attacks."

"We need to debrief you on those files."

"Okay. I'll start writing down some notes."

"Good idea. But we're worried he may try to stop you from telling us more."

"How can he?"

Donovan paused. "His men may be searching for you now."

She froze at the thought that Hasham might be coming after her again.

"So, as an extra precaution, Agent Manning is sending over two FBI agents. They'll take you and Lindee to a safe location until this is over. They'll arrive shortly."

"All right . . ." she said, wondering if they were being overly cautious. A guard was already posted outside Lindee's door. On the other hand, she remembered how enraged Hasham was because he thought she stole the two flash drives. Rage drove the man. Rage might drive him to come after her again.

Donovan said, "We'll drive Jacob, his mom, and Mia from LaGuardia to the safe location where you and Lindee will be."

"I can't wait."

They hung up.

Nell told Lindee what Donovan said.

Lindee nodded, then brought over two glasses of chilled Chardonnay.

"To my older, wiser sister!" Lindee said, handing her a glass.

Nell paused, closed her eyes. "*Un-wiser . . .*"

Lindee stared at her. "What? Why?"

"My career . . ."

Lindee continued staring at her.

"My career led us all to this, Lindee. It's led my family, you, me, and thousands of innocent Americans to this horrifying deadly situation."

"That's not true! Hasham did! You said he would attack whether he'd abducted you or not."

"Yes, but I helped make his weapon more effective."

"Because he threatened Mia's life!"

Nell shrugged. She'd done what seemed right at the time. Helped him so she could maybe find a way to stop him. But she didn't find a way. Still, she would always wonder if she could have done something more to block his attack. And even if she had refused to help him, Hasham's VX weapon would still kill thousands.

"Anyway, when this is over, I've decided to change things."

"How?"

"Find safer work outside Aberdeen."

"Will you be happy doing that?"

Nell thought about that. She wasn't sure. "Probably not to start. But maybe I'll grow happy with time."

"I know what'll make you happy now," Lindee said, smiling.

"What?"

"What we were doing before you were so rudely interrupted."

"What's that?"

"Our Broadway Shop-Till-We-Drop-Athon!" Lindee said.

Nell smiled. "That beautiful brown Michael Kors purse still calls out to me. But by now someone snatched it up."

"Someone did!"

Lindee reached behind the couch, lifted out a *LEATHER TRENDS* bag, took out the purse and handed it to her.

Nell grinned like a lottery winner.

"I was looking at this when . . ." Nell ran her fingers over the soft leather, smelled its sweet scent. "Lindee. This is the most awesome-est welcome home gift in the entire history of the universe."

"Actually sis, you are . . ."

Nell hugged her sister and it felt wonderful.

She sipped more wine, then began to tell Lindee everything that happened in the cabin, Hasham's threats to sell Mia into slavery, Aarif's attempt to rape her. As they talked, they packed small suitcases to take to the safe house. When they finished, they sipped more wine and Nell felt herself begin to relax. Mia was safe. Jacob was safe. She was safe.

The apartment's lobby phone rang.

Lindee grabbed it and spoke to the lobby guard. "Send them up, John."

Lindee turned to Nell. "Donovan's two FBI men are coming up to take us to the safe house."

A couple of minutes later the apartment doorbell rang.

Nell checked through the peephole, saw the two male agents in coats and ties, then opened the door. They smiled and flashed their FBI badges.

"I'm Agent Dutton, ma'am," the tall blond man said. "And this is Agent Witkowski." He gestured toward a shorter, muscular, thick-necked man, who nodded.

"Please come in."

They entered.

"Are you both ready to leave?" Agent Dutton asked.

"Yes," Lindee said.

"These suitcases go?"

"Yes, please."

"I've got them," Agent Witkowski said, picking them up.

Lindee set her apartment alarm and they stepped out into the hall.

"Where's the agent who was sitting out here?" Nell asked.

"Agent Davies is on his way to the safe house. You'll see him there," Agent Dutton said.

"Okay . . ."

They walked down the hall, entered the elevator and descended.

"How's the search for Hasham going?" Nell asked.

"No luck yet."

"He's a dangerous man," she said.

"Number One on our list!" Agent Dutton said.

The elevator passed the lobby and went on down to the basement.

"We're leaving through the basement?" Nell asked.

Dutton nodded. "Safer than the front entrance."

"But I saw a police car out front."

"It's still there, but they told us the basement rear exit in back has less exposure."

Nell nodded, but then remembered the basement door also exited onto an exposed street.

Agent Witkowski bent down to grab the suitcases and she noticed a swastika tattoo creep above his gray collar.

A swastika tattoo? And a ponytail. And white socks. Would the FBI hire a guy with a large Nazi tattoo? Maybe for undercover work. But would the FBI condone a long-barrel handgun tucked loosely in Agent Dutton's belt? Agent Manning had a holstered Glock. And Witkowski's gun was some other brand.

She knew FBI agents dressed more casually than back in J. Edgar's day, but Witkowski's green plaid sport coat, missing shirt buttons and a SmackDown Wrestling belt buckle the size of a coffee saucer - all seemed too relaxed even for today's more relaxed FBI dress code. Drew Manning and his fellow agents wore dark sports coats and dress shirts.

Nell remembered how quickly Dutton and Witkowski flashed their FBI badges. Maybe too quickly. And the agent who'd sat outside Lindee's door promised he'd tell them if he went anywhere. But he didn't. And she thought his name was *David*, not Davies, as Dutton said. Nell was picking up bad vibes. Her instincts were usually right in situations like this.

The elevator jiggled to a stop. They stepped into the basement and she saw no one else there. More bad vibes. Something told her these men weren't FBI agents. And Donovan had warned Hasham's men might try to grab her again.

"Oh . . . damn!" Nell said, stopping.

"What's wrong?" Agent Dutton said.

"I forgot my cell phone. I'll run up and get it." She'd go up, call Donovan and verify these two FBI agents' names.

Agent Dutton looked at Witkowski, then her.

"Another agent will bring your phone to you," Dutton said. "You really need to come with us now."

"I will. But first I need to phone my daughter. She's been traumatized. It's very important that I talk to her. Calm her down, you understand."

"Use your sister's phone."

"She doesn't have my mother-in-law's number and I don't remember it off hand. It's in my phone's Favorites List."

She started back toward the elevator.

Witkowski grabbed her arm and showed her the business end of his handgun.

SIXTY THREE

"Comcast, AT&T, and Time Warner are back up!" Agent Manning shouted across the conference table. "Other service providers will be operational in minutes."

Donovan felt a glimmer of hope. "Keep blasting warnings on them all the time! Use language subtitles and signers."

He still couldn't believe Hasham's brilliant, synchronous strategic plan. The man allowed *ChocoYummy* media warnings to go out on the Internet so all police groups would focus totally on *ChocoYummy* – and then when he launched his primary attack, the deadly IRS checks – he disabled cable servers to block the IRS warnings to the public.

Obviously, Hasham had highly skilled hackers and Internet cells involved in all aspects of his coordinated attacks . . . cells that had metastasized nationally like cancer.

* * *

"Finally!" Mildred Greenacre said to herself.

Her cable TV had been down, but *Wheel of Fortune* just popped on, even though it popped on to a Viagra commercial. At eighty-four she probably wouldn't fiddle with many more erections. But a woman could hope.

She stood to fetch the mail and noticed her stride was getting shorter, like her time on Mother Earth. The smart-ass neighbor kid had asked if she dated Abe Lincoln. She shouted back "His *father!*" and flipped the little turd the finger. Hadn't seen him since.

Back in the house, she sorted through the junk mail. One offered to clean her septic tank, another'd clean her colon, and another'd shrink her prostate thank God.

Mildred noticed a white envelope addressed to her. In the window she saw *Mildred Greenacre*. The return address read: *Internal Revenue Service*.

What's this? I already received my $205 refund check and spent the money. It looked like another refund check. Impossible. She looked through the envelope window.

Pay to the Order of Mildred Greenacre . . .

She ripped open the envelope and took out the contents.

She was holding an IRS refund check payable to *her* - in the amount of - holy crap –

$4,600!

"Jesus Christ and Mary on the handlebars!" she shouted, her heart pounding louder than the *Wheel of Fortune* buzzer.

Was she dreaming?

Was this really *her* money? She looked at the name on the check. *Mildred Greenacre*. She looked at the address. *Hers!* The letter said that the IRS recalculated her taxes in the last six years and she was now entitled to this refund.

"Whatever you say!"

Should she call and verify the check? No damn way.

I'll deposit this baby! Then I'll pay off some overdue medical bills, before they realize their mistake and demand the money back. The IRS wouldn't demand it back from a poor old widow, would they? Of course they would.

$4,600! A Godsend!

Her phone rang. It was her best friend, Myrna Faye.

"Myrna, I just got an IRS refund check for $4,600. I'm taking you to dinner at *TGI Fridays*. The quesadillas and key lime pie are on me!"

"Why'd you get the refund?"

"Because I'm a highly distinguished and deserving US citizen!"

"And I'm Doris Day!"

The two women laughed, chatted a bit and hung up.

Mildred set the check down on the coffee table as an *"Urgent News Bulletin"* interrupted *Wheel of Fortune*. She saw Lester Holt.

Please, Lester, not another school massacre.

As she started to grab her IRS check again, Lester said something about "IRS checks." She turned up the volume.

> *"We have an urgent nationwide alert from Homeland Security. There are fake IRS refund checks which contain the deadly poison VX arriving at homes in the mail . . ."*

As she listened, Mildred felt her entire body go rigid. She looked at the envelope, letter and check on the television, then at hers on her coffee table.

Identical!

She raced to the bathroom and washed her hands and face with soapy lather. Then she washed them again.

Her heart pounded! How long did she hold the check? A few seconds? No, *several* seconds. *Where* did she hold it? The middle?

The corners maybe? Did she hold the envelope by the flap or corners? She couldn't remember.

Mildred hurried out her front door and headed toward the *24 Hour Walk-In* clinic two blocks away. *Long* blocks.

Her adrenaline kicked in. She grew tired as she walked. Her heart seemed to pump harder than normal. *Why? Because I'm walking faster . . . or because I'm old, or because the poison . . .*

She took a deep breath. Her lungs felt tighter, like something was squeezing them. Or was she imagining it? She slowed down.

She saw the clinic one block ahead.

Can I make it?

SIXTY FOUR

Their hands flex-cuffed, Nell and Lindee sat in the back seat of the Lincoln. Nell couldn't believe she was back in the grasp of Hasham . . .

Nell wondered how these two FBI imposters knew the real FBI agents were coming to Lindee's apartment. Clearly, a phone tap or apartment bug. Or worse, a police informant told them.

But by now, the real FBI agents had arrived at Lindee's apartment. They would have viewed the building security video, seen her and Lindee leave with the two men, maybe even seen them leave in the Lincoln, maybe got its license number, then organized a search.

She watched Dutton steer onto 39th and head west. Opposite her on a fold-down seat sat Swastika Witkowski, staring at her. He lowered the window and tossed the crushed pieces of Lindee's cell phone out into a sewer vent.

Donovan was right, she realized. *Hasham abducted me again to tell him which files I saw in the lab - and tell him what I told the FBI.*

———

He also wants me to admit I stole the two flash drives, even though I told him at the bottling plant I did not. And when they body-searched me at the plant and didn't find them, he accused me of hiding them in the forest near the cabin.

And he was right. She'd hidden them under a log and retrieved them after the FBI team rescued her at the gas station.

Hasham's rage about the flash drives proves their value to the FBI. They could contain information about imminent attacks, maybe even names of people who would implement them. If so, Hasham might be forced to cancel or alter future plans. And his jihadist cell members may be forced to run for their lives. And if the FBI tech specialists could extract more data, lives could be saved. All good results.

But would Hasham somehow know when the flash drives were opened? Would opening them trigger an alert to him so he could warn his jihadists to flee.

Now, incredibly, Hasham's men had grabbed her again. He would insist she'd stolen the flash drives. She'd deny it. He would not believe her. Then what? Torture. *Me* for sure. *But probably Lindee to make me talk.* The thought sickened her.

Nell checked Lindee. Her sister looked terrified, and Nell feared this abduction might trigger a relapse of Lindee's depression after being attacked in her apartment last summer.

Suddenly the car went dark.

Nell saw they'd driven into the Holland Tunnel. Two minutes later, they emerged into brilliant sunlight in Jersey City. They turned onto Palisade Avenue heading north, driving parallel with the Hudson River. Some time later, she saw broken store windows, darkened buildings, abandoned warehouses, some homeless men clustered in alleys.

Dutton answered his phone, spoke fluent Arabic, said "Hasham" a couple of times.

Nell was angry with herself. She should have asked Donovan for the names of the two agents coming to the apartment. She should have inspected Dutton's FBI badge more closely. She should have called Donovan and double-checked the agents' names. And because she didn't, her sister's life and hers were now in grave danger.

After all, Hasham had ordered Aarif to kill her. But she killed Aarif instead. Then she'd escaped, twice, giving Hasham even more reasons to kill her.

SIXTY FIVE

BRONX

Hasham Habib was delighted. His IRS checks had already harvested one hundred eighty-nine infidels . . . with hundreds more in so much pain they were begging to join their deceased brethren . . . and soon would.

Yes, some were children who drank *ChocoYummy*. Yes, some were women and men who'd held the IRS checks. Yes, they died like thousands of Muslim men, women and children died from infidel attacks over the decades.

Like my innocent family died.

Do you understand yet, America?

But now, I must leave your shores . . . Nell Northam gave authorities his name. The FBI, Homeland Security, the police, the CIA, and the NSA with their sophisticated software and resources were searching for him and his aliases. It was only a matter of time before they discovered, if they were lucky, that one of his older aliases could lead them to the Bronx apartment where he was now. Perhaps they already knew and were on their way.

Hasham hurried to his bedroom closet, knelt down and removed a floor panel. He reached down and punched in the code to unlock his security safe. He removed four sets of passports, drivers' licenses, and credit cards. He also took sixty thousand dollars in cash and placed everything in a leather satchel. He put his Beretta in his shoulder holster and stuffed several thirteen-round clips in the satchel.

He walked into the living room and stared at Abdul, the youngest member of his New York cell. Abdul was a brilliant NYU chemistry major with great potential for the cause. The bearded, devout Muslim lived in the apartment and monitored all police, FBI, and Internet activities for Hasham's network of US cells. Abdul also coordinated with cells throughout Europe.

"What's our latest total, Abdul?"

Abdul checked his computer. "*Many* more deaths than CNN and FOX report! Another hundred or so more according to social media. Your IRS jihad is a great success, Hasham!"

"Most gratifying!"

"Wait - Hasham! *Look!*" Abdul pointed at the screen.

Hasham turned and saw the *US Terrorist Watch List* site.

"They just announced *your* name! Look – your photo, too!"

Hasham looked and grew concerned. The eight-year-old photo had been age-enhanced to an amazingly accurate degree . . . like they'd snapped the photo of his face yesterday.

"Check CNN and FOX!"

Abdul checked. Both networks showed the same photo captioned: *Hasham Habib. Wanted By Police! Extremely Dangerous. Call 911.*

So they're onto me. It had always been a matter of time.

Still, Hasham felt his pulse kick up a notch. He hurried to a closet and took out his small portable theatrical kit with several disguises.

———

He would use them until the Abu Dhabi plastic surgeon gave him a new face in three weeks. He placed the kit in his satchel.

He checked his watch. By now, his two FBI imposters were driving Dr. Nell Northam to meet him. He would force her to admit that she took the flash drives. He would also force her to tell him exactly what she told authorities about the confidential file folders she'd seen and read in the lab. Based on what she told authorities, he might alter plans.

He'd been too lax with her in the lab and cabin, simply because she was never supposed to leave the cabin alive.

She'd also tell him that she'd seen his most closely guarded secret plan - his orange file. Even though the file was in code, she might have deduced it dealt with a weapon that would render an important US city uninhabitable for seventy years.

The hidden flash drive she'd stolen was also critically important. It contained plans, plus the aliases and birth names of many cell members now active in America. If the FBI hacked into that flash drive, his people would be hunted like vermin, many killed by drones or CIA assassins.

Even though he'd been assured that the FBI and NSA tech people could never crack through the series of passwords and encryption codes on the flash drives, he knew better. American analysts had sophisticated code-breaking and eavesdropping technology no one else even knew about.

Whatever the case, Dr. Nell Northam would tell him everything she told the authorities. If she refused, torturing her sister would loosen Nell's tongue.

Then, after she gave him the answers he wanted, he'd do what Aarif failed to do.

Kill her.

"Hasham, I think the NSA might have listened to Bassam Maahdi's phone calls to you."

"It's possible."

"How else could they learn your name?"

"From the woman, Nell Northam. In the cabin she heard Aarif call me "Hasham" a couple of times.

Abdul shook his head. "Most unfortunate."

"Yes."

"Still," Abdul said, "poor Aarif died a martyr for our cause."

"Yes." *But a stupid martyr.*

"What should I say if the police ever come here?"

Hasham knew they would come here soon.

"Don't worry. They don't know about this place yet, Abdul. But to be safe, you must now start destroying all evidence here. All computers. Drill holes in hard drives, files, backup files, flash drives, smash the throwaway phones, destroy the SIM cards. Destroy everything now!"

Abdul looked concerned. "Everything?"

"Yes. Later, you can retrieve data all from your Cloud folders, right?"

"Yes. Fakhir and I can."

"Good."

Abdul began smashing computer hard drives and emails and shredding some paper files.

Hasham made a phone call and activated his backup escape plan. He watched Abdul hammer flash drives and shred old backup disks and files. Minutes later, when he finished, he faced Hasham.

"I have destroyed all sources of our metadata. All files and drives. All sources of information."

"Excellent, Abdul. But you forgot one."

"Where?" Abdul turned and looked around the room for it.

Hasham shot him in the back of the head.

Abdul slumped in his chair, then collapsed onto the floor. He did not move.

"I'm sorry, Abdul," Hasham whispered. "It was not supposed to end like this. But it had to. You know what I know. You know of our glorious plans for America and Europe. You know my backup escape plan. You know who I'm meeting in Rome and where and when. And you know the police would have tortured you to get all that information."

How could we risk that, Abdul? What choice did we have? You understand . . . You are a martyr for our righteous cause.

Hasham looked down at the young man again, blood pooling around his head. Abdul's eyes were fixed, staring outside at the heavens . . . where he'd believed seventy-two virgins awaited him in Paradise.

If he'd had a son, he would want Abdul to be that son.

Hasham felt a rare tinge of sadness. But reminded himself that a jihadist was always required to do the right thing. And the right thing at this time was to send Abdul to Allah.

Hasham hurried to the hall closet where he took out a jerry can filled with gasoline. He splashed the gas around the rooms. He took a fifteen-minute military fuse, lit it, and hurried from the apartment.

In minutes, flames would engulf the rooms. All evidence would vanish from the apartment.

And I will vanish from America . . .

SIXTY SIX

D onovan's phone rang: Bobby Kamal from the NSA.
"What's up, Bobby?"

"Possible address for Hasham."

Donovan stood up. "Where?"

"The Bronx. 3489 Matthewstone Street. Apartment 3F. Gray brick, four-story building. One block south of the railroad tracks."

"Anyone inside?"

"Not sure. We just found it. We'll start monitoring communications to and from the apartment."

"Manning and I'll head there now."

"One more thing. Hasham plans to meet with the main guy behind this attack."

"Wait - *Hasham's* not the main guy?"

"Apparently not."

"Who's the boss?"

"The guy in Yemen who's been phoning Hasham. The Yemini calls himself Mr. Jones. His birth name is Bassam Maahdi. But we

---

255

call him Fatty Warbucks because he's a major money-man for ISIS and al Qaeda, and because he's fat. CIA and Interpol have targeted him for years. Clever bastard, multiple aliases. Outstanding arrest warrants in seven countries. The guy always hides below radar."

"When is Hasham meeting him?"

"Three days from now."

"Where?"

"Rome. Small backstreet hotel. The Largo."

"Good work, Bobby. If we miss Hasham here, we'll nail both at the Largo."

"How's the search for Hasham going?"

"No leads yet. TSA, anti-terrorist FBI teams and police are watching for him at airports, bus and train stations. So far, no luck. Hasham has vanished. We age-enhanced his eight-year-old photo and emailed it to all TSA personnel and anti-terrorist teams. But Hasham uses disguises."

"And aliases," Kamal said. "We're monitoring four now. An old one led us to his Bronx apartment."

"Any luck with Hasham's phones?"

"All burners. Uses them once or twice and destroys them."

"Keep us looped in, Bobby."

"Will do."

They hung up.

"Some good news," Manning said. "More cable server networks are back up broadcasting IRS check warnings."

"Good," Donovan said. "But still, thousands missed the warnings. Some who heard them won't believe them and will try to deposit the checks."

Manning nodded. "Like the two men who just dropped dead demanding the bank tellers take their checks. The tellers tried to warn them."

"Greed trumps brains," Donovan said.

* * *

Donovan felt nauseated as he and Manning raced toward Hasham's Bronx apartment. The death count had rocketed to one hundred sixty-seven. Most deaths occurred in Manhattan and the surrounding boroughs, but many died in New Jersey, Connecticut, and Rhode Island.

Manning answered his phone, listened, then slumped against his seat as though he'd been shot. His face turned bone-white.

What now? Donovan wondered.

"Im-fucking-possible!" Manning whispered as he closed his eyes.

Donovan didn't want to hear this. "What . . .?"

Manning swallowed, shook his head. "Nell and Lindee . . ."

"What?"

"They were . . . just . . . *taken!*"

Donovan felt like he'd caught a line drive in the throat. He swerved over to the curb to avoid hitting the truck ahead. He gritted his teeth. "How the hell - "

" - two guys posing as our FBI agents escorted Nell and Lindee from the apartment building six minutes before our two agents arrived to pick them up."

Donovan couldn't speak.

"Hasham's guys bugged Lindee's apartment phone. Heard your call to her and sent two fake agents over. They showed the lobby guard FBI badges, went up, then left with Nell and Lindee through the basement rear exit."

Donovan squeezed the steering wheel hard enough to bend it.

"But we posted an agent right outside Lindee's apartment door."

"Unconscious, tied up and gagged in a janitor's closet. He should recover."

"We had an officer in back."

Manning lowered his eyes. "Found his body in a dumpster. Shot in the head."

"Jesus . . ." Donovan's rage rocketed.

"We have a very grainy video of the two fake agents taking Nell and Lindee through the basement. They drove away in a black Lincoln Town Car."

"License number?"

"Taped over."

Donovan exhaled hard. "Every time we gain traction on this bastard, he skates. I want him bad!"

"I want him *dead*!" Manning said, his face crimson.

Donovan nodded. Nell will feel Hasham's rage even more for escaping the bottling plant, taking his flash drives, and looking in his files. He'll torture her for what she told us. Then he'll kill her."

Manning looked numb. One of his agents had been killed, another badly injured. Donovan knew Manning would swab the floor with five-foot-six Hasham if he got his hands on him. And Donovan would help.

"Which means the files and flash drives are extremely valuable to him, and therefore to us," Donovan said. "We've got to extract the data on them. Get the best hackers working on it. Freelance the best. Whatever it takes! No political game playing. Tell everyone to share info. If they don't, I'll name names to the president."

"It will take time."

"There's no time for time."

SIXTY SEVEN

Nell looked out the Lincoln window as the limo drove them through New Jersey. Swastika Witkowski activated the kid-locks, preventing them from jumping out at red lights.

He rechecked their flex-cuffs, put on his ear buds and tapped his foot to the Grateful Dead's *Truckin'*.

Lindee leaned close to Nell and whispered, "What do they want?"

"To know what I told the authorities," Nell said.

"Will you tell them?"

"Some . . ."

Lindee looked terrified.

Nell touched her sister's hand and whispered, "Everyone is looking for us, Lindee. They'll see the security video of us leaving through the basement and - "

"Shut the fuck up!" Witkowski shouted, pushing his cold gun barrel into Nell's neck.

She said nothing.

The car's tinted windows made it difficult to see any landmarks. But based on the sun, Nell knew they were driving north, somewhat parallel to the Hudson River, which she glimpsed from time to time.

The limo bounced into deep chuckholes, passed abandoned stores, a burned-out church, an older strip mall, an *A-1 Liquor Shoppe*, a *Lady Nails*, a Mexican discount grocery . . . and a young man with a sign that read *Need Help.*

Me too . . .

A minute later they drove inside the loading area of a sprawling two-story cinderblock warehouse. The garage door thudded down behind them.

Witkowski gestured for her and Lindee to get out.

They stepped out. Nell smelled grease and exhaust fumes. She saw four of the gray delivery trucks she'd seen at the bottling plant. But the signage on the trucks had changed. It no longer read - *Ask Mummy for ChocoYummy.*

The trucks now read - *J. Smith Medical Supplies.*

Men were changing the trucks' license plates. More misdirection, Nell realized. Hasham wanted police wasting time searching for *ChocoYummy* trucks that no longer existed.

Nell watched a long black limousine drive into the garage and creep to a stop a few feet from her.

A tall, thick-necked, muscular man stepped from the passenger seat and stared at her. A chauffeur got out and opened the rear door. A small man stepped out, turned around, and faced her.

Hasham Habib.

Angry.

He walked toward her slowly, his eyes seething. He stepped close, glared at her, then slapped her face so hard she fell back against the car. Her cheek stung and her eyes flooded with tears. She wobbled a bit and Lindee steadied her.

"That's for taking my flash drives! Including the one *hidden* on my computer!"

"But I told you . . . I didn't see any flash drives! I had to run from the cabin because your men were coming inside!"

"Liar!" He started to hit her again, but stopped, took a deep breath. "But . . . you will tell me the truth soon enough, won't she, Musa?" He looked at the huge muscular man beside him.

"Yes, she will." Musa's thick lips bent in a grin.

"Musa, please escort these two women to our limo."

"With great pleasure," Musa said in good English.

Musa led them, still flex-cuffed, over to the long black limousine and into the back seat. Hasham got in front, Musa sat in back in the flip-down seat, facing them. The chauffeur drove out of the garage and continued heading north along the Hudson River.

Minutes later, they pulled into the parking lot of the *Lincoln Bay Yacht Club,* a sprawling marina on the Hudson.

"I trust you are not afraid of sharks," Hasham said.

She was terrified of sharks.

"I love them. They go through 30,000 teeth in their lifetime."

She said nothing.

"They love to attack in less than six feet of water."

She said nothing.

"One man caught a massive 2,700 pound Great White right where we're going. Imagine that."

She felt her throat tighten.

"Now, as we walk through this marina to my yacht, you will not speak to anyone. You will not look at anyone or signal them in any way. You will keep your heads down and walk beside us like we're two happy couples going for a cruise. You will do exactly as I say, do you understand?"

Nell and Lindee nodded.

"If you don't, you will bleed. If you bleed in the water, the sharks will find you fast. A school of feeding sharks can devour two women your size in under sixty seconds."

Musa cut their flex-cuffs and led them from the limo.

Despite Hasham's warning to keep her eyes down, Nell glanced around for someone to signal on the dock or the yachts.

She saw no one.

＊ ＊ ＊

The FBI Suburban skidded to a stop. Donovan and Manning jumped out and hurried toward the burning Bronx building. Donovan saw thick gray smoke pouring out through the blackened windows of Hasham's apartment and spilling down onto the street. Donovan felt like he was breathing tar.

He and Manning flashed their badges as they hurried past three NYFD fire engines. They stepped over black hoses fat as pythons. The hoses pumped heavy shafts of water into the apartment windows. The fire had destroyed Hasham's apartment and the one above, but now seemed mostly contained. Frightened tenants shouted for fireman to save their adjoining apartments.

Manning introduced Donovan to a skinny young male FBI agent near the door.

"Anyone in Hasham's apartment?" Donovan asked, praying they hadn't found Nell's and Lindee's bodies inside.

"One body. Male. Young."

Donovan's shoulders relaxed a little.

"His name is Abdul Sanwari. NYU chemistry major. Muslim."

"Caught in the fire?"

"Caught a bullet in the head first."

"Probably Hasham eliminating a link to himself," Donovan said.

Manning nodded, "What else is in there?"

"Fried computers, drilled hard drives, smashed cell phones. Everything hammered and destroyed *before* they were burned! Lots of disks and flash drives demolished. Scraps of letters from Abdul to his parents in Teheran. We found this in a metal cabinet drawer."

He held out a sales flyer for the Largo Hotel in Rome.

Donovan nodded. "That's where Hasham plans to meet his

Yemeni money man, Bassam Maahdi, aka Fatty Warbucks, in three days. We'll set our people up in the Largo now. Be ready and waiting."

"Our tech guys are bagging everything here," the young agent said. "One question. . .?"

"Ask away . . ." Manning said.

"Does this have anything to do with those IRS letters killing people?"

"*Everything.*" Donovan said.

SIXTY EIGHT

After a double shift waiting tables at *Bob Evans*, Emma Stanton grabbed her mail and walked into her 745-square-foot Newark home . . .

. . . her home for two more weeks.

That's when the landlord would kick her and her two young daughters out - and into the back of her ancient 120-square-foot Chrysler minivan.

She refused to stay with her ex, Karl Gene, an alcoholic, deadbeat-child-support father who lived in a filthy, booze-bottle-strewn two-room apartment that smelled like a urinal cake.

Emma and her daughters were alone in the world. Which was fine with her since they were her world.

She heard their school bus hiss to a stop.

She looked outside as Ashley, eight, and Lily, six, her popsicle-skinny blondes, hopped off the bus. Seeing them filled her heart every day – and broke it every day because she couldn't offer them more in life.

She hurried outside, and swooped them into her arms. She loved inhaling the sweet scent of their warm young bodies.

"Mommy, can we watch SpongeBob?" Lily asked.

"One SpongeBob! Then homework."

"Okay . . ."

She watched them run into the tiny den, heard the TV pop on with a commercial for something called *ChocoYummy,* then heard the familiar SpongeBob music.

Emma grabbed the stack of mail. Mostly junk. People complained about junk mail coupons. She survived on them. She flipped through an *eHarmony* and *Match.com* dating flyer, three bills - then froze when she saw the next envelope. From the IRS. Her name in the window.

No way! Can't be another IRS check . . .

She'd already received her $360 refund four weeks ago, and made a partial rent payment to the landlord who complained "ain't nowheres near enough to stop me from evictin' you and yer two little brats!"

She ripped open the envelope and stopped breathing.

An IRS check!

Pay to the order of Emma T. Stanton!

$4,650!

"Sweet God in Heaven above!" she said.

Was she hallucinating? She couldn't believe it.

The check was real. The letter was real – the refund was hers!

Ashley and Lily ran from the television room.

"Mommy *DON'T!*" Ashley shouted.

"Don't what, honey?"

"*Don't touch the Irish mail today!*"

"What Irish mail?"

"The SpongeBob man said don't touch the Irish mail today!"

"The SpongeBob man is just a make-believe *TV* man."

"No. The *real* man came on *SpongeBob*. The real man told us to go tell our mommy and daddy that the Irish mail today will make us very very sick if we touch it! He told us to tell you right away. Don't touch the Irish mail, *please* mommy!"

"I didn't get any *Irish* mail . . ."

Then it hit her – *the Irish mail is . . . the IRS mail.*

Emma dropped the check like it burned her fingers.

On the radio, Beyoncé's *Single Ladies* was cut off and an announcer said . . .

> *"We interrupt this program for an urgent bulletin from Homeland Security about deadly IRS checks arriving in today's mail . . ."*

She listened in disbelief to the warning . . .

"Mommy, is this the Irish check? Ashley reached for the check. *"Don't touch it!"*

Emma snatched it by the corner and put it, the letter and envelope on top of the bookshelf.

She ran to the bathroom and washed her hands for several minutes, dialed 911 and was told the police would arrive in minutes to retrieve the check. Then she sat down and prayed, waiting for the police . . . and waiting for the symptoms to hit her.

Her throat felt raspy. *Was it raspy before I opened the IRS envelope?*

She couldn't remember.

Minutes later, she felt tightness in her chest and grew terrified. Was that a symptom? Probably. The girls were going to watch her suffer and die right in front of them. They'd remember it forever. *Please God, don't let that happen. And please don't let Karl Gene get custody! Please . . .*

The doorbell rang.

She jumped up, opened the door. Her jaw dropped open when she saw the policeman.

This is all a dream! Has to be . . . It's just too bizarre!

The policeman was Ethan Miller. Nice, gentle Ethan, her prom date years ago, whose family moved to Florida with him three days *before* the prom. Ethan who then got posted to Afghanistan. Ethan now standing at her door . . . *Has to be a dream!*

"Hi Emma . . ."

"Ethan . . . I thought you were in Afghanistan."

"Got back two months ago. I heard your 911 call at the station. You feeling okay?"

"I think so."

"How long ago did you hold the check?"

She checked her watch. "About seventeen minutes ago."

He smiled that same beautiful smile that melted her heart in high school.

"That's a real good sign, Emma!"

"I think I only held the corners of the check."

"Where are the check and letter?"

She pointed.

Wearing latex gloves, Ethan placed the check, letter and envelope in a large zip-lock bag.

"Emma, . . . you look terr – "

" - terrible, I know."

"I was going to say *terrific*."

"Oh . . . " She felt herself blush. She couldn't remember the last time a guy said she looked terrific.

They smiled at each other. *Ethan Miller – the good guy that moved away.*

"I've been thinking maybe I should call you," Ethan said.

"Why?"

"That Sadie Hawkins Dance at the VFW hall. Wondered if maybe you'd like to go . . . kinda make up for that prom we missed?"

"I'd love to. Maybe get those gossipy tongues wagging."

SIXTY NINE

Hasham Habib strolled along the bridge of his 72-foot Hatteras, the *Leyla,* gazing at the ocean, hypnotized by the gentle, rolling waves. The only waves he'd seen as a child in Iraq were heat waves shimmering above the searing sands near Kirkuk.

He'd long dreamed of cruising through oceans of blue water, and now he was, thanks to Bassam Mahdi's oceans of money.

My beautiful Leyla, he thought, admiring the yacht's sleek lines and rich appointments. *An appropriate remembrance for my wife's ultimate sacrifice. And the perfect getaway for evading my pursuers. How many jihadists escape in a million–dollar yacht?*

"Let's question the woman," Hasham said to Musa Igbal, two hundred thirty pounds of steroid-pumped muscle, walking beside him.

"I would like that very much."

Hasham met Musa years ago at an al Qaeda training camp where the big man jogged wearing a fifty-pound knapsack. His pulse rate never rose above sixty-eight. What he lacked in formal education he made up for with brute strength, street smarts, and his very special gift: eliciting information from uncommunicative people. He called his gift "enlightened persuasion." Everyone else called it torture. For men, Musa preferred carving *M U S A* on their genitals. He bragged he'd never made it past *U*.

An equal-opportunity torturer of men, women, and sometimes children, Musa's instruments included fingernail pliers, electric drills, hammers, breast hooks, and the occasional drops of sulfuric acid. "Slow pain gets fast answers," he often said.

Hasham smiled as he remembered how the US Army idiots released Musa from Guantanamo, thinking he'd lead them to bigger al Qaeda fish. Instead, Musa led the two CIA agents tracking him to their beheading in a Yemeni souk. Three weeks later, he was back in Dallas sipping Starbucks coffee with Hasham and doing Allah's work.

America the Stupid.

He and Musa walked down below decks where they'd locked up Dr. Northam and her sister in a cabin.

"Do you have your tools?" Hasham asked.

"Never leave home without them." Musa's held up a purple velvet bag, bulging with sharp angles.

Musa slid the key in the cabin door.

✶ ✶ ✶

Nell watched the door handle turn. Her muscles froze as Hasham and Musa walked into the bedroom and stared at her and Lindee sitting on the bed. Hasham's eyes burned with revenge, Musa's glowed with eagerness.

Hasham walked up to Nell. She leaned back, fearing he'd slap her again. Her jaw still ached from his earlier blow.

"Your people opened one of my flash drives twenty-three minutes ago!" Hasham said.

So opening it triggered an alert, she realized, but said, "The police must have found the flash drive in the cabin rubble."

"Impossible. Everything in the cabin was totally destroyed by the fire and explosion."

She said nothing.

Hasham stared out the porthole window. Over his shoulder, Nell saw the coast maybe two miles away. They were cruising south. Did the authorities have any idea where they were? Probably not. Did the authorities have any idea they were on a yacht? Probably not. Did the authorities have any chance of finding their bodies if they were dumped overboard? Probably not.

"What else did you tell the FBI and CIA?"

"I told them what we worked on in your lab."

"The VX."

"Yes."

"Did you tell them about my unique delivery system?"

"How could I? You never told me what it was."

"But you told them all about the bottling plant. And *ChocoYummy?*"

"Yes. We thought *ChocoYummy* was your unique VX delivery system."

"Why?"

"Because it was so different. Like you said.*"

He puffed with pride, then stared at her as though waiting for her to finish. "And then . . . ?"

"And then they discovered only *some* bottles contained VX."

"Correct."

"But enough bottles to kill many innocent children," she said with raw anger. "*Innocent, helpless* children - !"

"- mere casualties of war," he said with the emotion of a coma patient.

She said nothing.

"Then what?" he asked.

"Then they wasted a lot of time pursuing the *ChocoYummy* bottles in stores."

A bent smile. "Exactly as planned."

"But they soon realized many bottles did *not* contain VX."

"Correct."

She said nothing.

"And then you finally told them about the printers, correct?"

"I told them I saw some printers."

"You told them about the IRS checks."

"No. I never saw any IRS checks. I never saw what your printers printed."

"So how'd they learn about the checks?"

"FBI technicians puzzled together tiny scraps of the checks. Tests confirmed the checks contained VX."

Hasham paused, then nodded. "My compliments."

She said nothing.

"And did they discover my secret substance that we blended with the VX?"

She nodded. "DMSO."

"Good work. And do you know why I blended DMSO with VX?"

"Faster VX absorption into skin. Faster death."

"My compliments again." He looked out the window, then ran his finger along the shiny brass porthole sill as though checking for dust.

"You told them about many other things you saw in my laboratory. Like my file folders."

She thought *yes,* but said "No."

"Folders you should not have looked at, but did. They contain certain attack and weapon scenarios. And my special plan for Washington DC. You told the FBI about my DC plan, didn't you?"

"No. I never saw it. I only saw some closed file folders. I couldn't read them because you were always with me."

"Not always . . ."

271

"And I was always so busy blending, trying to measure up to your extremely challenging specifications. They required my total concentration, as you well know. I was very focused! I worked to meet your demanding deadline! I had no time to read files."

"Good Christians do not lie."

She couldn't hold back. "And good Muslims do not murder thousands of innocent men, women, and children just because they're Americans!"

His face turned beet-red and he stepped toward her as though he would hit her again.

She stepped back and he stopped.

"As I told you - *all* Americans are guilty by association."

She said nothing.

He turned and faced the ocean. "You will tell us everything you saw in the lab and in the cabin . . . everything you told the authorities in detail. It's very important that you remember everything you told them. Musa is going to help you remember."

"I've already told you everything."

"What do you think, Musa?"

"She lies . . ." Musa's grin revealed gobs of green *khat* stuck on his yellow-brown teeth. He, like Aarif, probably used the amphetamine-like substance to stimulate him for what he was about to do to her.

Hasham dabbed his nostril with a clean white handkerchief.

"In Guantanamo, Musa laughed at what the Americans called torture. He called it pat-a-cake pat-a-cake. Love taps. So he developed his own special interrogation technique. Show them."

Musa held up the vial of liquid.

Nell leaned away from it.

"Know what this is?" Musa asked her.

She studied the liquid, suspecting it might be sodium pentothal, truth serum. But it looked too viscous for that.

"Sulfuric acid," Hasham explained. "Very nasty stuff."

She knew how nasty.

Musa smiled. "Eats skin faster than flesh-eating bacteria. I once poured some in a guy's ear. Guy screamed . . . begged me to kill him. So I pumped a nine-millimeter full metal jacket into the other ear."

"Like a mercy killing?" Hasham said with a smile.

"Yeah . . ."

SEVENTY

Donovan's hope sank as the deaths rose. Sitting in the CIA safe room, he tried to think of what more he could do. Only one thing made sense - more warnings. Many more.

But despite the non-stop warnings on television, radio, and Internet, the latest numbers sickened him.

191 deceased
104 critical

Hasham was winning.

And incredibly, some people, despite hearing the warnings, were still trying to deposit their deadly IRS checks. Minutes ago a Brooklyn man dropped dead insisting a teller take his check. A Hoboken bank president tried "cleaning" his VX check with hand sanitizer and dropped dead a minute later.

Most bank cashiers now wore gloves and face masks. Some wore protective wraparound glasses. Many refused to touch any

IRS check until Homeland Security personnel verified it was safe. Cashiers called in sick.

Shrewdly, Hasham timed his VX-IRS checks to arrive in mailboxes when many genuine IRS checks arrived. Many people were expecting their IRS refunds. And those that weren't figured it was their lucky day. The urge to rip open the envelope and hold the IRS check in their excited fingers was overwhelming. Who can resist an unexpected windfall of thousands of dollars? And so far, all VX-IRS checks paid out thousands.

Many people refused to open their *genuine, authentic* IRS checks - until specialists tested them to be safe.

The door swung open and Special Agent Drew Manning hurried in.

"A young woman over in Weehawken saw two dark-skinned men in business suits with two women fitting Nell and Lindee's description."

"Where in Weehawken?"

"At the Lincoln Bay Yacht Club Marina."

"A yacht marina?"

Manning nodded. "The two women and men got out of a black limo, then walked toward the yachts."

Donovan wondered if Hasham would escape by water.

"I know . . . a yacht escape makes no sense!" Manning said.

"Maybe why Hasham would use it."

"Anything's possible with that bastard!"

"What exactly did the young woman see?"

"First, she saw Nell's and Lindee's photos and descriptions on CNN. Five minutes later she saw two women wearing the exact same clothes getting out of the limo. And she knows clothes. She works at Nordstrom."

Donovan nodded.

"Also the two women acted strangely."

"How?"

"Like they didn't want to go with the men."

Donovan grew more interested.

"One woman turned around as though searching for help, but the man kept pushing her along. The girl described Nell's face and Lindee's to a tee. And the small thin man matched Hasham's description. He even dabbed his nose with a white handkerchief. Bottom line: the women's clothes, shoes, and faces match. And Hasham matches. What are the odds?"

"Good enough to go check out now. Do we know which yacht?"

"No." Manning said.

"So it might still be docked."

"Yes. Especially if they don't think we're onto them."

"What about the marina manager?" Donovan said.

"He saw nothing. Been working in his office."

"Let's get over there!" Donovan said as they hurried to the elevator, headed down, and rushed outside into brilliant sunshine.

"Forget the car," Manning said, pointing at the sky.

Donovan looked up and saw an FBI Bell UH-1H helicopter descending into the nearby park, scattering sunbathers like autumn leaves.

Donovan and Manning boarded and soared up over Manhattan's concrete canyons. Manning alerted the New Jersey police, NYPD Harbor Police, and Coast Guard to be prepared for a description of the yacht. He also directed an FBI Rescue Team to meet them at the marina and prepare to board a yacht.

Minutes later, they landed on a small patch of grass on Harbor Boulevard near the Lincoln Bay Yacht Club. They deplaned and hurried into the manager's office.

Donovan saw a tanned, fiftyish man with a blond mustache look up from his desktop computer. His desk nameplate said *Ned Bruckner, Dockmaster.* His blue T-shirt said . . . *Beeracuda.*

"You guys from the chopper?"

Donovan nodded and flashed his ID.

Bruckner sat up straight. "Whatcha looking for?"

"These two women?" He showed him the photos.

Bruckner frowned at the photos. "Sorry, but like I told your fella on the phone, I haven't seen any ladies 'cuz I've been buried in here crunching budget numbers."

"How many yachts left in the last three hours?"

"A bunch. Sun draws 'em like flies. Let's see. Bruckner tapped his keyboard and the screen filled with a long list. "Thirty-nine departed. Small, medium, and large."

"Does a man named Hasham Habib have a berth here?"

Bruckner frowned like he'd never heard the name. He checked his computer, then turned back. "No Hasham Habib has a berth here at Lincoln Bay."

Donovan's hope sank. "A Mr. Smith?"

"Three Smiths. One's eighty-two, retired dentist. Cruised his new Sunseeker down to South Carolina two weeks ago. The second's a rich real estate fella. Been in the Bahamas five months. The third's a stockbroker lady."

"The yacht's probably in someone else's name," Donovan said. "This man, Hasham, is a very dangerous terrorist. He's abducted the two women. Killed many others."

"*Jesus!*"

The dockmaster stood up, looking very worried. "Sorry, but the Rollin' Stones been pounding in my ears as I worked. Didn't pay much attention to anyone outside."

"So they could have boarded and departed without you knowing?"

"That's right."

"How many yachts dock here?"

"Over a hundred."

Donovan knew it would take hours to search them all. His frustration grew.

Bruckner closed his eyes a minute. "What's this Hasham fella look like?"

"Short, thin, dark hair, dark-skinned. Sorta like a professor."

"Does he speak like . . . a foreign language?"

"Arabic," Donovan said, realizing he should have mentioned Arabic sooner.

Bruckner nodded. "I heard some fellas walk by my office speaking something foreign. Sounded like they were clearing their throats. Mighta been Arabic. They headed toward the last dock. I was on the phone. Didn't see them. Minutes later, I saw that Mr. Duncan's big Hatteras had pulled out."

"Mr. Duncan?"

"What's Mr. Duncan look like?"

Bruckner described Hasham Habib in perfect detail.

"Mr. Duncan told me he's in the medical supplies business."

Donovan thought of the new *J. Smith's Medical Supplies* sticker now on Hasham's gray trucks and looked at Manning who nodded back.

"Speaks with an English-accent. Quiet fella. Looks kinda middle-eastern I guess."

"Where'd he dock?"

"Last pier." He pointed out the window.

"Any other yachts launch from that pier today?"

Bruckner checked his computer. "Only his."

"What kind of yacht?"

"Huge Hatteras! She's a beauty!"

"What's it look like?"

Bruckner fingered through some desk drawer files, pulled out a photograph and handed it to Manning. "That's his actual yacht! A 72-foot Hatteras! Fully loaded with extras. Cost a bloody fortune."

Donovan and Manning studied the full-color photo of a spectacular, gleaming Hatteras yacht, plus a list of its luxurious appointments and engine specifications.

"What's the yacht's name?" Donovan asked.

Bruckner checked his computer. "Mr. Duncan's yacht is called the . . . ah . . . *Leyla*."

"Bingo!" Donovan said.

"What?" Manning asked.

"Hasham's wife's name is *Leyla*."

SEVENTY ONE

Donovan heard Manning phone in a BOLO for the *Leyla* to the Coast Guard and NYC harbor police.

"How long ago did the *Leyla* depart?" Donovan asked the dockmaster.

Bruckner turned to a bank of security monitors showing multiple views of the yacht club. He tapped in commands and the screen zipped back to earlier in the day. He hit *Fast Forward* and yachts skated across the screen like an old-time movie.

Donovan couldn't help but smile at some yacht names:

The Codfather . . .

Fish and Chicks . . .

Ship For Brains . . .

She Got The House . . .

"Lots of comedians!" Manning said.

"Look, there's the *Leyla!*" Bruckner said.

He pointed at a very large white yacht gliding into view. He freeze-framed the video.

"The *Leyla* departed here two hours and eight minutes ago." Bruckner said.

"Go back a few minutes earlier. Maybe we can confirm the women are Nell and Lindee . . . and with Hasham."

Bruckner reversed a few minutes earlier. The video showed two men escorting the two women onto the deck of the *Leyla.*

"That's Lindee and Nell," Manning said.

"With Hasham and a big guy," Donovan said.

On board, a small deckhand took the women below decks. Donovan scanned the *Leyla* and saw Hasham and the big guy standing beside the captain on the bridge. Hasham signaled the captain to depart.

Bruckner hit *Play* and Donovan watched the stunning, seventy-two foot white yacht ease into the Hudson River and cruise south . . . toward the forty-one million square miles of the Atlantic Ocean.

* * *

Nell cringed when a key clicked in the bedroom door. She watched the door open and Musa's huge shadow blacken the wall.

He walked toward her, all six feet four inches. He stared down at Nell and Lindee, sitting beside each other on the bed. He moved closer and checked that her hands were still bound.

He held the purple velvet bag with a gold drawstring. The bag bulged with what she assumed were the tools of his trade - torture.

Her heart pounded.

He sat in a chair beside Nell and smiled like a friendly neighbor stopping by for a chat.

"Hasham is too patient with you."

She said nothing.

"I'm much less patient."

"You speak very good English," Nell said, trying to flatter him, get him talking, buy time, maybe get lucky and find a way to talk him out of what was planning to do. It worked with Aarif. "Where did you learn English?"

"University of Guantanamo," he said proudly.

"You're really fluent."

"Yeah. I persuaded the military shrinks I was innocent. The fools released me. Now, I'm back helping Allah."

Does Allah's work include killing thousands of innocent people? she wanted to ask.

"Hasham wants to know what else you told the FBI and CIA. What else you saw in the laboratory."

She said nothing.

"He says you saw some file folders that contained information on plans for new chemical and biological weapons he's been working on. You saw them, didn't you?"

"I saw some folders on his desk. But they were *closed.* And Hasham had me too busy working to open them."

"Hasham says you looked in his orange folder on a lab table. He wants to know what you read in the orange folder."

"Orange? I didn't see any orange folder," she lied, remembering she'd glimpsed in it and saw it hinted at an attack on Washington DC.

Musa stared hard at her. "He says you couldn't miss it. He left you alone with the orange file once for a few minutes."

She shrugged. "I only noticed some beige files and two blue files on the wall shelf."

He shook his head, clearly not believing her and losing patience with her answers.

Slowly, he reached into the velvet bag, removed a pair of shiny long-stem gold pliers. He gazed at them dreamy-eyed, obviously remembering all the pleasure they'd given him.

He showed them to her. "Beautiful, aren't they. Custom- made. Solid 18-carat gold. Mother-of-pearl handles. A gift from Hasham."

She said nothing.

Holding the pliers, he walked toward her and stared down at her bound hands.

"You have beautiful hands." His eyes moistened.

———

She inched her hands back.

"My mother had beautiful hands . . . until your drone blew one off. She was just shopping for rice."

"I'm very sorry."

"Not as sorry as she was."

He looked at her hands again. "Maybe we should sacrifice one of your hands. You know, a hand for a hand. I could use my gold scimitar upstairs. The sharpest Arabian saber I've ever used. Cuts flesh like warm butter. And don't worry about the bleeding – I've cauterized hundreds of wounds."

She fought back a wave of nausea. *Do not vomit. Distract him, keep him talking . . .*

"How long were you in Guantanamo?"

"Long enough to learn America's goal."

"What's that?"

"To destroy Islam."

"But that's not true."

"It *is* true!"

"Then why are so many mosques thriving in America? And why are Muslims elected to the US congress? And why do we allow vetted peaceful Muslims to immigrate to America?"

He shrugged the facts off like fake news.

"What else did you tell the FBI and CIA?"

"Nothing else. That's all I saw." Her heart pounded.

"I don't believe you. Tell me now and you won't feel pain."

"Really. That's all I saw – "

He grabbed her left hand, and before she could react he clamped the pliers onto the nail of her index finger.

"Last chance!"

He smiled.

"Really - I saw *noth* – "

He yanked the nail halfway off her flesh. Pain shot up her arm like a bolt of electricity.

She screamed. Tears spilled down her cheeks. Every nerve in her body seemed to cry out. Beside her, Lindee wept.

Musa smiled at the nail. *"Tell me!"*

She couldn't speak, tried to catch her breath.

"But I saw *noth –* "

- he ripped the fingernail completely off!

The pain felt like a hammer blow! Like no pain she'd ever felt. She gripped her throbbing finger, buckled forward, pain radiating through her body.

Lindee tried to embrace her, but Musa pushed Lindee back down on the bed.

"Here's the good news," Musa said. "Your nails will grow back. They grow even after you're dead. Did you know that? And don't worry. The bleeding is minimal. Stops in ten minutes. Unless you're a bleeder."

She said nothing.

"One nail down! Nine to go. Are we having fun yet?"

Nell fought to keep from passing out. She had to stay awake. She had to stop him . . . but how?

"Okay . . . okay . . ." she said.

"Okay what?"

"I'll talk."

His eyes dimmed in disappointment.

"I'll tell Hasham everything else I told the FBI. But stop! My hand is hurting so much I can't even think straight!"

"No! Talk! Tell me *now!*"

"I can't. There's far too much technical information. I need lots of paper and a pen to write down some complex chemical formulas. Believe me, Hasham will want to know. Especially the research specifications I saw. You can't possibly remember them all. Hasham will want me to be very specific and absolutely accurate about what I saw."

He stared at her, trying to decide.

"I'll go get some paper and be right back. But if your memory fails again, we'll try another finger or two or three. And I just remembered – your sister has ten fingernails, too."

He left and locked the door.

Nell fell back on the bed, holding her throbbing, bleeding finger.

I'm going to die on this yacht.

SEVENTY TWO

Minutes later, Musa walked back into the cabin and Nell's muscles tightened.

He checked the ropes binding her hands and smiled at the washcloth soaked red with her finger blood. The bleeding finally stopped but the throbbing pounded on.

He walked toward her, looking eager.

She didn't see the paper and pen she asked for – and panicked. *Hasham gave him the green light to rip off more fingernails!*

Her heart pounded.

"Where's the paper and pen?"

He reached in his pocket and took out a small tape recorder and turned it on. "Hasham says you must tell him everything you saw in his laboratory. Writing takes too long. You will say everything into this recorder. You will give exact formulas. You will list files you saw and looked into. You will give details. You will tell the whole truth. If you lie, he will know."

Nell melted with relief that she might keep her remaining fingernails.

She took the recorder, closed her eyes and began listing certain files and research folders she'd seen in the lab. She mentioned the obvious folders Hasham had left on lab counters, and a couple of concealed files in drawers so he'd believe she'd been snooping around and was now telling the truth. But she didn't mention certain chemical and biological weapon documents he'd hidden beneath magazines in a drawer. Nor did she mention she'd briefly peeked into his orange file.

When she paused, Musa pointed at the recorder. "Hasham wants to know what *equipment* you told the FBI about?"

"I told them about *all* the sophisticated lab equipment. The hermetically-sealed containers, the centrifuges and bio-level 4 chamber and biocontainment materials. I told them about the vacuum ovens, the three spectrophotometers, beakers, pipettes, round bottom flasks, sterilizers, and the expensive Meiji-5000 microscopes. Everything set up for chemical and even biological agents!"

He nodded.

She took a breath.

"What else?"

She closed her eyes as though thinking. "That's all I saw."

He stared back. "I still don't believe you."

She knew Musa wanted a reason to torture her.

She said nothing.

"You forgot something."

"What?"

"The orange file on his desk. You told them about it, didn't you? You told them what you read in it."

"As I said earlier, I did not see an *orange* file. I saw three *tan-beige* files on the corner of his desk. And two blue files on a shelf. That's all."

He stared at her, then shook his head.

Slowly, he reached into the purple bag and pulled out his long stemmed gold pliers.

An acid taste rose in her throat . . .

"You know, I once went as high as seven nails before the guy talked."

She said nothing.

"But you know what - fingernails take too long. And we're in a hurry, right? So what's faster you may ask? Permit me to show you."

She said nothing.

Musa pulled out a vial of clear liquid he'd showed her earlier. It looked similar in color and viscosity to a chemical she'd once seen in her Aberdeen lab.

"My special sulfuric acid!" He smiled. "Very very strong. Nasty stuff. After I was released, I used it on my former Guantanamo guard, a cruel man. A few drops on his manhood and he screamed the answers I wanted. That night I rolled his head down Sherman Avenue near the base. You know what they say?"

"What?"

"Nothing rolls like a head." Musa chuckled.

He took out a Granny Smith apple and placed a single drop of acid on its green skin. The acid fizzled, puffed smoke, then began eating its way down inside the apple. He added another drop and the acid quickly sizzled and burned its way down to the core.

Musa seemed mesmerized by the acid . . . then he studied her face. "You have a very smooth complexion. Smooth as the apple skin. Perfect. Maybe too perfect. They say a scar adds character to a face. What do you think?"

She closed her eyes.

"I think your face could use some character. . ."

His phone buzzed.

He answered, listened. He hung up and stared at her, clearly frustrated by the interruption.

"Hasham is writing down some very specific and comprehensive questions he wants you to answer in detail. I'll be back."

He left, locked the door and headed back up on deck.

Nell exhaled slowly. Lindee put her arms around her and held her tight.

Again, Nell feared she and Lindee would not leave this yacht alive.

Unless they did something . . .

SEVENTY THREE

Donovan tightened his seat belt in the FBI Bell UH-1H helicopter as he, Manning, and the FBI Hostage-Rescue Team raced down the Hudson River toward the bay and the Atlantic Ocean.

Donovan couldn't shake his guilt for not preventing the abduction of Nell and Lindee. Even though the FBI had tactical responsibility for their custody, he had overall responsibility from the President, whose cousins, Nell and Lindee, had just been abducted from Lindee's apartment - *on my watch!*

Agent Manning insisted *he'd* take the bullet for their abduction, even though he'd followed all requirements and all FBI/Homeland protective-custody rules.

"We should have moved them to the safe house sooner," Manning said.

Donovan nodded. They'd underestimated Hasham's uncanny ability to block their efforts and threaten family members to get what he wanted.

"By now, he's torturing Nell to reveal what she told the FBI," Donovan said.

Manning nodded. "But if Hasham believes the FBI has extracted data from his flash drives, he might be forced to change or cancel certain plans. A good thing."

Donovan agreed. He looked out the chopper window at a row of yachts hugging the coast.

"And," Manning said, "if the flash drives reveal jihadist locations, many will be running for their lives."

"Nice thought," Donovan said, "But I'm worried we might force him to do something even worse."

"What?"

"Unleash future attacks sooner!"

"Like *now?*"

Donovan nodded.

Manning blinked. "Let's hope he's too damn busy escaping. The *Leyla's* photo is now with the Coast Guard, New Jersey Police, NYC Harbor Police, Yonkers Marine boats, and US Navy. Everybody's looking for it."

"But nobody's finding it," Donovan said. "The *Leyla's* two-hour head start gave him time to hide the yacht."

"But he may not realize we know about the yacht."

"He'll know any second. He'll have sophisticated police listening equipment. He'll hear Coast Guard bulletins, police radios."

Manning nodded.

"He could have headed out to some island," Donovan said. "Or hid the *Leyla* in a covered boathouse and escaped by car."

Manning stared east into the ocean. "Or raced out beyond the US territorial waters, beyond American jurisdiction."

"We'll pursue the bastard beyond all jurisdictions! He's involved in an active terrorist act."

Donovan stared down at some small yachts near the shore, then turned to the FBI tech seated behind him. "Any kind of signal from the *Leyla* yet?"

The tech shook his head. "They incapacitated GPS and their AIS, Automatic Identification System. Even their SeaKey."

"What's SeaKey?" Donovan said.

"Like GM's OnStar. It tracks the yacht's position. The *Leyla* came equipped with SeaKey. But Hasham has obviously disabled it. In fact, it looks like he's disabled or deactivated all electronics on board: sonar, depth sounders, all radar and trackable systems. Even their ship-to-shore and marine radio."

"So the *Leyla's* cruising dark," Donovan said.

"Like a ghost! We've got nothing to track unless he uses a phone."

"Then he'll have to stay within about five miles of a cell tower on shore," Manning said.

"Maybe not," Donovan said.

"Why not?"

"The *Leyla* might have one of those built-in mini phone towers. The mini tower links up with a shore tower. He can call from farther out at sea. If he has a mini tower and makes a call we can pinpoint the *Leyla's* location."

Manning asked an agent, "See if the *Leyla* came with a mini cell-phone tower. Or was retrofitted with one."

"Also," Donovan said, "check if the *Leyla* has a satellite phone. With that he could call from anywhere in the ocean."

He grew more frustrated as he looked out the window and saw Sandy Hook Bay below. Large, white yachts lined the docks. Many looked like Hatterases, Sunseekers and large Dutch-built yachts, but smaller than seventy feet.

"The Police and Coast Guard should be able to find a seventy-foot yacht named *Leyla*," Manning said.

"Maybe not."

"What. . . ?"

"The *Leyla* may not be the *Leyla*."

Manning stared at him.

"Hasham's name game. His magnetic stick-on names. He changed his trucks from *Zelda's Fresh Garden Flowers* to *Ask*

Mommy for ChocoYummy to *J. Smith's Medical Supplies.* Why not change the *Leyla* to something like – *The Proud American.*"

Manning nodded. "The bastard can't change *length*. We'll check all yachts over seventy feet."

Donovan's phone buzzed with a text.

He slumped in this chair as he read the latest IRS check death total . . .

Deceased: 396
Critical: 319

The attack grew worse by the minute.

But by now, Donovan hoped the half million people sent the deadly IRS checks had seen, heard, or read the media warnings. If so, the death rate should soon start slowing down.

But when would it *stop?* After a thousand people died? After two thousand deaths? Five thousand?

My most important assignment ever, Donovan thought. *My worst failure ever. The worst attack on American soil since 9/11. . . and the attack is still going on.*

Hasham was winning big - escaping to kill another day. The man had all the advantages.

And Donovan saw another one – angry black storm clouds rushing in from the southeast – the kind that could ground their chopper and the others.

SEVENTY FOUR

Nell looked out the window and saw the *Leyla* had cruised farther away from the US coast . . . deeper into the Atlantic . . . *heading to our final resting place . . . unless we do something.*

She sat back on the bed, then looked down at her bloody, throbbing finger. Her entire hand felt numb and she worried about infection. An absurd worry, since she was probably within hours of her death.

"Lindee . . .?"

"Yeah. . ."

"*We* have to stop Musa!"

"I know!" Lindee stood up and paced along the desk.

"But how?" Nell said.

"By first untying your ropes."

"With what?"

"These," Lindee bared her teeth.

She bent down, and began gnawing into the knot on Nell's ropes. After much biting and tugging, she loosened the knot a bit. She dug her fingers into the knot and unraveled it all the way.

Nell pulled her hands free, rubbed her wrists and felt warm blood flow into her hands. She then worked on Lindee's ropes using her teeth and good hand. Soon she loosened and pulled off Lindee's ropes.

"We need a weapon," Nell said.

They looked around the master bedroom, paneled with beautiful rose and cherry wood furniture, but saw nothing they could use. Everything was too big: chairs, bedside table, a small desk.

"The heavy stuff is bolted down," Lindee said. "And the clothes hangers are too light."

"Check the dresser drawers."

In the bathroom, Nell opened the medicine cabinet and saw tanning lotions, skin creams, and Advil. She swallowed two Advil, pocketed the bottle, then wrapped two Band-Aids around her bloody finger.

As she turned around, her elbow rattled a towel rack. The ends of the metal rack were small chrome pineapples. The pineapples, she noticed, screwed onto the ends of the rack rod.

She tried to twist one off, but it was too tight. She opened the cabinet beneath the sink and found cleaners, washcloths, Windex, 3-IN-ONE oil, and in back, taped to the water pipes, a wrench. She grabbed the pipe wrench, then oiled the pineapple where it screwed onto the rack end. Using the wrench, she tried to twist the pineapple off again. Still wouldn't budge.

She heard Hasham and Musa talking upstairs. Musa getting his list of questions for her. He'd come back down any second.

She wrapped a towel around the wrench to deaden sound, then whacked the pineapple hard. It loosened a bit. She thumped it again and the pineapple loosened more. She oiled it and managed to screw the pineapple off. Then she pulled the rack rod out of its wall brace and screwed the pineapple back on the end.

She was holding a three-foot steel pole with heavy metal pineapples at both ends. A seven-to-eight pound *bat*. She grabbed the second rack rod, oiled and unscrewed the pineapple, made a second bat and handed it to Lindee.

Lindee took a couple of hard swings.

"I'm swinging for the bleachers!"

"Start with his head."

Lindee nodded.

"But we have to bring him downstairs when *we're* ready for him. We need him totally focused on something other than us. Something he can't ignore."

Lindee grabbed a box of matches from the ashtray. "Fire!"

Nell nodded. "Perfect. Musa will have to come down to put it out."

"And when he's focused on putting out the fire - "

" – we knock his ass out!" Lindee's mood had changed. She looked and sounded angry. Lindee's anger surprised Nell. "Lin, you sound ready to do this!"

"I'm *very* ready!"

Nell realized something had transformed Lindee in the last few hours. She looked stronger that she had in months. Maybe this abduction had somehow ignited her survival instinct - her I'm-not-going-to-be-a victim-anymore reflex. Lindee looked ready to do someone serious harm.

They reviewed their plan, walking it though step-by-step a few times.

"And if we need extra uuumph . . .!" Lindee said, lifting a bed table lamp with a solid brass base. "It weighs over ten pounds."

"That could kill him."

"Works for me!" Lindee said.

Nell embraced her, praying they could pull this off.

"Let's do it!" Nell said, grabbing a roll of toilet paper and some magazine pages. She looked for a place where smoke would be drawn up through the ventilation system to the upper cabins and deck so the men would smell it. In the bathroom, she saw a metal mesh wastebasket and moved it directly beneath the ceiling vent in the far corner. Nell stuffed the pages and papers in the wastebasket.

Lindee lit a page, smoke curled up. Nell turned on the exhaust vent. Smoke spiraled upward and into the vent. In seconds the smell would reach the upper decks. Someone would race down to check out the cause.

"Let's hope only Musa comes," Lindee said.

* * *

Thump . . . thump . . . thump . . .

Footsteps.

Coming down the stairs.

Coming toward us, Nell knew. The smoke had filtered up to the men on deck.

How many are coming? If two, our chances are impossible – unless both men turn their backs to us to put out the fire - and we disable both with one whack each. Lousy odds.

If it was just Musa, he'd quick-check their hands were still tied. Then he'd turn his back to go put out the fire in the bathroom. When he did - they'd both strike with their bats from behind! Possible odds.

She heard someone opening and closing cabin doors in the hall, obviously searching for the source of the smoke. Footsteps of one man. Who?

Musa?

The small deckhand?

Hasham?

The man checked the room next to theirs, a mini kitchen, then closed the door and stepped toward their stateroom.

Nell had draped the bloody towel over the ropes around her wrists so he'd think they were still bound.

Click . . .

A key in the door.

Musa stormed inside, holding a small fire extinguisher and his handgun.

Only Musa.

His eyes were maniacal, his neck arteries bulged like computer cables. "Where fire?"

"*There!*" Nell nodded toward the bathroom door. "It smells electrical! We shut the door to contain it. We yelled "*FIRE!*" Didn't you hear us?"

"Engine too loud."

Musa glanced at the bloody towel covering Nell's loosely-roped wrists and then Lindee's roped wrists. Then at the smoke seeping out under the bathroom door. He opened the door and billows of smoke whooshed out, engulfing him. He eased into the clouds of the smoke-filled bathroom, looking for the source of the fire.

Musa stepped deeper into the thick smoke and sprayed the fire extinguisher, releasing even more clouds of white smoke. Then he paused and looked up at the ceiling vent.

"I turned the ventilator on so you'd smell the smoke." Nell said, moving up behind him, holding her heavy pineapple rack behind her back.

Musa inched closer to the source of the smoke.

Then he looked down and froze.

He sees the burning wastebasket . . . suspects our setup . . .

He started to turn back toward her -

– as Nell bashed the steel pineapple into the back of his head!

Musa wobbled, stunned, but didn't fall. He started turning his gun toward her - as she slammed the pineapple into his head again!

Musa dropped the fire extinguisher and slumped against the wall, shaking his head, his knees buckling . . . but still somehow standing.

Then, incredibly, he started turning toward Nell –

- as Lindee's cast-iron lamp bashed into his temple.

Musa dropped like wet cement, his forehead crashing against the toilet. He landed face down on the floor, unconscious. His gun skittered away a few feet.

Nell grabbed the gun. Lindee sprayed the fire extinguisher on the wastebasket fire, then turned off the ventilator so Hasham would assume Musa put out the fire. Quickly, they tied Musa's hands and ankles with their ropes, and stuffed a washcloth in his mouth. Nell couldn't tell if Musa was dead or alive, but preferred the former.

They had to move quickly. They opened the door, stepped out of the room and walked silently through the hall. Nell wanted to reach the rear deck where she'd seen their one and only hope of escape. But reaching the rear deck, depended on where Hasham, the deckhand, and the captain were now.

She looked at Musa's gun. A Beretta M9. Years ago, she fired an older Beretta during her Aberdeen training. She checked the full clip, then clicked the safety off.

She hoped the men were all up on the bridge, staring *ahead*, looking for Coast Guard vessels, or busy checking radar or radio traffic. If they were busy on the bridge, she and Lindee might reach the rear deck unseen. But if anyone glanced down, they'd see them.

It all depends on where the men are.

Only one way to find out.

Nell and Lindee climbed the stairs and peeked out at the rear deck. Nell saw no one. Then more good luck – looking up she saw the bridge extended much farther over the rear deck. So much farther the men couldn't see them unless they stood at the end of the bridge and looked straight down.

Quickly, Nell led Lindee onto the rear deck. Their one hope was ten feet ahead - the small life raft. She checked the bridge. Still, no one looking down.

They unfastened the raft and eased it into the water. The soft splash was muffled by the yacht's engine noise.

They climbed in the raft, released the rope, and drifted a few feet away from the big Hatteras. She checked the raft's small motor. No way she could start it until they'd drifted well out of earshot, several hundred yards at least.

She realized the raft had no lifejackets.

As they quietly paddled away, she saw Hasham, the deckhand, and the captain on the bridge, all staring straight ahead, scanning the horizon, probably watching for Coast Guard and police boats.

Keep staring that direction . . .

Just maybe, this is going to work.

Then slowly . . . Hasham started to turn around.

SEVENTY FIVE

"Hasham has too much head start and too much ocean to hide in," Donovan said, squinting at the empty Atlantic horizon stretching toward Europe, three thousand five hundred miles away.

Manning nodded.

Despite the enormous sea and air dragnet by the Coast Guard, Navy, police boats, no one had spotted the *Leyla*.

"How the hell can a snow-white, seventy-two foot yacht hide on dark-blue water?" Manning asked.

"Covered boathouse," Donovan said.

Manning nodded. "Just one more Hasham deception. Hide the yacht in a roofed boathouse and escape by car as authorities search a million miles of ocean."

"Possible."

"But we have people checking marinas, docks, and boathouses. Anywhere he might have moored and covered the *Leyla*. But that's a lot of marinas. So far, nothing."

Donovan nodded and looked down on Staten Island and the coast of New Jersey sweeping past below, then moments later, Perth Amboy, Morgan, Union Beach . . .

As they headed into the Atlantic, Donovan saw marina after marina, rows of yachts tucked like white piano keys against the docks. The sun glinted off the chrome deck railings.

Manning pointed, "None of those yachts has *Leyla* on their rear deck."

"None will if he renamed it," Donovan said.

Manning nodded as his phone rang. He answered, grew excited and hung up.

"Seventy foot white Hatteras near the Sandy Hook Bay Marina. Guy says the name started with an *LE*."

Three minutes later they were circling over Sandy Hook Bay Marina.

Donovan looked down and couldn't believe his eyes. He saw at least fifty yachts stuffed into the marina docks. All were white. Many appeared to be Hatterases, fifty to seventy feet or more.

"Problem," Manning said.

"What?"

"The yachts' names are *backed* up against the docks. Hard to read."

"We gotta try!"

The pilot banked right and swept down behind the yachts two hundred yards away. People on the rear decks stared wide-eyed up at the aggressive chopper racing over them. Some people waved. Most smiled. A body builder gave them the finger when the downwash blew his toupee into the water.

"There - the yacht with the *LE . . .!*" Donovan said, pointing.

The pilot swooped down behind the large white yacht, but Donovan's hope sank when he read -

L E E W A R D.

The pilot pointed. "More big yacht marinas down there."

The chopper rolled right and they swept down the coast to the *Marina on the Bay*. Again, Donovan saw maybe thirty yachts moored on long docks. Only two looked over seventy feet. One had several women sunbathing on the deck, the other was powder blue.

"What about all those yachts docked inland?" Donovan pointed at several long canals that stretched inland like watery fingers. Each was lined with hundreds of medium-sized to large yachts moored in front of rows of McMansions. Some yachts had long covered boathouses, big enough to hide the *Leyla*. Everywhere he looked – yachts, mansions. Hurricanes had not devastated everyone in the area.

"We're checking all of them," Manning said as his phone rang. He listened and hung up, excited.

"We got the *Leyla!*"

"Where?"

"Down near the *Gateway Marina*."

"Where's that?"

"Real close!" the pilot said, banking left and racing down the coastline at one-hundred-thirty miles per hour.

Two minutes later, they hovered over the yacht.

Donovan looked down and saw two policemen, guns in hand, slowly approaching the seventy-foot docked Hatteras. As the chopper drew closer, he thought the yacht looked like the photo of the *Leyla*. He saw three men on the deck.

Then Donovan slumped when he saw the yacht's name.

LEYLAND.

SEVENTY SIX

"Hasham is racing to get outside US jurisdiction," Manning said.

"Which puts him in CIA jurisdiction," Donovan said.

"Wherever he runs, we nail him!" Manning said.

"Nails are too kind."

The pilot pointed ahead where the dark blue water fused into a dark gray sky. "Nasty storm moving in fast."

Donovan nodded. "Has radar or AIS located any large yachts this far out?"

"Sixteen within eight miles of us," the pilot said. One fifty-footer, some over sixty, and most over seventy. The over seventy-footers are farther out, cruising deeper into the Atlantic where we're heading."

"How far can Hasham's Hatteras travel with a full tank?" Donovan asked.

Manning checked his notes. "The *Leyla* left the marina with a full tank. Three thousand gallons. Figure a half-mile to the gallon.

So depending on speed, wind and currents, they could cruise maybe 1,500 miles or more."

"So south to Florida or Bermuda . . ."

Manning nodded. "Or north to Nova Scotia or Newfoundland. Or to some small island we don't know about.

"Or for all we know," Donovan said, "Hasham could hook up with fuel tankers mid-ocean, refill his tanks, and cruise on to Europe."

* * *

Nell relaxed when Hasham turned his back to their raft. He never saw it because he was staring into the afternoon sun.

But now dark clouds had swept in, blocking the sun. So it was only a matter of time before Hasham, the captain or deckhand turned around and saw them.

Then what?

Then, Hasham would order the captain to bring the yacht around, race toward their raft, probably ram and deflate it. Without lifejackets they'd die quickly in the frigid water. Even with lifejackets, they'd die in the frigid water. But slower.

As they paddled the raft, Nell knew they were still too close to start the motor.

The yacht had slowed to an idle during the fire. But by now, Hasham must have stopped smelling the flow of smoke. He'd wonder why Musa was taking so long and maybe send the deckhand below to check things out. The deckhand would find Musa unconscious, gagged, and tied up. Maybe even dead. Everyone would search for her and Lindee, checking every nook and cranny.

Then someone would notice the missing raft. They'd scan the ocean and spot it –

- but not if the raft had drifted *much* farther away.

Nell and Lindee paddled harder.

Nell looked down at the Beretta. A two pound gun - against a fifty-five ton yacht. She checked the clip again. Nine bullets. She practiced flipping the safety on and off a few more times.

On the yacht, she'd briefly considered shooting Hasham and the others, but their AK-47 and Uzi would have sliced and diced her and Lindee in seconds.

And what about the deckhand and the captain? What if they were just hired boat workers? Could she have shot them? Were they jihadists? Both men had beards and dark complexions and seemed to know Hasham. And sometimes, like now, profiling could save your life . . . or put another way . . . *not* profiling could *end* your life.

She saw Hasham walk down from the bridge and head below to the cabins. He would find Musa. Alive or dead.

The raft was only about two hundred fifty yards from the idling Hatteras. Still visible from the yacht and still within hearing range of the motor. She estimated she should be well over three hundred yards before she started the small 25-horsepower Evinrude. By then she could be out of hearing range, maybe even visual range, unless the rolling waves lifted the raft high enough to be visible.

The big question was – *did she have enough fuel?* The gauge indicated half a tank. She had no idea how far that would take her?

She also had no idea if the small motor would even start.

"Look!" Lindee said, pointing back at the yacht.

Nell saw Hasham helping Musa onto the deck. Musa had a bloody bandage wrapped around on his head and seemed wobbly. Nell was amazed the man was alive.

Hasham, Musa, and the deckhand walked around searching for her and Lindee. After searching, they went back down into the cabins below, apparently to search some more.

Should she try the engine now?

No. Still too close. The noise would rocket over the water like a gunshot and alert the captain and deckhand. She and Lindee paddled harder. Just another eighty yards should do it.

She scanned the ocean for another boat to race to. She saw none.

A minute later, Hasham and Musa came back up on deck. Musa pointed to the empty brackets where the raft had been tethered. Both men spun around and faced the ocean. Hasham grabbed some binoculars, aimed them toward shore. Then he turned back and started scanning the horizon, moving slowly in their direction.

He locked on their raft.

Hasham pointed at them and said something to Musa.

Musa hurried into the bridge and came out with a rifle. He steadied it on the deck railing, aimed, and fired.

Bullets splashed into the water about one hundred feet short of the raft.

Nell pushed the raft's starter button.

Dead.

She tried again.

Dead.

She saw Hasham signal the captain to turn the big yacht around and head toward them. Slowly, the *Leyla* turned in an arc.

She hit the starter button again.

A sputter, then nothing.

The yacht headed toward their raft.

She hit the starter.

Silence.

Dead battery? Clogged fuel line?

Bullets splashed twenty feet from the raft.

SEVENTY SEVEN

"Where in the hell is the *Leyla?*" Donovan said.

Manning shook his head.

"It's gotta be one of the remaining seventy footers farther out," Donovan said.

"Makes sense," Manning said. He briefed the FBI Hostage Rescue Team seated behind them to get ready to board the *Leyla*.

The Rescue Team, highly skilled at both land and water rescue, looked eager to deliver the women to safety and Hasham to the fires of Hell.

Donovan noticed the pilot pointing at the dark thickening storm clouds they were flying into – then at a large white yacht.

"Seventy-footer. Hatteras profile," the pilot said.

Donovan nodded but couldn't read the name on the yacht's rear deck where three men sat in chairs.

They pilot flew closer and Donovan relaxed when he saw the luxury yacht's name: *McCue DealerShip*. One man raised his mug

---

of beer toward the chopper. Donovan would kill for a cold one right now.

"*There!*" said the pilot, pointing. "Another big one. Two miles out. Ten o'clock."

Donovan fixed his binoculars on the area, and the long white yacht's profile.

"Have the Coast Guard check its GPS."

Manning made the request.

Moments later, "GPS and all electronics are functioning!" Manning said.

"Maybe he turned everything back on," Donovan said. "Let's check it out anyway."

The chopper swept toward the big white yacht. Donovan saw two middle-aged men fishing off the rear deck. Two women brought them a tray of sandwiches.

One woman looked similar to Maccabee. He suddenly worried that Mac might not have reached Dr. Dubin's office safely. He'd check later.

* * *

Nell watched the huge Hatteras race toward them.

She pushed the raft motor's starter button again. It sputtered and died.

She tried again. Two sputters-stops. She pushed again. The motor rumbled, sputtered, and went stone silent.

Frustrated, she whacked the motor hard with her hand - and it roared to life!

She cranked it to full throttle and the raft chugged ahead.

But the Hatteras raced toward them. It would soon ram them. Musa's bullets ripped into the water ten feet behind them.

Another bullet speared the water even closer.

Nell aimed the Beretta and fired back at the yacht without hope of hitting anyone because of the rolling waves. But Musa and Hasham heard the shots and ducked behind a counter.

She shot again, splitting off a chunk of counter – and the two men ducked down like Whack-A-Moles.

But the yacht kept coming.

She searched the horizon for some other vessel. She saw none.

The *Leyla* closed fast, just two hundred yards away. She fired off another shot that hit below deck.

Musa fired back, his bullets ripping the water three feet from the raft. A large wave pushed the raft to the side.

Musa's bullet tore into the raft's motor. The motor sputtered, spewed black smoke, groaned and died.

She aimed at the *Leyla* and pulled the trigger.

Nothing. The gun jammed.

A second later, two bullets ripped into the fabric of the raft – and air whooshed out though the holes. Lindee held her hand over them, but the escaping air pushed her fingers away.

Musa pointed to the raft and grinned, obviously delighted with his marksmanship.

Then Hasham surprised her.

He signaled Musa to stop shooting. This clearly angered Musa, who obviously wanted revenge for his head wound.

But Hasham turned and signaled the captain to idle the yacht. The big yacht coasted to a halt about one hundred fifty yards away.

Hasham stared at the raft for several moments, saw her and Lindee failing to stop the air leaks. Satisfied the raft was deflating and sinking, and that the motor was dead, he signaled the captain to turn around and head back.

The Hatteras cruised away.

Hasham was going to let them sink.

Nell understood. No bodies on his yacht, no evidence of crime. No problem.

She felt the raft sinking fast. The motor was dead. They had no lifejackets.

In minutes, they'd be freezing to death in the icy water.

———

SEVENTY EIGHT

Donovan peered into ugly black clouds as they flew deeper and deeper into the Atlantic.

He pointed at a white yacht hurrying back toward shore. "Big one at one o'clock!"

The pilot banked toward it.

Donovan checked the deck and saw two doctors and some nurses with kids in wheelchairs. A long banner said, *St. Jude's Floating Hospital.* The smiling kids waved up at them. Donovan waved back.

Manning pointed at another enormous white yacht much farther out – racing farther out into the Atlantic and into the storm. The angle made it difficult to estimate length, but it looked at least seventy feet.

"Look," Donovan said, "that Coast Guard cutter is rushing toward the same yacht! A mile away. Closing fast. Maybe they know something."

"The cutter should reach the yacht when we do," Manning said.

"Can you get a GPS reading on the yacht?" Donovan asked.

Seconds later, Manning, eyes wide, said, "No GPS! No AIS. Electronics all *off!*"

Donovan's heart shifted into overdrive.

He watched the big yacht – a Hatteras - speed at full throttle toward the middle of the Atlantic. Why race toward Europe 3,500 miles away with enough gas to get you only a third of the way?

Or was it a drug runner escaping from the Coast Guard cutter?

The chopper quickly closed the distance to the big yacht.

Donovan locked his powerful military binoculars on it. He saw three men on the deck staring up at the chopper. The short thin man appeared to fit Hasham's size and description. The other two men had beards and dark complexions. One huge man had a bloody bandage wrapped around his head.

Donovan saw no sign of Nell or Lindee.

He tried to read the yacht's name on the rear deck. But the ocean swells kept hiding it.

Then he glimpsed an "*L*" and his heart pounded into his throat. He leaned forward, squinting at the yacht.

A huge wave suddenly lifted the rear deck up high and Donovan shouted, "The - *Leyla!*"

"*Confirmed!*" Manning said, fist-pumping the air and signaling his FBI rescue team to get ready.

The chopper raced toward the *Leyla* and leveled off behind it.

Donovan heard the FBI team preparing to board, checking body armor, weapons, helmets, and mics.

On the yacht's deck, the three men watched the approaching chopper as though waiting for it to get closer. When it did - they yanked out guns, ducked behind counters, and fired at the chopper.

The pilot anticipated the shots and dropped beneath the rising bullets.

The FBI team returned fire, scattering the terrorists for better cover.

The chopper swept around in front of the yacht and dropped low, compromising the terrorists' shooting angle.

The FBI team unleashed their Heckler & Koch assault rifles, their bullets eating chunks of counters as the three terrorists took cover.

To the right – the Coast Guard cutter raced to within one hundred yards, blasting its horn across the water and then unleashing its ear-drum-bursting warning.

> *"This is the US Coast Guard. HEAVE TO . . . HALT and prepare to be boarded! I repeat: HALT! This is the US Coast Guard. We are going to board your vessel! Do you understand?"*

Apparently not.

Incredibly, the terrorists shot at the cutter and kept racing ahead at full throttle.

Bad decision.

The sailors unleashed their powerful M2 50-caliber machine guns. The finger-sized bullets tore into the rear deck, shredding cabinets, Plexiglas and wood panels like they were papier-mâché. Within seconds, the side of the yacht looked like Swiss cheese.

Donovan prayed the bullets didn't penetrate the cabins below where the women might be.

The FBI team members roped down onto the bow, crept along the *Leyla* sides toward the rear deck, firing non-stop – flushing the terrorists from their hiding spots.

The terrorists ran, shooting back.

But the FBI team bullets ripped into them. The large man with the bloody head bandage fell to the deck and didn't move. The captain and small deckhand dropped their weapons, staggered, slumped to the deck floor and went still. Blood saturated their clothes. They would bleed out in minutes.

But where was the short thin man - Hasham? Donovan saw him get shot in the arm. Saw blood on his shirt. Saw him walking fast.

But now he'd disappeared. The FBI team searched the deck and bridge for him, then headed down below deck.

Donovan prayed for some sign they'd found Nell and Lindee alive below.

Two minutes later, the FBI team leader came up on deck, looked up at Donovan in the chopper, shook his head and spoke into his mic. "No hint of the two women. Or Hasham!"

Donovan's gut twisted. He signaled the pilot that he wanted to board the yacht. Seconds later he and Manning roped down to the deck. Together with the Rescue Team and Coast Guard sailors, they rechecked the yacht, the bridge, rooms, closets.

They did not find the women.

Or Hasham Habib.

Hasham *had* to be on the yacht. Donovan saw the man's bloody arm, saw him hurry in the direction of the stairs heading below deck. But at that moment, the chopper banked left and when Donovan looked back, Hasham was gone. Where? Down the stairs? Hiding below deck? Secret compartment?

Two more FBI team members came back up on deck.

"The women and Hasham are not anywhere on the yacht!" the leader said.

"Where are the women?" Manning asked.

Donovan turned and stared at the answer . . . the vast, icy Atlantic Ocean.

SEVENTY NINE

Donovan walked across the deck, sat down on a bench cushion and tried to visualize what might have happened to Nell and Lindee. He'd seen a bloody towel in a cabin below. Was it Nell's blood? Lindee's? Or the big guy with bloody head bandages?

And where the hell was Hasham? He'd vanished after being shot. No one saw him fall overboard. No one saw him put on a diving gear and jump in. No one saw him escape in some kind of James Bond mini-sub, which he could easily afford.

Did he jump in to commit suicide and prevent the FBI from interrogating him about future plans? Possibly. But if he jumped in bleeding, where was the bloody water? And where were the sharks?

Or did he put on a weighted vest that dragged him straight down several fathoms?

Donovan's gut told him no - Hasham was alive and hiding somewhere on the yacht.

Donovan recalled what he saw. Hasham walked past this deck area, hurrying toward the stairs that led below. Did he go down the stairs and hide in some secret storage area that we still haven't found yet? The FBI had examined each storage closet and tapped the walls and floors for hidden spaces. Hasham was not found.

Frustrated, Donovan gripped his seat cushion and squeezed. His fingers felt wet. He looked down and saw they were wet with blood.

Did I get hit or cut? He checked his body and saw he was not bleeding anywhere. He knew Hasham and the others were dripping blood as they ran past here.

Donovan looked down and saw blood splatter all over the deck, and on chairs and seat cushions. Then he noticed a straight line of blood droplets leading directly toward his seat cushion. He ran his fingers beneath the lip of the seat cushion again and picked up much more fresh blood.

How does blood get *under* the cushion lip?

When bloody fingers lift it . . . to crawl beneath the cushion into the storage bin below.

Is this bin large enough to hide a small thin man?

Donovan looked down and quickly realized it was.

The more Donovan thought about it, the more he sensed Hasham might be hiding in the storage bin beneath him. Donovan noticed three clear fingerprints on the cushion lid where someone would lift it to climb in.

Donovan signaled Agent Manning and pointed to the blood drops leading to the cushion, then to the bloody fingerprints on the cushion lid, and then to the storage bin below.

Manning stared at him and mouthed, "Hasham?"

Donovan nodded.

Manning signaled four FBI team members to positions around the storage bin.

Donovan stood up slowly, walked a few feet away from the cushion, turned around and aimed his Glock at the storage bin cushion, then nodded to Manning.

"Hasham Habib!" Manning said. "This is the FBI. Step out of the storage bin *NOW!* Lift the lid and come out with your hands up!"

Silence.

"Hasham Habib. *Get . . . out . . . NOW . . . with . . . your . . . hands up!*"

Silence.

Then Donovan heard something . . .

Behind him!

He spun around in time to see Hasham spring from an identical storage bin on the other side of the deck, aim his gun and shout *"Allahu – "*

"*- Akbar -*" never left Hasham's mouth as Donovan's bullets ripped into his throat. FBI bullets shredded the rest of his face and body – knocking him back so fast he flipped backward over the deck railing and splashed into the water below.

Donovan walked over and saw blood pouring from holes in his chest. He looked like was wearing a red polka-dot shirt. The blood pooled around him. A huge wave swallowed him.

Within minutes, sharks would.

A squad of Coast Guard sailors climbed to the bridge, and took control of the yacht.

Donovan turned to the FBI rescue team leader, "One last search for Nell and Lindee. The team split into two groups, one headed downstairs, the second scoured the deck and bridge.

Minutes later they met on deck.

"The women are not on board!" the team leader said. "But they were here!"

He held up a Lindee's purse.

EIGHTY

Nell could no longer feel the saltwater stinging the cuts on her back. She not feel her bone-white fingers. She could not feel anything except the ice-numbing cold.

Another wave slammed into her eyes, blurring her vision.

She knew it was just a matter of time before she and Lindee froze to death in the freezing water.

Their only hope was to cling to the deflated raft and pray. But clinging grew harder as each strong wave loosened their grip on the slippery rubberized fabric.

Her body heat was being pulled out to warm her skin's surface . . . but dropping her core body temperature dangerously low. Hypothermia was claiming their bodies, inch by inch.

A big wave slammed her and she swallowed some seawater. She coughed most out, knowing swallowing too much would kill her. But the heavy waves kept smashing her mouth open.

Barely conscious, she and Lindee hugged the nearly deflated raft, ninety percent underwater, like their bodies. Only their heads and chests lay atop the squishy raft. Their legs dangled like icicles in the glacial water.

She couldn't stop shivering. Beside her, Lindee looked gray as a cadaver.

"Lindee . . . can you hear me?"

Silence.

"Lindee . . .?"

"Yes . . ." she mumbled as a huge icy wave washed over her.

"Stay awake, Lin, hang on . . . please hang on . . ."

Long pause. "Tryin' . . ."

How long can we hang on? Nell wondered. She seemed to remember that the ocean temperature around New York at this time of year was around fifty degrees. At that temperature, she knew hypothermia would set in probably in an hour or so. They'd lose consciousness and freeze to death soon after. But she had no idea how long they'd been clinging to the deflated raft since her watch had stopped. She guessed at least an hour. Maybe much more.

"Behind you," Lindee whispered.

"A boat . . .?"

"No."

Nell turned and stared.

She saw black fins circling.

EIGHTY ONE

Donovan's gut churned like the waves below as the chopper circled the Hatteras. He saw no sign of Nell and Lindee. No sign of a life raft. Maybe a good thing. Maybe they'd escaped and were rescued by another boat. Maybe not.

They'd been on the Hatteras. Lindee's purse, the instruments of torture, and the two sets of ropes, one set bloody, plus bloody towels were proof.

Best-case scenario: Hasham had offloaded Nell and Lindee on shore where they were now being held. But why would he do that? Very unlikely.

Or Hasham set them free in the raft. Also unlikely. What's two more dead women when you're murdering thousands?

Or they escaped in the raft. Also unlikely. How could Nell and Lindee sneak past four men and escape in the raft? And if they did sneak past, someone certainly would have spotted the raft in the water.

A more likely scenario - Hasham killed them, dumped their bodies overboard, and maybe released the raft to make it look like they'd been picked up by another boat.

Whatever happened, if they were now in the water, Donovan feared they were not wearing lifejackets, since he'd seen four lifejackets in the storage bin near the raft's mooring brackets. Maybe they had no time to look for the jackets.

The chopper rescue team continued searching the horizon. They saw no rafts. No lifejackets. No bobbing heads. No bodies. But they felt blasts of wind. The gusts buffeted the chopper as they circled wider and wider around the *Leyla*.

Fat black storm clouds hovered over them now. A lightning bolt ignited the ocean farther out. The pilot glanced at the storm clouds and shook his head, looking more concerned with each minute.

Yachts and boats raced for the safety of shore.

"Weather alert!" the pilot said. "We're grounded in five minutes."

"It doesn't look that bad," Donovan lied, thinking it looked like the end of the world.

Donovan hated to give up. Always had. Charging ahead, pushing through problems, not stopping, not giving up, persistence, that was his strength people told him. It was also his flaw, he often told himself. He sometimes pushed himself regardless of the risk and wound up with bad results. Like the time he was running the Pikes Peak Marathon at 7,000 feet altitude, tripped from exhaustion, and broke his wrist. Or when he kept working 120-hour weeks despite his fatigue, and the growing tightness in his chest forced him to bed with walking pneumonia.

Maccabee warned him that his not-giving-up tendency might catch up with him some day. Maybe it would today. Maybe he should call it off and head back.

Or maybe he owed it to Nell and Lindee and the President to search a bit more. If weather forced the pilot back to shore, he'd use his presidential mandate for a few more minutes to search. But no more than that. He would not risk the lives of Manning, the pilot, and the FBI rescue team beyond that.

The wind sideswiped the chopper hard to the left – then to the right.

"We're ordered back in three minutes!" the pilot said.

Donovan looked at the pitch-black sky, then leaned toward the pilot. "Just give me five."

The pilot stared ahead at the storm, then turned toward Donovan. "You're nuts! But you got five, unless lightning or wind-shear kills us first!"

"Thanks."

Vicious crosswinds whacked the chopper hard again. But it managed to level off seconds later.

Donovan focused his binoculars on a large fishing boat heading northeast about a half mile away. The name read - *Kathryn Marie & Hunter Scalloping Enterprises.* Fishermen hoisted aboard a large net bulging with scallops and placed them on deck.

Lightning flashed beyond the *Kathryn Marie*, and Donovan thought he glimpsed something tiny in the water.

"This wind is *brutal!* We gotta head back!" the pilot said.

"I saw something!"

"What?"

"Like a speck . . . no . . . *two* specks. Look - bobbing in the waves."

"Small markers, buoys maybe?" Manning said.

"No."

"Where?"

He pointed. "Eleven o'clock - beyond that *Kathryn Marie* boat!"

Everyone focused binoculars on the area.

"I don't see anything," Manning said, as lightning flashed nearby.

"I don't either," the pilot said. "We're ordered back *now!*"

"No wait - waves just blocked our view."

A big wave collapsed and again he glimpsed the two specks

in the water. He squinted into his binoculars, and his heart started pounding.

"Sweet Jesus – those are heads!" Donovan pointed.

Manning squinted and leaned forward. *"I see 'em!"*

"Me, too!" the pilot shouted.

Manning directed the Coast Guard cutter over to the location.

As the chopper raced closer, Donovan saw the heads were female, their upper bodies slumped over a nearly deflated raft, their legs dangling in the water.

The women were not moving.

The pilot said, "The water temperature is fifty-one degrees! Death occurs in one to two hours."

Their motionless bodies already looked dead, like they might slide off the submerged raft any second.

The *Kathryn Marie* lifeboat would reach the women first.

Seconds later, Donovan watched two *Kathryn Marie* fishermen lift the limp bodies of Nell and Lindee aboard and race them back toward the *Katherine Marie*. The women still had not moved.

We're too damn late . . .

Donovan watched their bodies for any signs of life. He saw none. A fisherman began CPR on Nell. Nothing. He kept pushing down on her chest. Nothing. Another fisherman began CPR compressions on Lindee. No response.

"They're dead!" Manning said.

Donovan closed his eyes. *How will I tell Jacob?*

He opened them – still nothing.

Seconds later, he saw water explode from Nell's mouth. Her hand jerked and she twisted her head back and forth and more water poured out.

Donovan couldn't speak.

Slowly she reached over and touched Lindee's arm. But Lindee did not react. Nell shook Lindee's arm harder, still no reaction. Lindee looked gray.

Beside him, Manning shouted, *"Come on, Lindee!"*

A fisherman pumped CPR a bit faster. Water spilled from Lindee's nose, but no response.

Then suddenly – a gusher of water erupted from her mouth and nose. She twisted left and right, coming out of it. More water erupted from her mouth and her arms jerked.

"BREATHE LINDEE BREATHE!" Drew Manning shouted.

Lindee's eyes pealed open and she saw Nell. She reached over and touched her sister's arm.

Manning high-fived Donovan and the pilot.

Donovan swallowed the lump in his throat.

"Tell Jacob," Manning said.

Donovan called Jacob Northam and said, "Nell and Lindee were just rescued. They're fine."

"How are they?" Jacob asked.

"Wet," Donovan said, deciding not to elaborate. "But fine. Gotta go . . . I'll update you in minutes."

Moments later, Donovan and Manning roped down to the deck of the *Kathryn Marie & Hunter*. Donovan smiled down at the two shivering women who managed teeth-chattering smiles.

The big Coast Guard 760 pulled alongside the *Kathryn Marie*. Two female sailors boarded, checked the women, and had them carried aboard the cutter to treat their hypothermia.

Donovan and Manning were pulled back up into the chopper.

"More good news!" the pilot said. "The storm eased up. We just got green-lighted to fly fifteen more minutes."

"We need it!" Donovan said.

"Why?" the pilot said.

"To get Hasham's DNA. Snuff out any rumors he escaped."

The pilot nodded and raced at full speed back toward the bullet-riddled *Leyla*. They began searching for Hasham's body in the surrounding water, moving in wider and wider circles around the yacht, seeing nothing human . . .

Donovan looked for a pool of blood. But the waves and swells climbed higher now, making it difficult to see between them.

Minutes later, he saw an odd distortion in the wave pattern about a thousand yards north of the *Leyla*. He zoomed in on the distortion and saw water splashing and swirling . . . caused by several jet-black fins twisting, jerking something under water.

As the chopper drew closer, he saw a group of sharks in a feeding frenzy, ripping into what looked like part of a human torso.

He saw Hasham's head. It dangled loose on a long twelve-inch tendon to his neck . . . like a yo-yo. Oddly, his glasses were still on. But his intestines were strung out several feet like a scrunchy garden hose.

Manning directed another Coast Guard boat to collect Hasham's body parts for DNA verification at the FBI's Washington laboratories.

"May he rest in pieces," Donovan said.

"Like his asshole mentor, Bin Laden."

EPILOGUE

TWO MONTHS LATER

Donovan looked around at two hundred or more customers sitting in *Auntie Billy's ScallopoRama,* a sprawling, family restaurant in New Bedford, Massachusetts. People "yum-yummed" over their delicious seafood dinners.

On the walls, he saw ancient marine diving suits, fishnets draped over lanterns and sexy mermaids, and a massive bronzed anchor from the distinguished battleship, the *USS Miele.*

He and Maccabee sat at an enormous oak table with Nell, Jacob, and their daughter, Mia, who played with Donovan's daughter, Tish. Beside them sat Lindee and Drew Manning, shoulder to shoulder, making goo-goo eyes, very close friends now. Any closer, they'd have to get a room.

Nearby, sat the entire crew of the *Kathryn Marie & Hunter* fishing boat, the Coast Guard Cutter sailors, as well as the NSA's Bobby

---

Kamal and wife, and the Mobil gas station attendant, Mustafa, and his mother.

Donovan admired a magnificent Montague Dawson painting of a ship on treacherous waves like those Nell and Lindee were rescued from. Now the two women laughed like teenagers.

For Hasham Habib, the sharks had the last laugh.

The waiters walked in with heaping platters of scallop chowder, pan-seared scallops, bacon-wrapped scallops, Parmesan-crusted broiled buttery scallops, even scallop *carbonara* . . . all compliments of the *Kathryn Marie and Hunter Scalloping* ship.

Donovan tasted some scallop chowder and purred.

His phone rang.

The boss: Director of National Intelligence, Michael Madigan. Even at a celebration dinner, one didn't refuse a call from DNI Madigan. Donovan answered.

"Sounds like party time!" Madigan said.

"Yep. With delicious sea food."

"The bad guys are shark food!"

"Works for me," Donovan said.

"But one bad guy is missing his food."

"Who's that?"

"Fatty Warbucks, Bassam Maahdi."

"The guy we missed two months ago in Rome?"

"Yeah. But we just nabbed him."

"Where?"

"Rome. Hotel Largo. A hotel clerk tipped us off that Maahdi had checked back in a couple weeks ago. All thanks to Bobby Kamal's tip."

"Is Maahdi talking?"

"Faster than a strung out junkie."

"You use enhanced interrogation?"

"Nope."

"Sleep deprivation?"

"Nope."

"What?"

"Lamb deprivation! We lowered his eleven-thousand-calorie-a-day, lamb-stew diet to nine hundred fifty calories. No talk, no eat! Six days later, he sang like a Yellow Tailed Cockatoo. Just in time, too. His European cells were planning sequential suicide attacks in London, Paris, and Brussels. We grabbed his laptop, too. It's a treasure trove of cell names, aliases, phone numbers, addresses even."

"That's big!"

"True, but so unfortunately, is the final VX-check death total."

Donovan felt his stomach sink.

"Four-hundred eighty-seven people died from holding the VX IRS checks and letters. Sixty-one are still critical. Another three hundred or so will fully recover. Plus sixty-eight kids died from drinking *ChocoYummy*."

Donovan felt sick. "Sorry we couldn't stop this sooner, Director."

"How could you, Donovan? Think of it this way - your team's FBI and Homeland warnings helped prevent over *four hundred fifty thousand people* who received deadly IRS checks from opening them, holding them in their hands and probably dying. Those are *SAVED* lives! *That's* a huge win!"

Donovan felt some relief, but still anguished that he couldn't save more.

"We also froze Bassam Maahdi's assets in US banks," Madigan said. Over ninety-eight million US dollars. The President will sign an executive order redistributing the money as compensation for the families of those killed or injured by the IRS checks."

"Great. So what's next, Mr. Director?"

"A quiet White House ceremony. The President asked me to thank all of you for everything . . . and also for rescuing his favorite cousins, Nell and Lindee. He'd like to honor Nell, you, Drew Manning, and Bobby Kamal and Lindee and anyone else you think should come to the White House in a few weeks."

"They're here. I'll tell them."

"Good. We'll talk later."

They hung up.

Maccabee nudged his elbow. "Check out Drew Manning and Lindee."

Donovan looked down the table and saw them still making goo-goo eyes at each other. Donovan remembered how Lindee was attacked and left for dead in her apartment a year ago, and how Drew Manning's girlfriend died in a car accident three years ago and left him inconsolable for months.

Now, things were looking up for both of them.

"Methinks, the stars have aligned for those two," he said.

Maccabee nodded. "For us too," she said.

"How so . . .?"

She opened her purse and took out long blue stick and showed it to him.

"Is this . . . what I think . . . ?"

"Congratulations, Papa. Tish is going to be a big sister."

Know anyone who might enjoy reading...

breathe

If so, just call Bookmasters at 1 (800) 537-6727,
or go to Bookmasters.com,
Amazon.com
MikeBroganBooks.com
bookstores

ISBN: 978-0-9980056-7-6

Also by Mike Brogan

KENTUCKY WOMAN

As an infant, Ellie Stuart is adopted by a poor, but loving couple in Harlan, Kentucky. When she's sixteen, they die in an accident, leaving her completely alone in the world. In college she searches for her biological parents with the help of a law student, Quinn Parker.

But as she gets close to finding them, an assassin tries to kill her.

When they finally discover why – it may be too late – and Ellie and Quinn have to run for their lives.

Available at
1 (800) 537-6727
Bookmasters.com
Amazon.com
MikeBroganBooks.com
bookstorcs

ISBN: 978-0-9846173–9-5

Also by Mike Brogan

G8

Donovan Rourke, a CIA Special Agent, discovers a man named Katill will assassinate the world's eight most powerful leaders at the G8 Summit in Brussels in three days. The President asks Donovan to handle the G8 security. Donovan agrees…but reluctantly. His wife was murdered there, and he blames himself.

In Brussels, Donovan works with the European G8 Director, Monsieur de Waha, and a beautiful translator named Maccabee. They learn that Katill is the same man who murdered Donovan's wife.

They also learn that Katill has just penetrated the G8's billion-dollar wall of security.

Donovan sees the world leaders walking into Katill's deathtrap! He tries to warn them – but it's too late…and then his worst nightmare happens right before his eyes.

Available at
1 (800) 537-6727
Bookmasters.com
Amazon.com
MikeBroganBooks.com
bookstores

ISBN: 978-0-9846173-0-2

Also by Mike Brogan

MADISON'S AVENUE

First, she gets the frightening phone call from her father. Hours later, he'd dead. The police say it's suicide. But Madison McKean suspects murder – because her father, CEO of a large Manhattan ad agency, refused a takeover bid by a ruthless agency conglomerate. Madison inherits his agency – and his enemies. When she and her new friend Kevin zero in on the executive behind her father's death, they soon discover an ex-CIA hitman is zeroing in on them.

MADISON'S AVENUE takes you inside the boardrooms of today's cutthroat, billion dollar corporations – to the white sand beaches of the Caribbean – to the high hopes and low cleavage of the Cannes Ad Festival...a world where some people take the phrase 'bury the competition' literally.

Available at
1 (800) 537-6727
Bookmasters.com
Amazon.com
MikeBroganBooks.com
bookstores

ISBN: 978-0-692-00634-4

Also by Mike Brogan

DEAD AIR

D r. Hallie Mara, an attractive young MD, and her friend, Reed Kincaid, learn that someone has singled out many men, women and children to die in ten cities across the U.S. in just a few days.

But because Hallie has no hard proof, the police refuse to investigate.

When Hallie and Reed try to find proof, they unearth something far beyond their worst fears. And as they zero in on the man behind everything, the man zeros in on them. Barely escaping with their lives, they finally convince the police and Federal authorities that a horrific disaster is imminent. But by then there's a big problem: it may be too late.

Midwest Book Review calls DEAD AIR, "a Lord of the Rings of thrillers. One can't turn the pages fast enough."

Available at
1 (443) 918-7141
Amazon.com
AmericaStarBooks.com
MikeBroganBooks.com
bookstores

ISBN: 1-4137-4700-0

Also by Mike Brogan

BUSINESS TO KILL FOR

Business is war. And Luke Tanner is about to be its latest casualty. He's overheard men conspiring to gain control of a billion dollar business using a unique strategy – murder the two CEO's who control the business. The conspirators discover Luke has overheard them and kidnap his girlfriend. He tries to free her, but gets captured himself.

Finally they escape, only to discover that the $1 billion business is his company . . . and that it may be too late to save his mentor, the CEO. The story takes you from the backstabbing backrooms of a major ad agency to the life-threatening jungles of Mexico's Yucatan.

Writer's Digest gave BUSINESS TO KILL FOR a major award, calling it, "the equal of any thriller read in recent years . . ."

Available at
Amazon.com
MikeBroganBooks.com
bookstores

ISBN 0-615-11570-5

ABOUT THE AUTHOR

MIKE BROGAN is the *Writers Digest* award-winning author of BUSINESS TO KILL FOR, a suspense thriller that *WD* called, "the equal of any thriller read in recent years." His DEAD AIR thriller also won national awards, as did MADISON's AVENUE.

His years in Kentucky, gave him a unique perspective in writing KENTUCKY WOMAN…as did the amazing, but true story that inspired him to write this new mystery thriller.

And his years living in London and Brussels, narrowly escaping terrorist bombs on two occasions, gave him the experience and background to write G8 … and his latest thriller - BREATHE.

Brogan lives in Michigan where he's completing his next novel. To learn more, visit MikeBroganBooks.com